Violent Delights

S.B. Urquidi

"Si nos dejan," written by José Alfredo Jiménez translated by S.B. Urquidi

The cover was designed by Sarah Lorenzen.

This is a work of fiction. While, as in all fiction, the literary perceptions and insights are based on experience, all names, characters, places and incidents either are products of the author's imagination or are used fictitiously.

For Sarah

Also by S.B. Urquidi

Love in Fire and Blood

"Yet each man kills the thing he loves
By each let this be heard.
Some do it with a bitter look,
Some with a flattering word.
The coward does it with a kiss,
The brave man with a sword!"

—

Excerpt from Oscar Wilde's, *The Ballad of Reading Gaol*

ACKNOWLEDGEMENTS

I am very grateful to those friends and family members who collaborated with comments and suggestions to improve the book. First of all thanks to my daughter, Sarah Lorenzen, for her helpful comments and for the design of the cover. I am also indebted to Tricia Breen, Brian Breen, Erica Marin, Flora Botton, Nancy Rocha, and numerous others who cheered me on. Thanks also to my Tepoztlán writers group—Janet Dawson Clark, Magara Graf, Annabella Eatherley, Bridget Galsworthy Estavillo, and Lourdes Arizpe—for their constant encouragement and interest. I would also like to thank Susan Cajiga for her help in so enthusiastically promoting my first book. Verónica Bulnes is once again responsible for the delightful maps.

A very special thanks to Marina Urquidi who edited the book not once but twice with such loving care. Her suggestions and professional eye turned a sow's ear into a silk purse.

ÁVILA

to United States

to Nuevo Progreso

SIERRA MADRE

1. Colonia Alfonso García Robles
2. Historic Center
3. Santa Teresa
4. Commercial Center
5. Boston Clinic
6. San José Church and Convent
7. Railway
8. El Refugio
9. Rancho Los Encinos
10. Shopping Mall
11. Airport
12. Gabriel's apartment

to Mexico City

INTRODUCTION

*I*t is not easy to step into a different culture, particularly when a reader is trying to follow the threads of a plot which the author often has made intentionally obscure. There are two aspects of this book which have frustrated some readers: the long Mexican names and the Spanish vocabulary. Under Mexican law everyone (citizens and permanent residents) has to be registered with both their father and mother's first last name. Therefore, my friend, Silvia **López Gutiérrez**, uses López from her father (Jesús **López** Pérez) and Gutiérrez from her mother (Anita **Gutiérrez** Colón). Married women today rarely take their husband´s name because that would mean adding a third last name. If she would choose to do so, my friend Silvia would be Silva López Gutiérrez de Sánchez, quite a mouthful.

As far as the vocabulary in Spanish is concerned, I have provided a glossary at the end of the book. In most cases when I chose to use a word or a form of address in Spanish, it seemed appropriate and added to the authenticity of the story. Building the glossary was in some ways more difficult than writing the book as not all Mexican Spanish speakers and not all English speakers agree on the meaning of a word, nor is the Internet infallible. However, the challenge soon turned into delight as I became caught up in the complexities of both the Spanish and English languages.

S.B. URQUIDI

CHAPTER 1

*A*lma hesitates before ringing the bell at Sandra Wearing's front door. She's suddenly uncomfortable about her clothes. Looking at her reflection in the glass door, she thinks the outfit probably rates a C- at best. Her shoes and handbag look all wrong. In fact, they both have seen better days. Her jacket is a size too big. She bought it because she loved the color, but now the color is no longer stylish, and the jacket hangs rather limply around her hips. Her black slacks are decent, but she's forgotten the belt. She checks her hair in the glass. It's naturally wavy and thick so she doesn't need to bother too much with styling, but her fingernails? Better not even go there, she thinks, curling them into the palm of her hand. But then straightening her shoulders, she says impatiently to no one in particular, *órale*, and gives the cord for the doorbell a hearty tug.

The young maid who shows her into the parlor of the nineteenth-century marble palace is perfectly dressed. Her pink uniform is neatly starched; her white sandals, freshly polished. She has pulled her dark hair back in a professional chignon. Her only makeup is a little pink lipstick. Alma sighs again as she removes her bulky jacket and takes a seat on one of the uncomfortable Regency sofas that are scattered, with their accompanying chairs and tables, around the large room.

Sandra and Bob Wearing live in the historic center of Ávila, an unusual choice for an expat executive who manages one of the big automobile factories on the outskirts of the city. Most general managers live in one of Ávila's gated communities which offer golf courses, tennis courts, spacious club houses, and security police who regularly patrol the grounds. The Wearings, however, had fallen in love with a historic wreck, the restoration of which went on to become a decade-long project. The *cantera* stone exterior is now as lovely as it was the year the house was built. In the interior, the white marble floors, curved staircase, and stained-glass windows have been preserved, but the rest of the palace has been carefully modernized. The kitchen, lined floor-to-ceiling with antique Talavera tiles, contains appliances usually found in upscale restaurants. The four bathrooms, all glass and chrome, have saunas, sunken tubs, and power showers. Central heating and air conditioning make the high-ceiling rooms as pleasant in chilly January as in sweltering May. The back garden has a discrete lap pool, solar-heated all year round.

Alma feels as if she has been allowed to jump over the velvet rope cordoning off a display in a museum devoted to fine nineteenth-century furniture. The Wearings' parlor is certainly authentic enough. The gold-inlaid cabinets and silk chaise lounges are in perfect condition; each oil painting is a romantic vision of a bucolic Mexico now long gone. But the room has not a single personal touch: no family photographs, no paperback casually turned over on a table, no roses plunked in a slightly chipped vase. Alma amuses herself imagining bits of whispered conversation from the long-dead residents of the palace. She conjures up a ball in this room in the eighteen-thirties. She sees slim-waisted girls whose faces are partially hidden behind fans, casting dark-eyed glances toward handsome men in gold-braided uniforms.

Drifting back to reality, she thinks about the dozens of times she's been to this house. Usually she waits in the front hall tapping her foot impatiently while her son says a long goodbye to his best friend, Max. She hadn't wanted to accept Sandra's invitation today. Casual chit-chat over mid-morning coffee is a time-wasting luxury she can ill afford, but the woman had insisted, begged, even, for a few minutes of her time.

"Sorry, sorry," says Sandra as she rushes into the room. "I was on the phone to the States. Coffee or hot chocolate? The cook has just made a fresh batch of *churros*. Doesn't that sound delicious with a cup of hot chocolate? But let's move into the family room down the hall."

Since she arrived back in Mexico six years ago, Alma has become accustomed to the little niceties required in local conversations. First, one needs to ask after the other person's health, and his or her family's wellbeing. Next you might comment on the weather if unseasonable or the traffic if worse than usual. However, the real conversation shouldn't begin until it has been politely prefaced. Americans, to the consternation of their Mexican friends, usually skip the preface and jump straight to chapter one.

Poor parlor, thinks Alma, as she collects her things and rises to follow Sandra, even your owner doesn't like you. The family room with its shabby leather sofa, giant TV, and family photos is far more welcoming. When Sandra rings a discrete bell, the well-groomed maid reappears. She nods her head as her mistress orders their mid-morning snack. Sandra's Spanish, Alma reflects as she listens to the conversation, is grammatically correct, but it has the rat-tat-tat sound of a marching band; not, as it should, the softer rhythms of a string quartet.

A pretty blue-eyed woman in her forties, Sandra has the sleek build of a swimmer: broad shoulders, strong upper arms. Her blond hair has been tinted and cut in the upscale salon she frequents in Houston; her cashmere sweater and slim-cut slacks speak Neiman Marcus.

"I'll get right to the point," says Sandra, turning to face her guest, "I need your help, Alma. I know how busy you are with your articles for the paper and your family, but I couldn't think of anyone else to turn to."

Alma keeps her gaze steady and her face impassive as she listens to Sandra's problem, but her mind races ahead to how she can politely step away from any involvement in the woman's personal life. Her mood, however, improves with the arrival of the hot chocolate and the warm, sugary *churros*.

"You see," begins Sandra again, "the daughter of an old

friend suddenly appeared two days ago on my doorstep. You could have knocked me over with a feather when I saw Evelyn standing there. I barely recognized her; she's so grown up! Her mother had sent me a photo a few years ago, but I never expected to see the girl here and, what's more, all on her own."

Sandra sits back on the sofa and frowns. Her young visitor is running away from home, she tells Alma. She had walked across the border in San Diego and flown from Tijuana to Mexico City, then taken a bus to Ávila. Alma waits patiently for the punch line. Why hasn't Sandra notified the girl's parents or sent her home?

She's a clever girl, continues Sandra. Both her parents are away. The father, Nick Hammond, is on a honeymoon with his third wife somewhere in Africa, and the mother, June, is in Iowa taking care of her ancient father who broke his hip. So Evelyn seized her chance and hightailed it to Mexico.

Alma thinks about how late it's getting. She would like to peek at her cell phone to check the time. She doesn't see where this saga is going or how it could possibly concern her. However, to be polite, she asks why the girl had to sneak off to Mexico.

"Well," says Sandra settling back on the sofa, "it's a long story." Evelyn, it turns out, was born in Ávila fifteen years ago to a single mother. June and Nick Hammond adopted the girl informally and managed somehow to take her to the U.S. as their birth child. Until two months ago, she had no idea that she was adopted or that she had a twin brother who should have been adopted too but who had disappeared from the home the day of their birth.

Sandra stops and apologizes for telling the story so badly. She doesn't know many of the details of the girl's life, but also, she whispers, the girl makes her nervous. She's so angry and not a little spoiled. She threatens to start searching for the brother on her own even though she doesn't speak a word of Spanish or have the least idea how to go about it. "I managed to call June; she was distraught that Evelyn had run off to Ávila. Her daughter had promised to stay with friends in San Diego. She said she'd come to Mexico as soon as she could. Neither of us knows how to reach Nick. So I'm stuck with Evelyn for a couple of weeks. I'm terrified she's going to do something foolish. The last thing June said to me was 'take care of my little girl.' That's a huge responsibility!" Sandra's voice gives way to her pent-up irritation with the entire Hammond family.

Ah, thinks Alma, we're finally getting to the punch line.

"I guess I thought you might take pity on me and—," continues Sandra. "You know, kind of look into the matter, just ask around a bit until the parents can get here and take her home."

"But what is it exactly that you want me to do?" asks Alma, baffled.

"Find her brother, of course. Or pretend to find her brother. You're good at investigating things. I only need your help for a week or ten days. I'm afraid she'll disappear on me. Her mother is one of my oldest friends." Sandra's eyes now have an imploring look that Alma hasn't seen before.

"Sandra, I'm not a detective. I'm a reporter. You need to

hire a professional investigator. I wouldn't know where to begin," she lies.

"Evelyn has some information. Just talk to her, Alma, please. I can't hire a detective. The way she was adopted and taken to the U.S. is too delicate; Nick would be furious. I'm not asking you to really find the brother, just to do a quiet, quick little search to prove to Evelyn that the boy can't be found. It needs to look like I'm trying to help her until her parents get here and take her off my hands."

This is a totally insane request, thinks Alma, as she lifts her cup for one last sip of hot chocolate. "Sandra, honestly, my time is so limited, and frankly won't the girl be even angrier if we also begin deceiving her?"

The woman's eyes begin to fill with tears. Oh, God, thinks Alma, how do I get myself into these situations? She sits silently for a minute or two reflecting on how much she doesn't want to become involved with these people. But then the three pricey vacations that her son, Kurt, enjoyed with the Wearings cross her mind. She remembers his frequent overnight stays at their home when she's been caught up at work and the afternoons spent at their country club. She takes a deep breath and against her better judgment, says, "I'll talk to her, but I'm not promising anything."

Alma barely has time to pull a pen and a small notebook out of her bag before Sandra reappears with Evelyn. After the briefest of introductions, Sandra waves to her visitors and leaves the room closing the door quietly behind her.

The two women eye one another. The girl is slight, small-boned. She's dressed in black tights, a long flowing shirt, and knee-high red boots. Her dark hair is pulled back in a butterfly clip. Her eyes are her best feature: large, almond-shaped with hazel irises and long dark lashes. Her skin is so white it seems almost translucent. She wears no makeup. After hearing of her daring trip to Ávila, Alma had expected a more imposing figure.

"So," says Alma after Evelyn has seated herself at the other end of the sofa, "I understand you're here to find your brother."

"And my birth parents," the girl answers. "I'm not leaving until I find out who they are." She clenches her teeth and stares straight ahead. A "don't mess with me" gesture if there ever was one, Alma thinks.

"Sandra says you can help me, but I don't understand how."

"I'm a reporter on our local newspaper and have a background in investigation. I'm not a detective, but I'm good at tracking people down."

The girl looks dubious. "If you're going to tell me a bunch of lies like Nick and June have done my whole life, then don't waste your time. I've had a lot of practice lately in smelling a rat." Her adopted parents are no longer Mom and Dad, Alma thinks, they've become Nick and June, the enemy.

"Why don't you tell me your story, and I'll see if I can help or not," says Alma, projecting, she hopes, an air of calm authority.

Evelyn stares ahead, obviously weighing her options. She finally leans back on the sofa and begins to speak. Her delivery is fluid as if she had rehearsed the story, if only in her head, many times. It wasn't as if she had never felt different from her parents. She didn't look like either one of them. Her mother had said that Evelyn took after the "black Irish" in the family. That was the way genes worked, she'd said. Some black-haired Spaniard in the sixteenth century ends up shipwrecked on the shores of Ireland, marries a local lass, and his genes join the Irish gene pool; then generations later his dark hair shows up in a girl living in California. Evelyn had believed her because she had wanted to believe her. June and Nick had divorced when Evelyn was six, and it had been hard. Her father married again and just when she had gotten used to his new wife, that marriage had broken up. Now there is yet another stepmother. Her mother fusses over her too much, is overprotective. Her parent's one constant is their incessant fighting over Evelyn.

On her fifteenth birthday last May, she had received a strange e-card. She had opened it because she thought it had come from a boy she liked. It was a cute cartoon Mariachi band singing that Mexican birthday song. The message on the card had said, "Who is Evelyn Hammond?" She had deleted it and thought no more about it. Three months later she'd received another e-card. The same Mariachi band singing greetings, but this time the message said, "Are you really Evelyn Hammond?"

She'd shown the message to her mother, but June had brushed it off, saying she should be more careful about the e-mails she opened. She had mentioned the cards to Alice, her best friend. Alice had said every kid wished they were adopted at one time or another. Evelyn's parents would have told her when she was three or four if she'd been adopted. That's what her friend Heather's parents had done. There'd been a whole adoption story.

But just after Thanksgiving, the third card had arrived with the same happy motif, but the message had said: "Evelyn Hammond, you need to know the truth."

"The last message totally freaked me out," the girl says. Was someone trying to help her or just mess with her head? She couldn't talk to anyone about it, but she had started to think all over again about her so-called "black Irish" genes and many other odd things. How was it that she could sing anything, but her parents were tone deaf? Her mother was forty-five or forty-six when Evelyn was born; that was really old. Then there was her name which means "most wanted child."

A few days later, her mother had taken jewelry out of the safe where all the family documents were also kept. She'd left the safe open while going out for the evening with friends. Evelyn had found the brown manila envelope easily. Written on the front were the words, *Niña G.* She remembers slowly unwinding the red string that was twisted around the two small discs on the back of the envelope. She felt sick with anticipation. She wanted and didn't want to know. Inside were two yellowed hospital certificates: one for *Niña G* and one for *Niño G.* They were issued by a place called La Casa de la Esperanza and signed by someone called *Hermana* Fernanda. There was also a small bracelet made of white beads that said *Niña G.* and a sheet of paper containing the lines to what looked like a poem. It was titled *"Si nos dejan."*

She had waited up for her mother. June had arrived in an Uber around two a.m. humming the tune "When I'm Sixty-Four," but her mood had changed quickly when Evelyn had said, "The truth, I just want the truth."

June had collapsed in a chair and said, "Oh, sweetheart, I'm so, so sorry." In those brief seconds Evelyn had felt her life implode, dynamited like those unwanted buildings you see demolished on TV. That evening the emotional dust had settled very slowly. There had been many tears but not a lot of explanations. June had desperately wanted children, but none had appeared. They had put their name down in a dozen adoption agencies, but as they travelled incessantly, they always seemed to remain at the bottom of the lists. She was determined when they went to Mexico to come back with a baby. After several years in Ávila, Nick had come home one day and said that he had found a child: a newborn that would be available in a matter of weeks. She had been ecstatic.

June had no idea who Evelyn's birth mother was. Sister Fernanda had told them that the girl was young, only fifteen, but from a good family. Her family, however, had abandoned her, never visited. Someone had dropped her off at the home, and someone had picked her up. The nun had shown Nick a photo of the young woman, but he said he knew nothing else: no name, no address, no family history. When June had last talked to him he'd said that Evelyn today looked very much like the photo he had seen of her birth mother. The young woman had wanted the baby taken out of Mexico but had no desire to meet the people adopting her child. The father of the baby was never mentioned.

"But what about *Niño G*? You keep talking about 'a' baby but there are two certificates from La Casa de la Esperanza. Did the other baby die?" June had explained that no one knew until the day of the birth that the girl was expecting twins. She'd had no prenatal care. Nick had offered to pay for a doctor's visit, but she'd refused. The night of the birth her brother had been taken from the clinic by two men. The next day the mother had left. The nun had called to say that they had better pick up the girl baby as soon as possible.

"Why wasn't I adopted legally in Mexico?" Evelyn had asked her mother. "It's not so difficult. I checked it out. It just takes time." June had no idea why Nick was so anxious to leave Ávila. He'd spent a fortune to get her registered as their birth child. Did her mother know what the poem on the sheet of paper meant? June had shaken her head. She had found it tossed on the floor under Evelyn's small crib and for some reason kept it.

Evelyn had tackled her father the next day. He'd been furious with her mother. "Stupid woman," he had said over and over. The girl knew her father loved her, but she called him "her imperial dad." He barked orders to everyone. When she had said she wanted to go to Mexico to look for her brother, he shouted, "Are you crazy? Don't you listen to the news? Everyone knows that Mexico is practically a war zone." He promised he'd take her in the spring. She had to be patient. Why had he registered her as his birth child? He had his reasons; when she got older she might understand. End of discussion.

"Did you tell him about the Mariachi e-mails?"

"No," says Evelyn looking away. "He would have freaked out." Closets full of secrets in the Hammond family, Alma thinks.

"I've got about a week before my dad or mom can get down here. How much do you charge? I've got a little money."

Alma smiles for the first time that morning. "This is a favor for a friend, Evelyn," she says pausing for a moment, looking at the girl's expectant face. "You know," she says, "even if I do find your birth parents and your brother, they might not want to have anything to do with you. Or you might find out that they're awful people and want nothing to do with them. It could be tough, perhaps even tougher than the last two months. And by the way '*Si nos dejan*' isn't a poem, it's a popular song that has been around for a while."

The girl thinks for a moment. "A song, huh. That makes more sense if my real mom was a kid. I've thought a lot about the bad stuff that might be there if I do find my birth family. Don't think I haven't read dozens of shocking stories on the Internet, but I saw this video on YouTube about these twins from Korea who were reunited after being separated at birth. They couldn't stop holding hands and staring at one another. Maybe I'll be one of the lucky ones."

"Okay, let's get to work." Alma needs Evelyn to give her copies of all the documents she brought with her. Also, they need photos. Alma snaps several pictures of Evelyn in dim light. In several, her long hair covers part of her face.

The two women quickly scan the documents. "I'll call you

day after tomorrow," Alma shouts over her shoulder as she hurries out the door. *"¡Madre mía!"* she mutters as she opens her car door, why can't I ever simply say no?

*   *   *

The drive from the elegant historical center of Ávila where the Wearings' Porfiriano-era pink palace is located to the twentieth-century commercial center of the city should have been brief, but it is almost lunch time and schools are letting out. Snarled, Alma thinks, is the best word for our roads; they're tangled in knots early morning through late night. Delivery vans and gas trucks block some streets; school buses and parents' cars, others. There is usually a siren-blowing ambulance stuck in the middle of an intersection to add drama to the chaos.

It's curious, Alma thinks, that Evelyn and her birth mother both arrived at a crisis at the tender age of fifteen. Alma has a lot of sympathy with young women in crisis, having suffered one herself when she was in her early twenties. She knows what it feels like to be abandoned, betrayed. Your life collapses, and you can't see anything but the disaster that's pulling you under.

The word "disaster" jerks her mind back to Ávila and her surroundings. How different the newer buildings in this part of town are from their two- and three-hundred-year-old cousins in the older part of the city. The more ancient buildings have a classical grace; the newer constructions seem to have thrown style and beauty to the winds. Their peeling plaster invites the spray-painted graphics of the less talented graffiti artists of the city. She spies, however, several recent murals with political themes that show imagination; some concerning the new governor even make her laugh out loud.

Her thoughts drift back to Evelyn and her mysterious birth parents. A girl from a "good family" abandoned in a barebones home for single mothers, dropped off like dirty linen and then picked up months later? That's unusual in Mexico. No, she thinks, there must be more to the story.

When she finally pulls up in front of El Diario de Ávila thirty minutes later, *Don* Chencho, who has appropriated the public thoroughfare in front of the building for his private parking service, signals that even with cars double parked, he has no spaces left. "*¡Qué desmadre!*" mutters Alma, pulling back into the snail-paced traffic.

As she circles the block, she has to admit that as much as she loves street food, the gas tanks and sidewalk stalls add to the parking and traffic confusion. But who could live without the fruit vendor whose sculptured mangos are sold on small sticks or the man who squeezes fresh orange juice or the hawker peddling corn on the cob plastered with mayonnaise, *queso añejo* and *chili piquín*? Alma rolls down the car window and takes a deep breath. The smells, she thinks, are a mixture of the delicious and the repugnant. But it wouldn't be downtown without the scent of *tortillas* baking over burning charcoal or *jalapeños* and onions frying in a lump of lard. The day-old trash ripening in the sun and the smell of diesel waft uninvited into the mix.

To pass the time, she turns on the radio trying to catch the two o'clock news. The national headlines sound like a repeat of last month's or even last year's reports. The President of the Republic denies any corruption in his administration. Weeping mothers call for the government to find their missing children. On the local level Tepetlán's new governor, Humberto García Borresen, son of the murdered ex-governor, pleads for political unity. The state's economy needs to get moving again. She switches off the radio; even for a news junky, enough is enough.

Passing one more time in front of El Diario de Ávila, she sees a parking spot open up; she gratefully delivers her car to the faithful *Don* Chencho. The newsroom is buzzing. Today, she notices, all hands are on deck. Halfway across the room, she stops. There is that *cabrón*, Héctor Valdés, sitting at her desk again. His computer is open, and he looks like he might be working.

"Has your desk been donated to the Salvation Army?" she asks him, dropping her bag and her computer down on what she considers her property. She smiles at the man, but her eyes narrow in irritation.

"I need to speak to Ricardo urgently and, since you're not here much, I thought you wouldn't mind someone actually using the desk for a few minutes," he says leaning back in her chair.

Such a *fresa*, she thinks. Back in California she would have called him a yuppie with his slim cut shirt hugging his oh-so-thin torso, and that hair, so perfectly styled each morning to look casually chic. He's twirling the horn-rimmed glasses he's started sporting recently to make him look older, more intellectual. How pathetic.

At that moment, an office door a few feet down the hall

opens, and Carlos Núñez, the mayor of Ávila, walks out, followed by his cousin, Ricardo Núñez, the editor of their newspaper. Héctor tries to get Ricardo's attention, but before he can address him, Carlos spots Alma and rushes over to her.

"*Ay, mi* Alma," he says, giving her a bear hug, "how are you? Staying out of trouble, I hope? Your room at the Mayor's Mansion is ready whenever you need it."

Alma smiles and the two men walk off, talking in loud voices about tequila and nearby restaurants. Héctor slams down the lid of his laptop and marches off. He'll be back, Alma thinks; as soon as I leave, he'll be back.

Before checking her messages or examining the stories left in her in-box, she decides to look over Evelyn's documents, meager as they are. A preliminary birth certificate was issued in her name by a hospital called La Clínica Boston. Her official birth certificate has all the necessary stamps from the state of Tepetlán. The certificates issued by La Casa de la Esperanza simply give Ávila as the location of the home, no street address.

At that moment the oldest member of the staff, César Davila, walks by her desk. Since he has only a meager pension from the Seguro Social, Ricardo pays him a small salary which he collects once a week, using the visit to catch up on office gossip or to play a game of dominos. Today he is dressed in a freshly pressed blue *guayabera*.

"*Guapa*," he says winking at Alma as he perches on a corner of her desk. "Am I or am I not still the only *chingón* around here?"

"No one comes even close," says Alma smiling at the handsome old man. "Let me pick your brains. Do you by any chance know a home for single mothers called La Casa de la Esperanza?"

Cesar thinks for a few moments. His brow becomes furled. "Yes, if it's the same place, it closed down about nine or ten years ago. It was over on Calle Diez, but they tore down the building. The home only lasted a few years. It was started by that priest that got murdered, *Padre* Francisco." He pauses for a moment. Alma can see that his elderly brain is chasing a memory. Finally he says, "There was a stink about it." He rubs his thumb against his index finger and raises his hand to his nose.

"A stink?" says Alma. "What do you mean?"

"Things that weren't done quite right, like a lot of things in this state." He stands, leans over, and gives Alma a quick kiss on the cheek before winding his way to the cashier's office.

Alma busies herself next with downloading her photos of Evelyn and sending them to a photographer friend with the request that he turn them into black-and-white snapshots that look a little faded.

*   *   *

That evening when she and Kurt open the front door of their small rented house, all the lights are on, and good smells are coming from the kitchen. "Gabo is that you?" she shouts.

"Do you have another boyfriend that cooks?" says a loud male voice.

"What's for supper?" asks Kurt. "I'm starving."

20

"Your favorite dish, *sopa de sopa*," replies Gabriel.

As they sit down to eat at the battered but highly polished oak table that Alma found at a street market, Kurt asks, "How come this dish is called soup of soup?"

"I guess," explains Gabriel, "it's because pasta here is associated with soup. In Italy pasta is the first course like soup is here."

"But *sopa de sopa* isn't even a soup," says Alma. "Soup is watery, and this is dry."

"I wish," says Gabriel, "that I was at liberty to divulge our ancient family recipe, but I'm afraid I've been sworn to secrecy."

Kurt sighs as only a contented nine-year-old can do with his favorite meal. He piles his plate with another helping.

"What's for dessert?" asks Alma.

"Your favorite, Alma, *zapote negro*," answers Gabriel confident of the applause which he will soon receive.

"You're trying to seduce me all over again," says Alma when Kurt has gone upstairs to do his homework. "Why do we think that it's only men's hearts that are conquered through their stomachs?"

As they move out to finish their dessert and wine on the small back patio, Gabriel gives Alma a rundown on his last couple days of teaching at the law faculty of the Autonomous University of Tepetlán and the current cases in his law office. He's sorry that his small office can only take on a fraction of the human-rights cases that are out there. "Scrambling to pay the rent at the end of the month is a way of life," he says sighing, but he can't complain, he knew what he was getting into. He turns to Alma, "What's going on with you? Is Héctor still being his insufferable self?"

Alma waits a minute before answering. It is at moments like this that she marvels at her good fortune. What luck to have met this attractive, interesting, and just plain nice man. She can hear her mother whispering in her ear. Marry him Alma, he's perfect for you. One day, she silently replies; one day I hope I will, but I need a little more time. Well, I hope he waits around for you, comments Sofía. Me too, me too, she answers.

"Oh, we're going to talk about Mr. Entitlement. Let me think. Does he have any saving grace? Maybe, but it's buried so deep I can't find it. The rumor is that he has *palancas*, friends in high places. He certainly didn't work for a real newspaper before he joined El Diario de Ávila."

Gabriel smiles. He's now sorry he brought up Héctor; talking about him upsets Alma. "Any new stories you're working on?" he says changing the subject. "Are we still going to San Miguel de Allende this weekend?"

"Of course we're going. I'm looking forward to it. Kurt will be staying with his grandparents. You did tell me that you'd made a reservation at an Airbnb near the center of the town, didn't you? And yes, I do have a curious project that Sandra, Max's mom, has roped me into."

"Another school fund raiser?"

As Alma relates Evelyn's story, Gabriel's expression becomes more concerned. "Aren't you busy enough, *Flaca*?" he says. "Always trying to solve the world's problems."

"Look who's talking," she says beginning to laugh. "How

do you think they managed to register Evelyn as their birth child?"

"You said the father is a lawyer, what's his name?"

"Nick Hammond."

"What? Is he THE Nick Hammond? The lawyer to see if you've been extradited to the U.S. for drug smuggling or money laundering? If it's the same guy, he has many friends in high places who wouldn't mind doing him a favor."

"Sandra said that when he came here years ago, he was a corporate lawyer."

"Maybe so, but he picked up another specialty along the way. You're sure you haven't heard of him?"

"You sound as if you know him?"

Gabriel pauses for a minute choosing his words. "My ex-father-in-law, Linda's dad," he says, "tried more than once to get me a job with Nick Hammond. His firm was looking for experts on human-rights law because his clients felt their civil liberties were being violated in U.S. prisons. They were often kept in solitary confinement or denied access to their attorneys. Perhaps Hammond and his clients had a point, but that was not the kind of law I wanted to practice. Linda was very disappointed that I didn't sign on with him but—" Gabriel throws his hands in the air as if to indicate a divide no one could bridge.

"Anyway," he continues, "why do you want to get involved? It sounds like a thankless job."

"It's the girl," says Alma. "You and I are both only children although you have that lot of step-sisters, and I had my cousins in East Compton. Even so, I always desperately wanted a brother or a sister. Evelyn only has Nick and June, her parents. If anything happens to them, she'd be entirely on her own. That must be a scary feeling. We know where we came from. She doesn't have a clue. Can you imagine what it would mean to her to find a brother, a twin even?"

Gabriel stares at her for a moment, shrugs a shoulder, and standing up, starts to pick up the plates and glasses on the patio table. Alma stays seated. Yes, of course, she feels sympathy for Evelyn, but in her heart of hearts she knows that it's the strangeness of the girl's story that most intrigues her. The clandestine adoption, the abandoned teenage mother, the bizarre e-cards are puzzling enough, but it is César's comment about the stink associated with La Casa de Esperanza that has sucked her into what she now thinks just might be some kind of a story.

CHAPTER 2

The next morning, standing at the sink washing cereal bowls and a coffee mug, Alma gazes at the blue cloudless sky outside her kitchen window. Her life lately has been quite cloudless too. All the little and bigger bits of her day-to-day existence are humming along. Her family, her love life, her career, all seem to be in happy sync. She turns and raps her knuckles on the wooden kitchen table and then, laughing, gives a few quick knocks to the top of her head.

Her dad's bad back has become less painful thanks, she thinks, to their local soccer team's unexpected winning streak; no teacher, so far this term, has written reports on her son: less daydreaming and more attention to detail would improve Kurt's grades. Also, she's got a surefire idea for a series of articles on the new governor of Tepetlán. Her love life couldn't be better. Gabriel is as charming and attentive as the day they met.

She also has the small commission of looking into Evelyn Hammond's birth family. She feels sympathy for the girl's emotional turmoil. But it is the weirdness of the girl's story which has piqued her interest. Why did Nick Hammond feel so compelled to spirit Evelyn out of Mexico? Forging a birth certificate and lying to the U.S. authorities are felonies for which he could be disbarred in California. Then there's the identity of the birth mother. Why was it kept such a secret? The Mariachi e-cards bother her too. Someone is trying to unmask Evelyn's birth parents or perhaps wants the girl in Mexico but to what end? The lyrics of the song "Si nos dejan": What had they meant to Evelyn's fifteen-year-old mother? She had promised to send Evelyn a translation of the song today. And César's remark about the stink at the home for single mothers has also lodged itself in her brain.

Thinking of Evelyn, she realizes that it has been a good week since she's seen her own mother. "Dulce, we need a walk," she says to the small dog lying in a basket near the back door.

The fifteen-minute stroll to her parent's house through her *barrio*, the Colonia Alfonso García Robles, is... she grapples for the right word: instructive, amusing, disquieting; maybe it's all those things at once. Every house is singular; every block unique. It is certainly not beautiful, nor well planned. It has no interesting history or landmarks. The pavement is pockmarked; few trees shade the sidewalks. The water supply and the Internet are works in progress. But the streets teem with life. People are out on the sidewalks from sunrise to sunset: fixing a car, tending a garden, chasing a ball, talking to a neighbor. Not only talking, but exercising, shouting, swearing, singing, and occasionally even dancing.

Her neighbors' houses, like her parent's home, often change paycheck to paycheck: a new window here, a mended fence there. She teases Gonzalo about his taxi's new blue and pink paint job. "Can you believe it, Alma, the governor decreed that we had to paint our taxis powder blue and light pink? He's crazy. It's undignified. He says that if people see these baby colors on our taxis it will reassure them. Make them think our city is safe. *"¡Qué pendejada!"*

She briefly discusses with *Señora* Juárez this season's roses and with Manuel the best anti-crook locks for cars. Dogs, cooped up behind fences, bark at Dulce, but she pays them no heed. Alma notices that the yellow and black orioles are back from their summer sojourn up north. Music, drifting, and sometimes blaring, from car radios and out of kitchen windows amuses rather than annoys her. The morning is glorious: sunny with a cool breeze which rustles the blossoms on the bougainvillea vines. A perfect day, reflects Alma, as she walks through the front door of her mother's small *miscelánea*.

Sofía is on her hands and knees peering under one of the display cases. "What are you doing, Ma?"

"I just dropped a coin, and it rolled out of reach."

"Come on, Ma. You won't go broke if you lose a peso or two."

"Maybe not, Alma, but those pesos come hard-earned."

"Sorry," says Alma helping her mother to her feet.

"What brings you here so early?"

"I was missing you," says Alma giving her mother a hug and a kiss on the cheek.

"That's nice," answers Sofía returning the hug.

Pulling back from her mother and studying her for moment, Alma says, "Ma, did you ever think I should have put Kurt up for adoption?"

"What a thought! Of course not! What's he done now?"

"No," laughs Alma, "Kurt's just his normal nine-year-old self, but suppose I'd been a lot younger, like fifteen?"

"No, we would have been very disappointed, but no, we would have taken care of the baby and made you go back to school."

Sofía sits down on a stool behind the cash register. Years ago, she says, times in Ávila were a lot tougher. Women weren't so used to the pill. There were more unwanted pregnancies. In that case couples had to make some tough decisions. But today it's hard to find a baby to adopt. They're as scarce in Mexico as they are almost everywhere else. No big families anymore either; teenage single mothers? Yes, there are lots of those, but the children just seem to get folded into the family. Alma asks how she knows so much about it.

"Oh," says her mother airily, "I look at what's happening around our neighborhood, and I listen to the radio even if I don't read the newspapers much, except for what you write."

"Hey, the shop looks great," says Alma tiring of the subject. "Look at those cool desks with the three new computers! How's the new Internet business going? And look at the new showcase with the school supplies! You're quite the business woman."

"Don't make fun of me, Alma."

"I'm not making fun of you. I'm proud of you. But where's the sign over the front door? Did someone steal it?"

"No, no one took it. I had Papi take it down because *Maestra* Flor complained. You must know her. She teaches at the *Preparatoria número dos.*"

"She complained? What about?"

It turns out that the teacher hadn't really made a formal complaint. She had come in one day, and said she'd been walking past the sign for three years, and that it had bothered her every time she saw it. "Sofía," she had said, "the name *Mi premiecito* that you chose for your store doesn't sound right." Sofía had gotten worried thinking that the name might have a double meaning, but the teacher had said that it wasn't a bad word, just not a proper name for a store. Sofía had pointed out that her daughter who was a college graduate had thought up the name. The teacher had frowned, as if her authority was being called into question, and said that that name might have been acceptable to people in Los Angeles, but in Ávila where people named things properly, it sounded wrong.

"*Caray,*" says Alma, who is always a little uneasy about her written Spanish, "what are you going to call the store now?"

Her mother's mood brightens. "I decided to have a contest. I've asked the neighborhood children to submit names. The winner gets a few hours' free time on a computer. The *maestra* and I are going to pick the best name. You want to help us?"

Alma shakes her head. "But how's business going?" she

asks.

"The neighborhood kids come after school mostly to play games on the computers, and the school supplies are moving along. It's the snacks that fly off the shelf. I wish I didn't have to sell all that junk. Most everyone here has gotten too fat!" replies Sofía smoothing down the apron covering her slim figure. "Is Kurt coming over to lunch and to help me this afternoon?"

"Yes, but I hope he's really a help. Could he spend the weekend too? Gabriel and I would like to go to San Miguel de Allende for a couple of days. We both need a break."

"Of course, Kurt can come for the weekend. Didn't he used to live here? And how is Gabriel? We haven't seen him for weeks. But you'll be missing El Día de la Candelaria. Didn't Gabriel promise to bring the *tamales* again?"

"Yes, he did, but we're so busy that we haven't spent much time together. Couldn't we postpone the *tamales* 'til next Monday?"

"If you were married, you'd see each other every day," says Sofía giving Alma one of her more searching looks.

Alma closes her eyes and mentally kicks herself. Here we go again, she thinks. "Whoops, I'd better get going. I have an appointment at the paper. Can I leave Dulce here? She gets lonely. I'll come back for her at lunch time."

Alma kisses her mother quickly and steps out of the door before she hears Sofía's views on marriage for the umpteenth time.

* * *

"I'm in luck today," Alma comments to no one in

30

particular as she crosses the newsroom: no problem parking and no sign of Héctor. She opens her computer and sets to work. For the next couple of hours, she is so intent on what she is writing that Ricardo Núñez's assistant startles her when she approaches with a message from their mutual boss. "He wants to talk to you," the woman says, and then walks away without waiting for an answer.

"You're good?" says the editor as Alma settles into the old wooden chair opposite his desk. "Gabriel and Kurt? Your parents?"

"Yes, everyone is fine," answers Alma, hoping that the conversational preface won't go on for long as she has a couple of hours of work ahead of her. Ricardo looks tired. He's lost weight, she notices. Also, his brown hair has been too closely cropped which gives him the air of a military man, a look she knows he would hate. He seems today to have aged. My God, she thinks, I hope he's not settling into middle age. He's just turned thirty-eight.

Ricardo loosens his tie and looks out the window for a few minutes. "Beautiful day," he says finally. "I don't think there's even much pollution. Did you go for a run this morning?"

What's up with him? Why this aimless chitchat? "I don't run, Richie. I walked over to see my mom earlier. Is there something in particular you wanted to see me about?"

He begins to line up the pens and pencils that are spread across his desk. Without any further prelude, he launches into a long explanation of the changes he wants to make in the newsroom. Alma only half listens. Her beat is local and state politics, and that isn't going to change.

"The position of assistant editor, I was just mentioning, I'd like to offer it to you," he says abruptly and then looks apprehensive. The smile is gone from his face.

"Why?"

"I thought with the other changes I'm making that you might have time on your hands, and you could help me out."

Now she is really baffled. "What other changes?"

"It's been decided that Héctor Valdés will be covering state and local politics. Alongside of you, of course."

The room becomes so silent that you can hear the buzz of traffic through the double-paned windows. Keep calm, she says to herself, but she can feel her face getting warm. She takes a deep breath. "Who decided that and why?"

"Héctor asked for the position, and I thought that it was the best thing right now for the paper. He wants to do a series of stories on our new governor."

"Ricardo," she almost shouts his name, "there is no one in Ávila who knows the Garcías better than I do. I can't say that Beto, our new governor, has much affection for me, but I am the local expert on him." She says the last four words with such emphasis that she thinks there might be droplets of spit on Ricardo's desk. "You want me to resign, I gather. Fine, I'll clear out my desk today."

"No, Alma, calm down. Of course I don't want you to resign. This is temporary I'm sure." Ricardo puts his head in his hands. Finally looking up, he explains that Héctor's father and uncle are the newspaper's majority shareholders. His great grandfather, along with Ricardo's, was one of the founders of El Diario de Ávila. "They're pressuring me to give Héctor a chance. They've never asked me for a favor before."

"Couldn't he start out like the rest of us did, covering weddings and the State Assembly?"

"No, because he thinks he's a world-class journalist, and starting at the bottom is beneath him." He's got money and power behind him, the editor adds, so he doesn't need to start at the bottom. If Alma can be patient, the guy won't last reporting on politics because despite what he thinks, he knows nothing about it. He believes that because he knows Beto García socially, he's going to get privileged access to the governor. What he's going to get is spin. "Wait it out, Alma. Just wait it out," Ricardo pleads, smiling his crooked smile.

"You know what I was writing up this morning? A proposal for a series of articles on the new state government. What Beto was going to clean up, and what he will leave alone and why. I guess I can dump that in the trash. Do I have to hand over my desk too?"

"No, of course not. Give me a month. I need to show his father and uncle that he's not ready for the big time, but he needs to fall on his face first."

"Okay, a month, but meanwhile, I'm updating my resume and keeping my eyes open."

"Come on, Alma. Don't be like that."

"Like what? Like someone who's just been demoted or rather, should I say kicked upstairs? Wow, just thirty-one and kicked upstairs. That should be one for the record books."

*   *   *

At lunch a few hours later, Kurt teases his grandmother

about what he calls their patriotic lunch. "First you served *crema de calabacitas*, a green soup. Then we had *chicharrón en salsa roja*, and you made *horchata* to drink, which is white. Red, white, and green: you served up the Mexican flag."

Sofía laughs. "I'll remember to repeat the menu on the *dieciséis de septiembre*," she says.

After Kurt goes off to watch over the store, Sofía asks Alma why she was so glum during lunch. Knowing that her mother won't rest until she's learned the truth, Alma relates the changes Ricardo wants to make in the newsroom. "I didn't say this to Ricardo, Ma, but after I left the office I started to think about all the ads that the newspaper gets from the state government. Maybe Ricardo wants to go easy on the governor; maybe the paper needs the cash? He's never played up to a governor before but—?"

Sofía walks straight to the phone. "I'm calling Elvia, Ricardo's wife, right this minute." Alma groans. Her mother is on one of her missions. "You know we became quite friendly last year when Papi and I were at her ranch in Veracruz. She calls me at least once a month. I'll tell her that her husband is not thinking straight."

Alma begins to laugh. "Ma, you can't do that. Didn't you always tell me that I had to fight my own battles? But I do need you to use your influence with someone else."

"Me? Apart from Elvia, with whom could I possibly have influence? And don't think you're going to distract me. If I get a chance to speak with Ricardo's wife..."

"With *Padre* Rafael. You're his favorite altar lady, aren't you? I want you to ask him if he knows the whereabouts of a nun who was head of a home for single mothers. It was called La Casa de la Esperanza. Sister Fernanda is her name."

"Of course. I'd be glad to ask him, and at the same time, I could talk to him about Kurt's First Communion which you have been putting off for the last year or so." Sofía eyes Alma with a look that says, I've got you now.

Alma takes a large swallow of *horchata* and gazes at her mother with respect. She knows where and when to pick her battles, she thinks. We've been round and round Kurt's religious education for the last two years, but she's like a dog with a bone. She might have given up on my going to Mass every Sunday, but she got Kurt baptized, and now she'll see that he makes his First Communion.

"Okay, talk to *Padre* Rafael about the First Communion, too." If Kurt wants to be a Buddhist or a Mormon later in life, then he can fight it out with his grandmother. Alma also knows which of her mother's missions are worth going to war over.

Savoring her victory, Sofía moves on to further conquests. "And Alma, your clothes——. If you're going to San Miguel for the weekend, you need a new swimsuit. You should get a bikini and a sexy night dress and new underwear. Buy a few summer dresses too. What's happened to my pretty girl the last couple of months? All you think about is work."

Alma is stunned into silence: sexy underwear, bikinis, provocative night dresses. Is this her mother speaking? She begins to laugh. "What's come over you, Ma? I don't think this advice comes from one of *Padre* Rafa's sermons."

"No, it comes from common sense. I think it's important

for a man like Gabriel, a lawyer, to be seen with a woman who's not only smart but looks smart. They'll never change. Men, that is. He's a good man, but you've got to spice up the relationship; have other guys look at you; make him proud to be seen with you. You should also get your hair cut different, Alma."

Where is all this coming from? thinks Alma. Is my mother watching those make-over shows on TV? Does she think Gabriel is losing interest? "Is that how you held on to Pa?" she says smiling.

"Well, in my own time and in my own way, yes. Your dad was and still is a handsome man. You know in L.A. there were a lot of attractive women hanging around those houses they were remodeling. I kept myself up for him and for me. Also, have you seen pictures of Gabriel's ex?"

"You mean, Linda? No, how would I have? I couldn't ask him!"

"You could have gone online like your cousin Elena did."

Alma feels her face going red, indignation rising from the pit of her stomach. How dare they pry into her life and her relationship with Gabriel! She stands up saying, "I don't want to hear any more. Really, Ma. This is none of your business."

As she closes the front door pushing Kurt ahead of her, she hears her mother's voice. "Linda Wilcox. Look her up. You'll be surprised!"

*   *   *

While tucking Kurt in bed that evening, Alma broaches the subject of his First Communion. He'd have to take a few months of religious instruction, and she'd have to consult his father in L.A. "Maybe Dad will come for the ceremony," says Kurt, his eyes lighting up. Although he sees his father every summer, it's obvious that he wants his dad to see his life in Ávila, and he wants his friends to see that he has a dad.

"Then should *Abuelita* talk to the priest?" asks Alma kissing him good night.

"It would be so cool if Dad came for a visit," is the reply she gets.

Back in her bedroom, she opens her e-mail account which somewhat cheers her up. The Dallas Morning News wants her to write an article on Texan expats living in central Mexico. One of the online news sites she contributes to wants an article on Tepetlán's new governor. So, there are people outside of Ávila who believe in her work. She'll give Ricardo a month to boot Héctor off her beat. Yes, a month is all the time he'll get.

Her photographer friend has returned the photos of Evelyn. They are now in fuzzy black and white. She prints them out on photographic paper and crops just the head.

Out of curiosity Alma looks up the information needed to register a child as an American citizen when he or she has been born outside of the U.S. The required documentation looks difficult to forge. She wonders how the Hammonds had been able to obtain: dated ultrasounds containing the name of the mother, laboratory test results, doctor's receipts, pictures of the mother pregnant, pictures of mother and baby immediately following the birth and during the hospital stay, baby and mother's hospital identification bracelets, crib card, discharge orders, and last but not least, paid hospital bills.

Maybe it was less stringent fifteen years ago or maybe Nick with his friends in high places hadn't needed to provide so much proof.

She picks up the sheet of paper on which the lines from the ballad *"Si nos dejan"* are written. She does a quick translation into English to send to Evelyn. The handwriting on the old piece of paper is precise; simple block letters. There are no corrections or spelling errors. Was it the work of a teenager? Who knew?

If They Let Us

If they let us,
we'll love each other for life
if they let us
we'll live in a new world.

I believe that we can see
the new dawn
of a new day.

I think that you and I
can be happy still.

If they let us
we'll search for a corner close to heaven
if they let us
we'll lie in velvety clouds.

And there
together you and I
close to God
will see our dreams come true.

She isn't entirely satisfied with the translation, but then again, you needed the melody to appreciate the longing expressed in the song. But most of all, Alma wonders who or what had been stopping this young couple from realizing their dreams?

Next, she studies the official hospital birth certificate which lists La Clínica Boston as the place of birth. Alma wonders if anyone associated with the clinic has ever set foot in Boston, particularly Doctor Geraldo Bernal de la Vega, who signed the certificate. She does a Google search for La Clínica Boston, Ávila. Up pops a two-story glass building. There are also photos of the interior of the building: a modern reception area, doctors and nurses in crisp uniforms looking seriously professional. The list of services is mind boggling. You can have your nose remodeled and Botox to shed your wrinkles. Breasts can be enlarged, shrunken or reshaped, bottoms too. You can have a vaginal refreshing if that part of you is tired out. Liposuction for thighs and tummies is also available. All services are under the expert direction of Doctor Geraldo Bernal de la Vega. So, Alma reflects, the doctor who signed Evelyn's hospital certificate is still around, but no more babies, just babes. She almost relishes paying Doctor Bernal de la Vega a visit although giving herself the once over in the full-length mirror in the hall, and despite her mother's comments, she doesn't think she needs his help.

But speaking of babes, she has to admit that despite the irritation she felt at her mother's prying, her own curiosity about Linda Wilcox is now getting the better of her. How had her cousin Elena tracked down the woman? Is Elena friends with Gabriel on Facebook? Yes, of course she is. In two minutes, she's located Linda with two mutual friends listed and, somewhat shame-faced, asks to be her friend. The positive answer comes back in a few seconds. Does she have any idea who Alma is? This could be very embarrassing. Meanwhile, she sees plenty of posts by Linda: at a beach wearing a tiny bikini; at dinner in a fancy restaurant with a group of girlfriends; at some stable with her horses. In all the photos, her long red hair is fashionably cut; her finger and toe nails newly painted. She has great legs and fills out a bikini to perfection, so much for Gabriel's brief description of his ex-wife as a redhead with freckles. No photos either of her second husband. Oh, well, thinks Alma, why should I worry about an ex-wife far away in Houston?

CHAPTER 3

*A*s she now considers herself a part-time political correspondent for El Diario de Ávila, Alma decides to take the morning off. First, she'll check out the Boston Clinic and its photogenic director, Doctor Bernal de la Vega, and then see what else takes her fancy. Located near the new mall at the edge of town, Doctor Bernal's parking lot, at ten to nine, is almost full. The receptionist couldn't be more cordial. Even without an appointment, the doctor will be delighted to see her. While she waits, she leafs through the fashion magazines spread out on the coffee table in front of her. Linda Wilcox could be one of the models in any of the photos. Alma sighs looking down at her last year's jeans, white tee shirt, and light blue sweater which is starting to get little nubby bits from frequent washings. They're clean but that's the best that can be said for most of her clothes:

serviceable but neither fashionable nor sexy. Perhaps a shopping trip with her cousin, Elena, isn't such a bad idea: a new swimsuit, a few dresses, and a power jacket to put Héctor in his place? A new hair style too, why not?

Fifteen minutes later, the receptionist signals that the doctor is now ready to see her. Doctor Geri, as he insists on being called, shakes her hand warmly. He's a man of medium height, probably in his late fifties. His full head of black hair is silver gray at the temples; his mustache has flecks of gray to match. His physique shows daily workouts. His nose, well, it's an advertisement for someone's surgical skills. No wrinkles either, Alma notices; no doubt Botox has done its job. As he accompanies Alma across the large office to his desk, his practiced eye skims over her body as quickly as the flick of a lizard's tail.

"Delighted to meet you, *Señorita* Jaramillo, how can we help you?" he asks smiling broadly. There is something more spider-like than lizard-like in the good doctor, she decides. She imagines his soothing words spinning a reassuring web around his anxious patients.

"I'm afraid I'm here under false pretenses. You see I'm trying to solve a mystery, and I think you can help me, Doctor." Doctor Geri's smile freezes, and he blinks his eyes lids several times. Could it be that a few ill-advised surgeries have made him cautious? She draws a copy of Evelyn's hospital birth certificate out of her bag together with one of her own business cards.

"Evelyn Hammond?" she says, "Perhaps you remember her as a baby? She's fifteen now and looking for her birth parents. I'm lending her a hand." She passes the certificate to the doctor.

"But Evelyn is with her parents. It says so right here on the certificate. Nicolas and June Hammond are her birth parents." Alma sits silently looking at the doctor. "Will that be all?" he says, rising slightly from his chair.

"Look, Doctor, I don't want to make trouble for you although if the authorities were to find out that certain illegal practices were followed here in the past, they could close down your very profitable clinic for months while multiple investigations take place. I just want a little information then I'll be off."

"How do I know this isn't a shakedown or that the story won't get into the press?" The toothy smile is gone. He glares at her.

"No one wants to put Evelyn's U.S. citizenship in jeopardy. I'm not taking notes, and I'm not recording anything. Do you know who delivered Evelyn and her brother?"

"I did," answers the doctor now dead serious. "It was a complicated situation. I had just started this clinic, and Nick Hammond was my principal investor. That's another long story. I'd never even been to La Casa de la Esperanza. I found out later that several of the nuns were midwives; they usually delivered the babies. However, the girl began to have serious problems with the delivery. Nick panicked. He was sure that the baby or as it turned out, babies, were about to die. He brought me to the clinic."

"Were the girl's parents there during the delivery? Did you

get any idea of who she was?"

"No, I never met anyone but the girl, and the nuns, of course. She was so young, only fifteen. She spent the whole time screaming in pain. She was terrified. She'd had no prenatal care, and no instruction on what the birth would be like. It was shocking. I felt very sorry for her."

"Did she say anything at all?"

"I remember that she kept saying, *padre*. I assumed she was calling for her father. After the second baby was born, I gave her a sedative, and she passed out. I told the nuns I would check in the next day, but when I went back she was gone as was one of the babies. Afterward, Nick got me involved in registering the baby girl as his birth daughter. Against my better judgment, I went along with it."

"Why were the babies in the mother's room? It seems so cruel when she was giving them up for adoption. Sorry, also do you have any idea what the 'G' stands for on the little bracelet Evelyn was wearing? And why didn't Nick just do things legally?"

The doctor gives a short snort. The home, he says, didn't have a nursery. It was a very simple place; forget your fancy maternity hospitals. It was a charity home. Nick faked the birth certificate because Mexico requires the birth mother to wait at least six months before permanently renouncing her parental rights. For reasons of his own, he was in a big hurry to get the child to the U.S.

"You must know how pushy some people are. They believe that rules and even laws are made for other people. The 'G' on the bracelet might have stood for the first initial of the mother's surname. From the way the nuns talked I had a feeling she wasn't from Ávila, but I have no idea who she was nor do I want to know. Can you excuse me now? I have patients to see."

"Sorry, one last question. Did you ever hear rumors about something strange, maybe illegal going on at La Casa de la Esperanza? A friend of mine said the place had a, well, had a stink."

"For God's sake, woman. It was a charity clinic. Of course it stank." The doctor rises and waves Alma out of his office.

*   *   *

"I'm calling you *Señorita Metiche* from now on," Alma jokes as she gives her cousin Elena a hug at the front entrance to the mall. "But I'm so glad we can spend the afternoon together."

Elena smiles and taking Alma by the arm, starts walking her toward the Estética Beauté. "Being a busybody is what I'm really good at. And it works. Look, didn't I get you to call me?" When they enter the salon, Elena says to the receptionist, "She needs the works."

Four hours later as Alma is paying for a new swimsuit, a miniskirt, two low-cut summer dresses, some sexy underwear, and a few pairs of new shoes, Elena says, "We should do this more often, Almita. You've got a great figure and you're tall. You can wear all this weird fashionable stuff." Alma checks herself out in one of the store's mirrors. The auburn highlights and shorter more layered haircut somehow make her brown eyes seem larger; her skin tone, warmer. She squeezes Elena's hand. "I needed this. It's been fun. How about a coffee?"

"So, I told Ernesto—," begins Elena as they settle into a booth at Sanborns.

The buzzing of Alma's cell phone interrupts her. *"Flaca,"* says Gabriel sounding out of breath, "I'm on my way to the airport. I just got a call from a lawyer in Austin. He's finally located a witness I need to depose for a big case. The guy has asked for asylum in the U.S. If I don't get his statement immediately, I'm afraid he might get frightened and disappear. I'm sorry about the weekend."

"How long will you be gone?"

"Probably not more than a couple of days. I've paid for the room in San Miguel. So you go. Take Elena. I'm going to buy a U.S. cell phone when I arrive. I'll call you as soon as I can."

"It won't be the same," says Alma, "and you won't get to see my new look."

"What? I love the way you look."

"I'll send you a photo, so you can see what you're missing." Putting away her phone, she says to Elena. "You want to spend the weekend in San Miguel de Allende?"

*　　　*　　　*

As Alma walks across her parent's threshold, their *"¡Qué guapa!"* shouts can be heard, she is sure, half way across the neighborhood. Her mother says she hopes that Elena is putting up a photo on Facebook. "Your new shoes are cool," is Kurt's only comment. When the supper dishes have been cleared away, her mother comments, "Oh, I almost forgot. You need to call *Padre* Rafael before eight o'clock tonight. He needs to talk to you about that nun you want to see."

The gist of the conversation is not particularly promising. *Padre* Rafael wants to see her before she meets with Sister Fernanda. He needs to explain a few things about La Casa de la Esperanza. He has contacted the convent where Sister Fernanda is now living. As a favor to him, she has agreed to see Alma, but he wants Alma to know that the favor is really for her mother. There follows a three-minute discourse on her mother's virtues. He also expects to see Kurt in his catechism class next week. "Oh yes," the priest adds before hanging up, "Sister Fernanda, when she entered the cloister, took a vow of silence, but I'll explain all about that when I see you in the morning."

*   *   *

She has agreed to meet *Padre* Rafael the next day after morning Mass at the Chapel of San Juan Diego, their neighborhood Catholic Church. While he is changing into his "civilian" clothes, jeans and a sports shirt, Alma gazes around the chapel. She thinks about the silver merchants who several centuries ago built the Baroque-style cathedral and churches in the historic center of Ávila. Not only did they have different tastes but also far more ample budgets and, she reflects, hundreds of talented artisans working for slave wages. The current residents of her *barrio* had constructed this chapel by the sweat of their own brows. But the people's need to honor their God and saints seems to Alma no different now than it had probably been three hundred years ago.

The small chapel that her family and neighbors have

constructed from cement blocks has a single spire, which is somewhat taller than warranted with a brass bell that is somewhat smaller than needed. The outside of the church is finished with white stucco. The iron grill gates to the chapel are locked at night with a thick chain and padlock; no massive wooden doors needed for this church.

Inside, bricks have been laid to form a *Bóvada* style ceiling, at the top of which is a small skylight. The walls at the sides of the altar are painted with pastel scenes of saints ascending into the heavens accompanied by their cherub guides. At the back of the altar, God the Father, Christ, and the Holy Spirit are painted in a heaven of fluffy clouds. Statues of the Virgin Mother and La Virgen de Guadalupe stand on pedestals beside the altar, their alabaster white skin and fine features speaking of Spanish origins. The altar itself is a long, highly polished table made of white pine. The altar cloth embroidered by the local women looks to be linen. The dozen pews, purchased second-hand as funds became available, are somewhat worn. The large glass jars that have been placed on the tile floor around the altar perfume the entire space with the scent of white tuberoses.

A man in his early sixties, *Padre* Rafael is several inches shorter than Alma. His strong build speaks of his daily commute by bicycle between the several churches for which he is the sole parish priest. Warm, intelligent brown eyes soften his otherwise blunt facial features. As they sit down on an iron bench covered by blue flowers from the spreading branches of a jacaranda tree, he says, smiling, "So, Alma Jaramillo, what's Sister Fernanda ever done to you? I hear her name has come up in an investigation you're pursuing."

"As always, Father, you are absolutely right," she says smiling in return. "But it's not a story for the newspaper. It's a personal inquiry I'm making on behalf of a girl who's looking for her birth parents."

"*Ay, ay, ay*, one of those painful stories, I bet. Can you tell me any of the details?"

"Some of it is confidential but here's what I can tell you." After relating Evelyn's history without the details of her birth certificate, she says to the priest, "Neither the doctor who delivered the twins nor the girl's parents seem to have any idea of who the birth mother was. My hope is that Sister Fernanda will take pity on Evelyn and give me the name of the mother."

"The birth parents' right to privacy, Alma, doesn't that concern you?"

"Yes, of course, but my first concern is for the girl and her right to know where she comes from. The parents can always refuse to see her, but at least she'll have a name to hold on to."

The priest stretches out his legs and clasps his hands behind his head. He asks if Alma is interested in a short history of La Casa de la Esperanza. She nods her head. The founder, he says, was an extraordinary, but controversial priest. Some people couldn't stand him. Even his name shows how complicated he was. When he was ordained, he chose the name Father Francisco Javier, not after the famous Jesuit missionary, but rather after the Italian Sister Frances Xavier, Mother Cabrini, the patron saint of immigrants. *Padre*

Francisco grew up in the state of Tepetlán. His mother, he had told *Padre* Rafael, was unusually devout but also very liberal. He said his parents, who were teachers, revered Pope John XXIII. They wanted the Church to be closer to the people: that is, the Mass in Spanish, folksy hymns, altar girls, less splendor.

After studying for the priesthood at a seminary in Puebla, he traveled to rural Brazil and discovered Liberation Theology. Like many priests in Latin America, he came to believe that the Church should return to its early teachings. That it should focus on poverty, human rights, and social justice. The rest of his life was dedicated to those ideals. He worked for a couple of years in Guatemala and Honduras but came back to Ávila in the late nineteen-nineties. "That's when I had the privilege of meeting him," says *Padre* Rafael. "We weren't close friends, but I admired him. Still do."

"A colleague of mine told me he was murdered. What happened?"

The priest's shoulders slump; he sighs. *Padre* Francisco was killed ten years ago, he says, but he hasn't been forgotten. If Alma came to church more often, she would have heard how the priest's spirit lives on. Unfortunately, in the few years Francisco spent in Ávila, he had managed to make some powerful enemies. Many of those who opposed his work were members of conservative organizations like Los Militantes de Jesús or were in the gangs that preyed on immigrants.

The priest's first task in Ávila had been to build a hostel for migrants from Central America. Some of the town fathers didn't want poor transients being housed in their city, but the Bishop had supported the project. A year later, he had started La Casa de la Esperanza, which most people supported, but there were always the pious few who grumbled about abetting immorality.

"He was just thirty-five when he died," says *Padre* Rafael finishing his story.

"Did they find the person or persons who murdered him?" asks Alma.

"He was shot in the head late one evening, sitting in his car in front of the migrant center. He'd apparently just arrived from a meeting having to do with fundraising. No witnesses. Someone found him an hour or so later. The medical examiner said he'd died instantly. There were so many people at his funeral, they had to block off the streets around the Cathedral. No, no one has ever been arrested for the murder. The police pursued the case for several years but as far as I know, never came up with anything; the Church authorities, however, refuse to let the *Procuraduría* close the case."

"What happened to his projects?"

"The hostel still keeps going, but La Casa de la Esperanza closed a few months after he died. I understand the dioceses destroyed all the files. I think you might be wasting your time seeing Sister Fernanda, but you decide. You have the address of the convent."

The priest's expression now turns still more serious. "You must know the saying, Alma: '*Agua que no has de beber, déjala correr.*' Perhaps you're meddling in something best left alone. You could be opening a can of worms." He laughs when he sees Alma thrust out her chin. "Can't stop you I see, but I will reserve the right to say I told you so if there's trouble."

The priest starts to stand, but Alma takes hold of his arm. "*Padre*," she says, "this isn't a nice thing to say, perhaps, but a colleague of mine hinted that there was something amiss at La Casa de la Esperanza, maybe even something illegal going on. Did you ever hear any rumors?"

The priest sits down again and looks Alma straight in the eyes. "What exactly did this person say?"

Alma looks embarrassed. "He said that there was stink about the place. He's an old man and couldn't remember why it was but the comment bothers me."

"I don't listen much to gossip, Alma. I don't have time with four parishes under my wing. My friendship with *Padre* Francisco was superficial, but the man I knew had great integrity. He was devoted to his causes. He seemed, however, to believe that most men were as well intentioned as he was. I did hear at the time that some of his secular friends were more worldly." His eyes have a besieging look. "Don't bring him down, Alma. In this work we need our heroes."

Alma nods, and as they say good-bye she offers *Padre* Rafael a ride to wherever he's going but he hops on his bicycle. "Don't forget Kurt's catechism classes," he shouts as he rides off, "and watch your step."

*   *   *

Located on the edge of the city's historical center, the Church and convent of San José look several centuries old. The building is painted a cheerful yellow, the window trim in chalk white. Not knowing what to expect from an interview where one of the parties won't speak, Alma pushes the buzzer at the side of the ancient wooden door with some apprehension. She is met by a young woman dressed in a short cream-colored habit who introduces herself as a novice in the order of Las Hermanas de Santa Margarita. Half expecting to meet Sister Fernanda behind a screen or in a confessional, Alma is relieved to be shown into a sunny sitting room.

Sister Fernanda enters the room so silently that Alma gives a start when a figure appears in front of the sofa where she's seated. Instinctively, she rises to her feet and curtsies, which she realizes immediately is ridiculous, but the gesture comes straight from her childhood. The nun smiles broadly and beckons Alma to sit down. Gathering her brown habit around her, Sister Fernanda pulls a chair opposite Alma. The nun smells of Camay soap. The smooth skin on her face and neck, broad forehead, and bright, alert brown eyes belie her age. She must be at least sixty, Alma thinks, but she looks ageless.

"Sister," begins Alma, "I realize what a great favor it is that you've agreed to see me, and believe me I wouldn't have bothered you if I had any other way of helping this young person." Taking one of the photos of Evelyn from her purse, she presses it into the nun's hands. The reaction is immediate. The nun's shoulders jerk back; she begins to shake her head from side to side. Her eyes fill with tears. Getting to her feet she hands the photo back to Alma and turns to leave the room.

"No, please," says Alma rising also, "I've upset you; I'm so sorry. The girl in the picture is Evelyn. She's the daughter of a girl who I believe was once in your care. She was taken as a baby to California but is here now trying to find her birth parents and her brother." The nun's face is pallid; her mouth quivers. About to say "can't you tell me anything about the family," Alma realizes that of course the nun can't say anything. Instead she says, "The girl is lonely. I feel it would put her mind at ease if only she were to find her brother."

The nun walks to a table in the middle of the room where a number of pamphlets are spread out. She carefully selects a brochure, hands it to Alma, and pointing a crooked finger to a painting of Saint Michael on the cover of the pamphlet, swiftly leaves the room.

"Whatever can that mean?" mutters Alma as she lets herself out of the convent. She tucks the leaflet into her purse and, somewhat discouraged, heads home to pack for her trip to San Miguel de Allende.

*   *   *

When Alma picks up Elena that afternoon, her cousin practically dances out of her front gate. Throwing her suitcase in the trunk, she says, laughing, "Quick, get a move on before they know I'm gone."

"Does Ernesto not want you to go away for the weekend?"

"He's thrilled, as are the boys. They can eat junk food all weekend and watch twenty-four hours of soccer if they can find games on cable. The boys will stay up 'til midnight, have stomach aches and be exhausted on Sunday night."

"So why are you sneaking out?"

"Because I heard my five-year-old shouting that he couldn't find his soccer shorts which reminded my seven-year-old that he couldn't find his tennis shoes and the three-year-old that just on principle he needs his mom. Come on, get going!"

Alma laughs just as she had all through high school when she and Elena had shared a room. Elena is the daughter of Alfonso and Julieta, the relatives who had lent Alma's father the money for the traffickers who had guided her family across the U.S. border. She and her parents had lived for four years with Elena's family before moving to Los Feliz where Jesús, her father, had become the super in an apartment building. When it came time for Elena to go to high school, Julieta had sent her across town to go to Immaculate Heart High School with Alma.

The girls had become as close as sisters. Leaving high school, Alma had gotten a scholarship to study journalism at UCLA, and Elena had chosen to become a massage therapist studying for a year at Kaplan College. Then, on a trip to Ávila to visit relatives, she had met and later married Ernesto, becoming, as she advertised in her brochures, Ávila's only licensed therapeutic masseuse.

Driving on the new highway to San Miguel de Allende, both women relax. "You're the first to know, *Flaca,*" says Elena grinning, "Ernesto and I are getting married."

"What?" says Alma glancing at her cousin obviously confused. "You are married."

"We were married in a civil ceremony by a judge, but we weren't married by a priest in the Church. For our mothers you know that's what counts. Ernesto and I are not really married in our parents' eyes."

"Yeah, you're right. My mom is always saying. 'Thank God you didn't marry Kenny in the Church.'"

"So now that my parents are moving to Tijuana for good, my dad can come here and walk me down the aisle. My brothers and their families can visit because they've all got passports."

"What do Ernesto and the kids think about it?"

"They love the idea because it will mean a bunch of new clothes and a big party with the whole family. You know my husband, how he loves parties. My only problem is my dress. What to wear? I don't want a traditional wedding dress. That seems sort of silly. So the challenge this weekend is for us to find Elena's perfect wedding outfit. And the perfect one for you too. Because you're going to be *la dama de honor*."

Alma laughs. "That's me, always the bride's maid, never the bride."

"Get off it. You know you could marry Gabriel any time you want. He's crazy about you."

Alma is silent for a minute. Could she marry Gabriel anytime she wanted? If so, why didn't either one of them ever talk about marriage? Was it because she'd had her heart broken by Kenny, Kurt's father? She had fallen in love in Los Angeles with an American teenager's dream, a blond rocker, only to be slammed back to earth when he'd left her for his band's female manager. But that was years ago, surely she was ready to move on.

Then too, there were Gabriel's wounds. His brief marriage

to a young, affluent Texan had been a disaster, he'd said. He'd happily walked away from it. Alma had to smile. Both of them had dipped into unfamiliar worlds for partners and had promptly gotten a reality check.

"Can I use your phone?" says Elena breaking into Alma's thoughts. "I forgot to remind Ernesto about Guillermo's guitar lesson." As she searches through Alma's purse for the phone, she pulls out Sister Fernanda's leaflet. "What's this? Are you changing parishes?"

As the miles roll along, Alma relates Evelyn's story and her attempts to find any information about the girl's birth parents. "Didn't you say that that the nun had been the head of the home for single moms?" asks Elena.

"Yes."

"Well, then she's a smart, responsible person who got fed up with talking. And didn't you say that Doctor Geri suggested that the girl probably wasn't from Ávila? So, Sister Fernanda is telling you something with this brochure. Saint Michael is the patron saint of San Miguel de Allende, Alma. Duh."

"Elena, do you want my job? You're on the short side, but I'm sure you could whip Héctor into shape. But now I'll have to do a little work over the weekend. Hey, look up on Google if there are any Catholic girl schools in San Miguel. I can start there."

"Before I do that I have a little surprise for you. Do you remember Danny Sullivan?

"The *guapísimo* captain of our high-school football team? He's not easily forgotten. Why?"

"We're having dinner with him tomorrow night," says Elena, giving Alma a sly look.

"What, where, how did that happen?"

"Danny Sullivan and I are friends on Facebook. When he got transferred to Mexico, he contacted me. He's the acting manager of the Lakewood Resort in San Miguel. I've been dying to go there forever." Elena's small, pretty face lights up with delight. "So where are we staying?"

"Gabriel booked an Airbnb which isn't too far from the Jardín. So, it should be close to downtown. You can shop 'til you drop."

"And that's what I'll be doing while you do your Good Samaritan thing."

CHAPTER 4

Casa Belinda, their Airbnb, is hidden behind a tall stone wall on a narrow cobblestone street. Maggie Carpenter Torres, the current owner, greets them with a friendly kiss on the cheek. She's a large woman, obviously over sixty, but how much so is difficult to tell. The colorful *huipil* that she wears cascades over her abundant bosom. Her thin too black hair is pulled back in a tight chignon. Thick makeup covers the tiny broken veins in her red cheeks. Her voice has the huskiness of a longtime smoker; her Spanish, the perfection of a lifelong resident.

"Oh," Maggie says after reaching for Alma's and Elena's small bags, "but where's Gabriel? He seemed so nice on the phone; I was looking forward to meeting him in person."

"Business trip," says Alma, shrugging her shoulders.

"In that case you'll have to come back. He sounded like a handsome devil," the older woman says, ending her sentence with the most raucous laugh Alma has ever heard. It starts with a chuckle in the back of her throat and then turns into great roaring peals of high-pitched hooting.

Casa Belinda is a warren of small rooms built around a central patio. The smell of gardenias greets the women as they walk toward their room. There are pink azaleas and camellia bushes, also in the patio; a twisted frangipani tree stands at the center of the space. Their room at the end of the courtyard is large; the bathroom modern; the furnishings, if not the latest fashion, comfortable. "Come have a glass of wine with me after you settle in. I have some soup and good bread if you're hungry."

When Elena and Alma are seated around the kitchen table, a glass of wine in hand, Maggie asks, "What have you single ladies got planned for the weekend?"

Elena immediately engages their hostess in a conversation about the best shopping in San Miguel. She wants to see the markets, of course, but also, she'd like to visit gift shops and boutiques. When Maggie turns to Alma, she says she has a little work to do. In fact, does Maggie know anything about high schools in San Miguel?

"That's the first time a tourist has asked me that question." But as it turns out Maggie is probably the best person to answer the question, having grown up in San Miguel. Alma shows the older woman a picture of Evelyn. "She looks sort of familiar, but no, I can't say who she is. You say she might be from a good family and attended a Catholic girl's school? Then she went to El Colegio del Reino de Dios. It was girls only until ten years ago, when they started accepting boys. It's on the road to Celaya. I think the principal is a priest, but most of the teachers aren't nuns anymore. You might find someone there on a Saturday."

*　　　*　　　*

At nine-thirty the next morning Alma finds herself on the road to Celaya listening carefully to the instructions from Waze on how to find El Colegio del Reino de Dios. It will probably be a wild-goose chase, but she can spare a few hours. She'd left Elena eager to hunt down the best markets and boutiques for them to explore tomorrow. She begins to think how she can gain access to the school. On the Internet site, the school's facilities appear to be if not exactly luxurious, then very well appointed. There are photos of basketball courts, soccer fields, a library, a chapel, and of course classrooms with new desks and computers. When she stops at the front gate of the school, she flashes her press credential at the guard on duty. She tells him she's researching a story on the best schools in the area.

"Nobody's here today except the coach of the soccer team and the librarian."

"I'd love to talk to the librarian," says Alma. "I can come back on Monday to talk to more staff."

An obliging sort, she thinks, as the man gives her a visitor's pass and tells her how to get to the library. She waits a moment at the open door of the library, watching a young blonde intently logging new books into a computer. The large book-lined room with study tables certainly beats anything she has seen in Ávila, including the British Academy where her son goes to school.

The young woman looks up from the computer screen.

"Buenos días," says Alma flashing her friendliest smile.

The girl's face turns bright red. "No Spanish, sorry, not yet!"

"Don't worry," says Alma, "my English is pretty good. I guess you've just arrived in Mexico."

The girl looks relieved. "Yes, I've only been here a week. My university in Boston has a program with this school. I'm majoring in Library Science, so they put me to work right away." She extends her hand toward Alma. "I'm Rosemary. Are you a teacher or a parent? How can I help you?"

The story Alma has dreamed up is, she thinks, plausible, if not brilliant. A couple of weeks ago, she tells Rosemary, her car broke down late at night near the school. A couple about her own age had mercifully stopped to help. While the man had gone for a mechanic, she and the woman had chatted. The woman had mentioned that she had attended El Colegio del Reino de Dios. Alma in her nervousness about her car problem had forgotten to ask the couple's name. Now she wants to thank them properly, send them flowers or something. Would it be possible to look at the school's yearbooks? Rosemary, happy to help out, leads her to the section of the library that houses what looks like twenty yearbooks.

The search goes quickly as the classes twelve, thirteen years ago, when Evelyn's mother would have graduated ,were small, twenty girls at most. She places Evelyn's photo on the table in front of her. She reviews the three or four most likely graduating classes, but finds no one who even vaguely resembles the girl. In one of the older year books, she decides to leaf through the lower grades. The photo of a girl in Freshman year makes her stop and stare. The picture is fuzzy but perhaps, yes, it could be, she says to herself. A small girl in the last row isn't identical to Evelyn, but she has those large almond-shaped eyes, dark hair, and the same pale, translucent skin. At the bottom of the photo it says her name is María Teresa. That's useful, but Alma needs a last name.

She pulls out her cell phone and takes several photos of the class, the girl, and the other children's names. Flipping through the year book, she finds the names of all twelve members of the Freshman class. The only María Teresa has the last name Gómez y Velasco Aragón. Alma stares at the name for a few seconds and then remembering the "G" on the little bracelet, exclaims in a loud voice, *híjole*. The librarian turns around and puts a finger to her lips.

She's almost sure now that she's found Evelyn's mother. In her excitement she does a little dance. She stares at the name again. Gómez y Velasco Aragón, sounds very upper-crust, she thinks; there's certain to be a history behind those names. She also makes a note of the name of the girl standing next to María Teresa in the Freshman class photo. She's Lucero Sánchez León; three years later Lucero is in the graduating class but in that photo, there's no María Teresa.

On the way out of the building, Alma spots a poster for a school production of Shakespeare's *Romeo and Juliet*. She wonders what the students at this *colegio* will take away from the cautionary tale of young love gone terribly wrong. At the bottom of the poster is a quote from the play:

These violent delights have violent ends
And in their triumph die, like fire and powder,
Which, as they kiss, consume.

She studies the quote and wonders if María Teresa had read the play before meeting the father of the twins. Had her teacher explained as Alma's had done that Shakespeare used the word "violent" to mean "impetuous"? Impetuous delights: few fifteen-year-olds, herself included, could resist them. Sadly, the end of whatever triumph the girl had felt had been violent; she had apparently lost both her children.

Alma's thoughts turn to Gabriel. Was there any powder in their relationship to be set alight? Could something or someone blow it up? No, she doesn't think so; they're older, wiser; any impulsive behavior a thing of the past.

As she moves toward the exit, she sees a plaque with the names of the principal donors for the twenty-year-old building. The Gómez y Velasco family is number three on the list. She has no doubt that Maggie will know all about them.

*   *   *

As Alma parks in front of Casa Belinda, Elena practically pulls her out of the car. "We have to hurry, or we'll miss it."

"Miss what?" At that moment Maggie steps out of the front door. She has in her arms her *Niño Jesús* dressed in a white crocheted cap with white satin ribbons, a white hand-embroidered silk gown covers the doll's life-sized body; two tiny white leather slippers grace his feet. He is lying on a white blanket in a small carved cradle. "Of course," says Alma. "It's El Día de la Candelaria. How could we have forgotten?"

"Maggie has asked us to be the *madrinas* for her *Niño*. I said we'd love to be His godmothers," says Elena. As they walk toward the Parroquia de San Miguel Arcángel, they are joined by dozens of other women and men, each carrying their *Niño Jesús* to the Cathedral. Brass bands and fireworks soon become part of the procession.

"Since you two weren't raised in Mexico," says Maggie, "you probably don't have a clue about the origin of Mexico's Candlemas Day."

"I know that it celebrates the end of the Virgin Mary's forty days of rest after the birth of Jesus. In the Jewish tradition, it was the day the child was taken to the temple," says Elena.

"The name comes from the candles that are lit in Christ's honor on this day celebrating the light He brought to the world," adds Alma.

"That's only half the story," says Maggie. She explains that February second also has pre-Hispanic roots. It's the day in which villagers bring corn to be blessed as it's the last day of the new cycle for sowing seeds. This explains, of course, why *tamales* and *atole*, both made from corn, are served after Mass. It is also an important day in the Aztec calendar when certain gods were celebrated. Oh, thinks Alma, how fascinating, old gods hiding within new rituals. As they stand in line after Mass waiting for the priest to bless Maggie's *Niño Jesús,* a woman about Maggie's age appears next to her with two beautifully dressed dolls.

After Mass and the blessing of each Baby Jesus, as the three women walk back along the narrow streets toward the

Casa Belinda, the same woman passes them carrying her twin dolls. The dolls bring Alma's thoughts back to María Teresa.

"Do you know a family here in San Miguel named Gómez y Velasco?" she asks Maggie.

"You're taking an interest now in our local gentry. Yes, of course, everyone knows them or knew them. The wife died many years ago, and the patriarch, *Don* Hernán, I understand, suffered a stroke six or seven years ago."

"But wasn't there a daughter?"

"I know there's a son but a daughter, I can't remember. Perhaps. I used to see them at Mass in the old days. My family has been here for three generations, but families like the Gómez y Velascos go back practically to the time of Hernán Cortés. They keep to themselves and don't mix much except with people who have the same pedigree. They go to the same schools, belong to the same clubs, go into business together, and then marry one another. We ordinary mortals only get to peek into their lives if someone gets married or dies. They're not like the society people with newer money who came after the Revolution. Those people love to be photographed in gossip magazines. *Don* Hernán, they tell me, is also *muy mocho*."

After persuading Elena to continue her shopping, Alma easily locates the Gómez y Velasco home a few blocks from the town center. The shutters on the ground floor of the large stone house are closed, the heavy curtains on the second and third floors shut out all light. The house, in fact, looks deserted. The large wooden front door is formidable; no modern interphone here but high up on the archway there is a tiny painted arrow which points to a small buzzer. When Alma pushes the button, she hears a faint sound ringing in some distant part of the house. A dog barks. She waits two minutes in the busy street before ringing again. A curtain in a second-floor window stirs slightly. She waits five minutes and is just about to walk away when a tiny window covered by an iron grill opens in the door and a brown eye appears. The area around the eye is cross hatched with wrinkles. "*Dígame,*" says a deep voice. She can't tell if it's a man or a woman.

Alma holds Evelyn's picture up to the window. "I'm trying to locate this girl," she says. The sound which comes from behind the door is more a gasp than a scream. The small door slams shut. Alma rings the bell again, but the door stays shut. She looks at her phone, it's three-thirty. Down the block and across the street, she spots a small café. She can afford to wait an hour. Perhaps someone in the house will have to run an errand. She settles into a chair near the window and proceeds to see what she can find on Google about the Gómez y Velasco family. *Genealogies of New Spain* looks promising. The heading of the article says *Short Studies of Prominent Mexican Families:*

> *The Gómez y Velasco Family*
>   *According to genealogical records,* * *the first member of this illustrious family to reach Mexico, via a short sojourn in Cuba, was Pedro Gómez y Velasco Sáenz. A hidalgo (son of a noble but untitled family), Don Pedro was barely twenty-two when in 1689 he set foot in the city of Veracruz. He proceeded almost immediately to the state of Guanajuato, hoping to find his*

fortune in silver mining. Thanks to his foresight, he was able to buy the rights to a mine, La Coruña, which secured the family's fortune for the next 200 years. In August of 1803 the eminent German explorer and naturalist, Alexander von Humboldt, visited the mine, pronouncing it one of the finest in the region.

Having secured his future, Don Pedro married María Catalina López de Peralta Lara, the only child of the owner of one of the principle haciendas near the town of San Miguel de Allende. A portrait of Doña María painted by Juan Rodríguez Juárez now hangs in Mexico's National Art Museum.

One of the descendants of this fruitful union was General Manuel Gómez y Velasco who fought valiantly alongside of his commander, Agustín de Iturbide, during the Mexican War of Independence. General Gómez y Velasco was aide-de-camp to General Iturbide during the formulation of the Plan de Iguala. General Manuel's oldest son, Hernán, accompanied General Antonio López de Santa Anna to Texas where their forces were unfortunately defeated in 1836 by Sam Houston's ragtag army.

Disillusioned by the anti-Church policies of the liberal government, which included Benito Juárez, Hernán joined with conservative forces in 1857. Almost immediately, a civil war began, which lasted three years. The conservative forces were repelled but rejoiced a few years later with the arrival of the French Army and the Emperor Maximilian. The family quickly moved to Mexico City and were incorporated into the life of the royal court. Don Hernán had hoped that his loyalty not only to Emperor Maximilian but also to the Catholic

Church might induce the Vatican to grant him the title of Conde, but his untimely death from typhoid fever in 1868 ended that dream. His widow and most of his children moved back to San Miguel de Allende.

One of Don Hernán's granddaughters, the beautiful María Eugenia, married a nephew of Porfirio Díaz in 1902. The family prospered briefly during those years, but that alliance proved costly when the Mexican Revolution broke out in 1910. Most of the family's haciendas were subsequently confiscated.

The Cristero Movement of the late 1920s and 30s saw the family once again come to the defense of the Catholic Church, both as members of the clergy and as defenders of the Faith. The present patriarch of the family, Don Hernán Gómez y Velasco Santiago, is the grandson of one the brave leaders of that movement.

*The genealogy of this family comes from an oral history compiled in 2012 by Hernán Gómez y Velasco Santiago.

That's quite a family history, thinks Alma. Should she be treading more cautiously? She's barging into a world where people live deliberately behind high walls, people with wealth and influence who know how to protect their privacy.

She barely has time to digest that thought and to pay for her coffee when the front door of the Gómez y Velasco home opens. She gathers up her notes and closes her computer just as a small figure disappears around the corner. She is sure it's the same woman she saw in the morning with the two dolls. With a gray and black silk *rebozo* wrapped around her head and shoulders, she is easy to follow. She wears a dark blue sweater and a gray skirt that hangs down past her knees. Wooly black stockings cover her legs. The comfortable Oxford shoes she wears look new.

In a few short blocks, they are at the Cathedral. The woman enters and goes up the right-hand aisle where Alma can see a painting of La Virgen de Guadalupe and an almost life-sized statue of Juan Diego kneeling at the foot of the painting. The woman lights a candle and kneels to pray. Alma waits in one of pews at the back of the church. How should she approach the woman? Showing Evelyn's photograph had been a mistake. As the woman leaves the church, Alma steps in front of her. "Please just one minute of your time." The woman bows her head and tries to step around Alma. "María Teresa's child is looking for her mother. She's desperate to find her brother."

The woman steps back and look up into Alma's eyes. "Who are you?"

"I'm a friend of Evelyn, María Teresa's daughter, the child who was taken to the United States. She's fifteen now. Can you help her?"

The woman sighs. "The *patrón* needs his meal. I could meet you tomorrow in the Parque Benito Juárez. Do you know where the children's playground is? I'll see you there after Mass." With that, she skirts around Alma and walks briskly away.

*   *   *

Elena's purchases are scattered around the room: football shirts for Ernesto and the boys, new wine glasses and hand-painted serving plates for the house. "What about you? Did you find the perfect dress?" asks Alma.

"I didn't dare buy anything because I needed you to tell me that the neckline is too low, or the miniskirt is too mini, or that the seams are a mess. It's no fun without you. But speaking of fun, here's the e-mail from Danny about tonight's plans." The message with its barebones bullet points looks like a memo to the staff: meet-up reception area 6 p.m., tour of the facilities 6:15, drinks roof terrace 7:00, dinner dining room 8:00, disco 9:30.

"Super organized guy! Was he a marine by any chance?" asks Alma.

"I don't think so," says Elena. "But he hasn't exactly gone native either."

We do look good, thinks Alma as she and Elena enter the foyer of the Lakewood Resort at ten after six. Alma has chosen one of her new flowered prints, a dress with a neckline just low enough and a skirt just high enough to show off her curves and long legs. Elena, dressed in a sleeveless white sheath and red stiletto heels, draws approving glances from the doormen. But then our host doesn't look too bad either, reflects Alma as she spots Danny Sullivan across the hall. His dark gray suit, light blue dress shirt, and silk tie fit his six-foot-two well-toned body to a tee. "Does weights every day," she whispers to Elena. The face is more mature but just as handsome as his yearbook photo. He glances at the large gold watch on his wrist before greeting them.

"*Muchachas*," Danny says planting a kiss on their upturned cheeks. Colgate smile too, thinks Alma, look at those white teeth. They chat easily as Danny leads them through the beautifully landscaped central patio of the hotel. They view the large heated pool with its individual canvas cabanas for the sun-weary and then the grass tennis courts nearby. Inside the hotel, they are greeted graciously by the reservation staff. A four-foot-tall multi-colored flower arrangement fills the center of the reception area.

The concierge asks the women if he can arrange a house tour for them tomorrow. They beg other commitments. Taken by a soundless elevator to the third floor, they tour the meeting rooms and finally the grand ballroom.

"Sorry, they haven't had a chance to clean up after the event we had here last night," says Dan. "It was the most spectacular *quinceaños* party I've ever seen. The family even got the Bishop to say Mass in our chapel. There were over two hundred and fifty people for dinner, a live orchestra, and a DJ. The eight *chamberlanes* came from some military academy in Maryland. They had on their full cadet gear. The dancing went on until after three a.m."

As they are leaving the ballroom, Alma notices yesterday's calendar board near the elevator. "The *quinceañera* was Verónica Gómez y Velasco?" she asks turning to Danny.

"Yeah, they're an important family here. They booked the date when we inaugurated the hotel. She's an only child, her mother told me; so no expense was spared. She's a nice kid despite the big bucks her dad must have. *Sencilla*, as you say here."

"I know this is weird," says Alma, "but do you know where they live?"

Dan lifts one eyebrow. "Are you doing a story on San

Miguel's high society? At least, I hope that's your excuse."

"Something like that. Please?"

"I delivered the contract for the event myself. They live around the corner from that boutique hotel, La Casa de Sierra Nevada. It's almost the first house in the *privada*. I think it's number four."

Putting his arms around the shoulders of the two women, Danny suggests that they continue to chat over cocktails. Arriving at the roof-garden bar, Elena blurts out, "I don't need a drink; I'm already dizzy from the view." San Miguel with a hundred points of light stands spread out beneath them. The floodlit *Parroquia* is a picture-postcard of neo-Gothic splendor. The lighted cupolas and spires of the other churches guide the eye around the town. Seating them at the best table, their host suggests that they try a Margarita made with *limas*, cucumber, and *mezcal*.

With the drinks arrives Chef Miguel, eager to present his plates of *antojitos*. "*Señor* Sullivan said that I'd better come up with some spectacular hors d'oeuvres because his guests were two very particular local gourmets. I think he also wanted to impress two beautiful ladies," the chef says bowing toward Alma and Elena.

Picking up one plate at a time, Miguel explains his creations: "First we have miniature casseroles of shrimp with fried *ancho* chili and just a touch of garlic; next, tiny *sopes* prepared with refried black beans, goat cheese and cream, and topped with a sauce of green chili peppers and *tomatillos*. We also made small *quesadillas* using blue corn tortillas filled with *flor de calabaza* or *huitlacoche*, accompanied by a spicy red sauce;

finally, you must try the *tostaditas* with fresh tuna and crispy fried leeks, and topped with a *chipotle* mayonnaise. The guacamole is for the boss because he isn't quite a gourmet yet, but I'm working on it." Chef Miguel adds quickly that except for the tuna and shrimp, all the ingredients have been grown locally.

"I hope this is dinner," says Elena, "because there is enough food here for an army of real gourmets."

As they chat, or rather as the two women listen, Dan relates his experiences in the hotel business. Alma's attention begins to wander. She imagines bringing Gabriel up to the bar, and what fun she would have ordering the fancy hors d'oeuvres. He would put his arm around her shoulders and ask if she was cold—.

"Alma, report back to earth. Dan has asked you twice if it's too chilly up here," says Elena.

"I'm sorry. I guess I got absorbed in the view," says Alma. She can see Elena raise a skeptical eyebrow.

"Wait a minute," says Dan, "here comes my favorite innovation to our cocktail hour. It's the man with the canary who picks out fortunes."

"Oh, good, *un pajarito de la suerte,*" says Elena. "I love this tradition."

The old man stops in front of their table. He unstraps the bird cage from his back and opens the door of the cage. A yellow canary steps onto the perch. "You go first, Elena," says Alma.

The man presents the bird with a tray divided into small sections; each section contains a number of cards. Elena closes her eyes and crosses her fingers. The bird hesitates for a moment and then with its beak, selects one of the cards. Silent for a few seconds, Elena bursts into laughter. "It says, *Más vale feo y bueno que guapo y perverso.* Ernesto is going to love that."

Dan looks at her blankly. "Ugly and good are better than handsome and wicked," she explains.

Alma sits still as the canary selects her fortune. "*Ojos que no ven, corazón que no siente,*" she reads and then tosses the paper aside. She glances at Dan. "It means 'out of sight, out of mind.' These fortunes are just silly superstition," she says rising from her chair. "Who's ready for dinner?"

"Let's do it," says Dan checking his Rolex again. When they enter the wood-paneled formal dining room, lit by crystal chandeliers, it seems almost full. The prosperous gray-haired patrons look to be mainly tourists. Cream-colored damask tablecloths and napkins cover the tables. The dinnerware is a special edition of Talavera blue and white pottery; the silverware, heavy and ornate. The conversation is less one-sided than it had been earlier in the evening. Elena takes control. "So, Danny, how did you see us in high school?" she asks.

"Well, you were kind of a mother hen; you were always trying to push the couch surfers onto bicycles, the fatsos onto veggie diets and the geeks onto the dance floor. I don't know how successful you were. Alma was trying to save the world, but she was hot, so she even had the football players giving their lunch money to her charities. I see that hasn't changed either."

Alma's face turns bright red. Elena laughs.

"And I understand you both got high marks as kissers."

"Slander," both women call out at once. "Who were your sources?" asks Alma.

"Like a good reporter, I never reveal my informants," says Dan. "How about a little dancing? I need to work off that dinner," he adds, rising from his chair.

In the disco, Dan orders another Scotch and water for himself. "Rum and Cokes for you two?" asks their host. "Just Cokes," is the answer. They dance for an hour, sometimes all three take to the floor, sometimes Dan asks one or the other to dance. At times the women dance alone. Alma begins to relax. It is turning out to be a fun evening after all, she thinks, glancing at her cousin doing a solo turn; the best dancer on the floor.

"I don't see a ring," says Dan taking her left hand and staring at her fourth finger.

Alma smiles. "But there is a guy and," she pauses for a minute, "a commitment."

"Come on," says Dan pulling her to her feet. "One last dance."

It's a slow number. She follows his lead but makes sure not to press her body too close to his. He is an excellent dancer. Relaxed, he moves effortlessly to the rhythm of the music.

He whispers in her ear. "I want to see you again soon. Can you give me a tour of Ávila next weekend?"

"Sure," she says laughing. "Gabriel and I would be delighted."

*   *   *

"I had a good time," says Alma kicking off her shoes.

"He's a bit full of himself, but he's a gentleman. I'm glad he sent us home in a taxi. My feet are killing me," answers Elena sinking down on her bed. "Hey, he seems pretty taken with the new sexy Alma. Are you going to see him again?"

"He asked me to give him a tour of Ávila, and I said Gabriel and I would be happy to oblige."

Alma, now in her pajamas, settles into her bed. "Are you happy, Elena?" she asks her cousin out of the blue.

"Alma, you ask the strangest questions at the strangest times. I guess it's the reporter in you."

Elena thinks for a few minutes before answering. When they were growing up in L.A., she says, she had never imagined living in Mexico. She wanted to be a ballerina and dance around the world. She definitely didn't want her mother's life: five kids and a back-breaking, boring job. When she was fourteen, she realized that she'd never be a dancer. She was too short, too hippy, and not talented enough. She also found out that her dad had to work an extra job to pay for the lessons. She'd got interested in yoga and in massage therapy, and thought she might see the world with those skills. Her first trip had been to Spain. Then a friend wanted to tour the colonial cities in central Mexico, and she went along to translate.

She had fallen in love with the country. It was so different from what she had expected. She became interested in traditional dance and in the medicine practiced by the *curanderos*. On her second trip her mother had insisted that she visit relatives in Ávila; the first day, she had met Ernesto.

"Okay, and the rest is history," says Alma. "But you haven't answered the question. Are you happy?"

"I'm getting there," says Elena.

Ernesto, she continues, is a great father. He adores his boys. He's ambitious and wants the same things she does: a nice house, education for the boys, maybe a trip to Cancún someday. His income is dicey. He's a salesman, so sometimes he's rolling in money, but mostly they just get by. Elena likes his family. They're a lot like her own. Besides being a great dancer, which is what really won her heart, Ernesto is a gentleman. Elena likes men with good manners who treat women with respect. He doesn't fool around behind her back either. At least she doesn't think so. No, he isn't perfect, but she isn't herself such a *"perita en dulce."*

"You're still evading the question," says Alma. Her voice filled with frustration. "You've only talked about Ernesto. What about your job, your ambitions?"

"Yes, okay, okay," says Elena picking up the Bible on the nightstand. "I, Elena, swear before my best friend and cousin, Alma, that I love being a masseuse. I love my husband and kids. I AM HAPPY, if a little overworked and underpaid." Elena begins to laugh adding; "Now it's your turn. Are you happy?"

"Just a minute. But you gave up your dream of traveling around the world. Doesn't that bother you?"

"I've got new dreams now, Alma. Haven't yours changed?"

Elena knows, Alma says, that all through high school and

college she had talked of nothing else but getting a job on the L.A. Times. But the big recession and her father's deportation had forced her back to Mexico. After a few miserable years, she had secured a permanent job at El Diario de Ávila and freelance assignments for a Mexico City daily and the Dallas Morning News, and now she was also contributing to an Internet news site. She has, at the moment, a few problems at El Diario, but in general her work life has lived up to her old dream. With Gabriel she is hoping she'll get the rest of the dream. They've been together for a year, and she can't imagine her life without him. He's funny, sexy, handsome, and can cook. They share the same interests. He's great with her son, too.

"Yes, yes," she says, "I'm ninety-eight percent happy. But there's only one thing, Elena. Sometimes Gabriel goes to a place where I can't reach him. It's like he's cruising around in some distant galaxy or living a different life in a different place. Like right now. Why hasn't he called me or sent me his new phone number?"

"*Ay, Flaca*, who knows, but there must be a good reason," Elena says yawning. "Sweet dreams."

CHAPTER 5

Sitting on a bench in one corner of the Parque Benito Juárez, Alma hopes that the woman with the black and gray shawl, whose name she still doesn't know, had meant that they meet up after the ten o'clock Mass. Neither she nor Elena had slept well. Too much food the previous evening. At breakfast, Maggie had been curious about the Lakewood Resort and its manager. The women had tried to remember every detail of the evening. When the large bouquet of flowers arrived from the Lakewood florist, their hostess read the card out loud. "Enjoyed the evening. See you soon, Dan."

"Those are for Alma," Elena had said, laughing.

"Was Dan your boyfriend in high school?" Maggie had asked.

"Oh my God, no! I was geeky. He hung around with the cheerleaders. Right, Elena?"

"Maybe he's another one whose dreams have changed,"

answered Elena.

Now surveying the park, Alma can see that it's jumping with vendors, dog walkers and couples with strollers. While she waits, she checks her messages: still nothing from Gabriel.

Before she can read her e-mails, she sees the small woman wrapped in the same gray and black shawl enter the park. Alma stands up; the woman takes her by the arm, saying in a low voice, "Not here." When they reach a more deserted spot in the park, she points Alma to a shady bench.

"I've only got a few minutes. *Don* Hernán's son and his family come every Sunday for lunch; I'm the cook."

"Doesn't the family have other help?"

"There's only me and my brother, Chucho. He's the chauffeur, runs errands, and fixes things." The woman lowers her voice and looks around her. "Chucho told me that *Don* Hernán isn't so well-off anymore. That's why he doesn't hire more help."

"I understand that he had a stroke some years ago," says Alma. "But could you tell me your name? I promise I won't tell anyone that I talked to you."

Her name is María de los Ángeles Rivera. She's worked for the Gómez y Velasco family for thirty-two years. She'd been hired to be María Teresa's *nana*. She had expected to work for the girl's mother, Leonor, but the woman had died giving birth to Tere. So Ángeles had been much more than a nursemaid; she'd practically raised the girl. Chucho had treated Tere like a daughter since *Don* Hernán, her own father, seemed mostly to forget the little girl existed.

What had happened when Tere was fifteen had torn the family apart. It was Tere's sister-in-law, Sonia, who had discovered Tere was pregnant. *Don* Hernán had ranted and raved. To hear him talk, Tere was heading for the fires of hell. The distinguished lineage of the Gómez y Velasco family went back generations, centuries; a child born out of wedlock was an insult to that history. "He's a proud man. He couldn't cope with what happened," says Ángeles moving her prayer book from one hand to the other.

"What is María Teresa like?" asks Alma.

The woman's face softens. "I always told Tere that she was the real Snow White. She has the same white, almost transparent skin; the same black hair and red lips. She's small-boned; she seems fragile when you first see her. The girl in the picture resembles her but my Tere is even prettier."

"Does María Teresa still live here or in the area?" asks Alma.

Ángeles looks all around again, double-checking that there are no prying eyes or ears. "When she turned eighteen, she inherited all of the Aragón money. Her mother left almost everything to Tere. She moved away as soon as she could after that. She came back once but—." The woman stops talking and starts to move her prayer book once more from hand to hand. "Please, I must get going. *Don* Hernán can't walk; he's in a wheelchair. He gets upset if I'm gone too long." The woman sits thinking for a moment and then takes an envelope out of her small purse. Alma notices the stamps. They look exotic.

"No one that I'm acquainted with knows where Tere is. I

received this postcard almost nine years ago." The woman draws the card out of the envelope and hands it to Alma. The front of the card shows an elaborate Hindu temple. The letters say, Parvati Hill Temple, Pune, India. On the back of the card is written in small, precise letters, the message, **"I'm at peace. Don't worry. Tere."** The card, which is addressed to both Ángeles and Chucho, has no date or return address.

Ángeles stands up. "It's a long story. Perhaps the *Señora* Sonia will tell you more. Could you let me have that photo of the girl? I never knew the babies." The woman tucks the picture into the envelope with the postcard.

"Just one more question, Ángeles, why did Tere have the babies at La Casa de la Esperanza? Surely her family could have found a better place?"

Ángeles's face is a mask. Her eyes are lowered. She wraps her shawl more tightly around her shoulders. "I've forgotten most of what happened that year. Chucho and me, we only talk about the good times when Tere was just a little girl."

What now? thinks Alma. She's found the name of Evelyn's mother, but she's nowhere nearer locating Evelyn's brother. Walking along the edge of the park, she spots the *privada* where María Teresa's brother lives. What does she have to lose? A door slammed in her face? A ferocious dog? And it's Sunday, so probably no maid will be running interference.

The pretty face of an adolescent girl peeks out of the small window in the weather-beaten wooden door. "Hi," says Alma pleasantly. "I'm looking for María Teresa Gómez y Velasco. I think she might be your aunt."

"An aunt? My aunts live in Italy, and they're Bianchis, not Gómez y Velascos. Maybe you should speak to my mother."

When the small door opens again, an anxious woman in her early forties says, "Who are you? What do you want?"

Alma states her name and says she represents Evelyn Hammond who's seeking her birth mother, María Teresa Gómez y Velasco. She holds up Evelyn's photo. The woman, who Alma assumes is Tere's sister-in-law, Sonia, shakes her head as if to clear the cobwebs. "You've got the wrong people," she says as she reaches her hand up to close the small window.

"I'm also a reporter for El Diario de Ávila. Neither Evelyn's parents nor I want this story to appear in the news, but to avoid that, the girl needs information about her birth family." Alma knows she shouldn't have said that. Ricardo would be furious if he found out she was using the name of the newspaper to further her own private investigation. And Héctor? How he'd love to find out something that might compromise her.

The woman gives Alma a hard look. "You need to speak with my husband. He's having breakfast with a business associate. Come back in thirty minutes."

When Alma rings the bell of the home a little later, a man in his mid-forties answers. He closes the door behind him and leads Alma across the street. There is something of Evelyn in an expression that from time to time flits across his face. His skin is pale and his hair, black. It is so black that she wonders if he colors it.

"Is it the girl and her family who want to blackmail us or is it you who's dreamed up the shakedown?" he says turning to Alma. His mouth is drawn in a thin line of irritation; his eyes dart up and down the street. He doesn't want nosey neighbors to see us, Alma assumes.

"Neither one, *Señor,*" answers Alma. "Evelyn's parents are wealthy, and they are as much against this search as you probably are. It's the girl who wants to find her birth parents and her brother."

"So it's you who's raking up a lot of old scandal that's better left buried. I should have guessed that the press would be involved. Looking for cheap shots to sell your rag, are you?"

Alma smiles. "I used my profession to get your attention. I'm not interested, nor is my newspaper, in publishing this story. The girl lives with her mother. The parents are divorced. She has no siblings. Is it so wrong to want to know who your birth parents are? To want to meet your brother? Wasn't compassion one of Christ's teachings?"

Raúl smiles but his eyes are cold. He stares at Alma. "Christ's teachings? Give me a break. You are one ballsy bitch. Stay away from us and tell that girl to stay away too. For me and my family, María Teresa Gómez y Velasco is dead. She has no children. End of story." When he approaches the door of his house, it's opened by the teenager who had first greeted Alma. Before closing the door, the girl gives Alma a long, appraising look.

*   *   *

"*¿Qué te pasa, Flaca?*" says Elena as they near the toll road that connects San Miguel de Allende to Ávila.

"Sorry to be off in la-la land, but I was thinking about the weekend. What did you make of it?"

"First things first. I got my dress for the wedding, which was priority number one. I loved meeting Maggie. I want to be exactly like her when I'm sixty plus. The *antojitos* at the Lakewood Resort were to die for. We found that great little restaurant for lunch today. So, I'm happy. How about you?"

"Your dress for the wedding is perfect, and I loved Maggie too. I'm happy I found the name of Evelyn's birth mother, but I've no idea what to do next since the family seems so hostile. I think I'll try and find María Teresa's schoolmate, Lucero, if she still lives in the area. The food at the Lakewood Resort was heavenly, but I wish I'd eaten less of it. Dan seems like a nice enough guy but—"

"He's not your type, is he?

"Really Elena, right now I'm just thinking about Gabriel. I'm worried that I haven't heard from him. He said he'd contact me as soon as he arrived in Austin. That was three days ago. Suppose that guy he was deposing was some violent *narco?*"

"You worry too much. Doesn't he have a sister who lives in Austin? He's spending the weekend with her, and she took him shopping. He'll probably be home before we are."

*   *   *

It is only ten-fifteen Monday morning, but the newspaper office already smells of tobacco and burnt coffee. Neither Ricardo nor Héctor seem to be around. *Menos mal,* thinks Alma as she begins to scan the articles her editor has left for editing.

"Can I get you some coffee?" says Ana Flores an hour or so later. The young woman is one of the interns who circle through the office periodically.

"Sure," says Alma, glad to have a break from a job she finds tedious.

When Ana returns, she perches on the edge of Alma's desk and sighs. "Is there ever going to be something in my professional life except baptisms and weddings?"

Alma laughs. "You're bored, are you?"

"Yes, I'm bored and frankly, lonely. No one seems to want my help."

Alma knows all too well that newcomers aren't particularly welcome in the newsroom of El Diario de Ávila. There are as many women reporters as men, but most of the journalists have worked together for years and view interns as little more than potential scabs. Alma is tolerated because her stories sell papers. Ana has, in addition to little journalistic experience, a personality that seems to ruffle everyone's feathers. She is perpetually cheerful, optimistic and helpful, while most of the older reporters are by nature or experience pessimistic, grumpy, or plain disinterested. The office mood can be cheerful and upbeat, but too often lately, journalists all over the state have vanished or been gunned down. After that kind of news, the chirping of a naive young staffer is met with stony silence.

Ana brings in home-baked cookies, takes up collections for orphans on Children's Day, and gives flowers on Secretary's Day. Her greatest sin, however, is that she's a tie straightener and a label tucker-inner. "Got your Dior on today," she will say brightly, folding the offending label into a colleague's collar. Irma, *"La Gordis,"* the overweight chain-smoking woman who manages the obituary ads, waves Ana away as if she were a disease-bearing mosquito. The tall, skinny sports writer who was ironically nicknamed years ago *"El Chaparro,"* routinely flees to the men's room if the girl is in the vicinity. Ricardo, their editor, retreats to his office if he sees her coming, lowering the blinds and locking the door. "I hate people who pick lint off the sleeves of my suits," he whispered to Alma one day.

If her clothes were more provocative or if she knew how to flirt, the men, at least, might be more forgiving. But no, she appears day in and day out in a pink or baby blue long-sleeved blouse with a big bow at the neck. It is tucked loosely into the elastic waistband of a pair of baggy slacks. The rumor is that she and a maiden aunt share an apartment and a wardrobe.

But Alma finds the woman, despite her quirks, intelligent, hard-working, and occasionally, even witty. She needs help digging into Evelyn's history. Why not take a chance on Ana? At least she wouldn't be gossiping about Alma's moonlighting.

"Could I hire you to do some research for me in your free time? I need someone to check the archives to see if there is any mention of a woman named María Teresa Gómez y Velasco Aragón; her brother, Raúl, same last name; her father, Hernán Gómez y Velasco Santiago and any other assorted family members who might turn up. Also, she had a classmate named Lucero Sánchez León. All these people reside or resided in San Miguel de Allende. I found something of their family history on *Genealogies of New Spain*, which I'll send you. Oh, also a niece of María Teresa's, Verónica, just had a spectacular *quinceaños* party in San Miguel. But," Alma pauses for minute eying the girl, "you need to keep this under your hat because it's a private matter, and I'd prefer that our co-workers are, well, kept out of the loop."

Ana's face lights up. "Oh good, a mystery. This'll be fun and, of course, everything I find out is top secret."

Alma continues to whittle away the pile of papers on her desk. When her office phone rings, she grabs it. Ricardo Núñez's assistant says, "Some woman on the line for you, Alma. Won't give her name."

"This is Sonia Bianchi, Raúl Gómez y Velasco's wife," the woman says in a low voice when Alma picks up. "I'm in Ávila; I've got a few hours free. I'd like to speak with you. Could you meet me at Sanborns in the mall?"

"I can be there in twenty minutes," says Alma grabbing her purse and heading for the door.

Sonia is in a booth at the back of the nearly deserted restaurant. She stands up as Alma nears the table. Attractive, thinks Alma. She's of medium height with a tennis player's slim build. Her brown hair is streaked with blond highlights; her fingernails painted a discrete light rose. She has the look of someone who just stepped out of a beauty salon. Sonia's light knit dress and designer sandals seem more Italian than local. There's a bottle of imported mineral water in front of her.

"Thank you for coming so promptly. We were very rude

to you yesterday, but you caught us off guard. My husband is normally not that kind of man. He loves his sister but the situation—."

"I apologize also," says Alma. "You're not the first people to have been shocked by that photograph. It's as if I'd introduced them to a ghost."

To be fair, Sonia begins, perhaps Evelyn does deserve a little information about her birth mother, but she begs Alma not to tell anyone from whom she got the information. *Don* Hernán would fly into a rage if he knew Sonia had talked to a reporter. María Teresa has not been seen or heard from for ten years. Raúl assumes that she's still alive because her lawyer says money is routinely withdrawn from her Swiss bank account, but he won't say or perhaps doesn't know where she is.

"When I first saw Tere, she was a young teenager." Sonia had met her husband, Raúl, twenty years ago at an international meeting of Catholic youth in Rome. They had married three years later in Italy, and Sonia had returned with him to San Miguel de Allende. Although Raúl had been fourteen when Tere was born, he had adored her. He had taken a great interest in her education. When Sonia had arrived in Mexico, she had wanted to be Tere's best friend; she had tried to get close to her, but the girl seemed self-absorbed, haughty. Sonia lowers her voice, "*Don* Hernán spoiled her rotten, you know."

Alma nods her head as Sonia takes a sip of her mineral water. She wants the woman to keep talking, but a small yellow light goes on her head. What is the message that this woman wants to send? Her account of Tere's childhood certainly doesn't jibe with what her nanny, Ángeles, had said.

"So," continues Sonia, smiling now, "I hope you didn't take Raúl seriously yesterday. We'd love to meet Evelyn. I don't think her mother would ever care to know the girl, but we'd adore being her Mexican family. Is she here in Ávila?"

The yellow light becomes a flashing red beam. What is this woman playing at? Why does she suddenly want to befriend Evelyn? "I'm so sorry. I didn't mean to get your hopes up. Evelyn's parents are against the hunt for her brother. My investigation is preliminary. Someday Evelyn hopes to meet you."

The woman looks annoyed and starts to get to her feet. "Just a minute more," says Alma. "Evelyn's main concern is her twin brother. Can you tell me anything about the summer Tere became pregnant?"

Sonia and Raúl had been away in Italy when Tere had turned fifteen. *Don* Hernán had sent the girl for the summer to a ranch outside of Ávila. She loved horses, and he believed that the couple who ran the property was trustworthy. She had sent several letters to Sonia during those two months telling her about the volunteer work she was doing at a nearby migrants' hostel. She seemed happier than she'd ever been.

Sonia had found out Tere was pregnant late in November when she returned to San Miguel. Ironically, she herself had been pregnant. Tere was four months along by then. Abortion was illegal in Mexico, and anyway, *Don* Hernán's religious beliefs wouldn't permit it.

Who had fathered the twins? Tere had never taken Sonia into her confidence, and the couple who ran the ranch was as surprised as anyone when they heard about the pregnancy. Yes, there had been a group of kids Tere had hung out with, but the couple had never seen a boyfriend. Had she been raped? The girl had gazed off into space when the family tried to question her. Sonia didn't know why Tere had given birth at La Casa de la Esperanza. *Don* Hernán had tried to send her out of the country, but Tere wouldn't go. She had remained at home until well into her seventh month.

Six weeks after the birth, Tere had been packed off to a convent in Spain where she stayed until the day she turned eighteen. Then all hell broke loose.

"How's that?" asks Alma.

"Tere became a rich woman."

Leonor Aragón, Tere's mother, had been the heir to a large fortune. No one doubted that the Gómez y Velasco name was older, but Leonor Aragón's father had been one of the richest men in Mexico. He had investments in land, agribusiness, mines, hotels. Leonor had inherited most of it. Unbeknownst to her husband when Leonor had learned she was carrying a daughter, she had written a new will. Raúl had inherited some land and stock, but everything else went to María Teresa. Not a penny to *Don* Hernán. At eighteen, a trust allowed Tere to draw a six-figure yearly income. At twenty-five, her income tripled. "We were thrilled for her, of course, but not surprisingly, she shut us out of her life."

With her inheritance, at eighteen Tere had made a beeline for San Francisco. She'd quickly been taken up by an unsavory group of hangers-on. Her father and brother had visited once and been appalled. Two years later, Tere had returned to San Miguel for a visit. She had stayed a few nights in a hotel before contacting the family. When she and her father had finally met, at first all seemed to go well. They were, Sonia said, like *"uña y carne,"* almost inseparable. But that hadn't lasted long.

Within a few weeks, at a family Sunday lunch, *Don* Hernán had suddenly turned on his daughter, asking her if she was repentant; if she had asked God to forgive her sins.

Tere had answered. "First you need to ask God's forgiveness for your sins, Papá."

Don Hernán had called her a *puta*, an infidel. "I think he said she was even worse than Jezebel." He had also said something that shocked everyone at the table. He had said that Tere was a harlot like her mother.

Tere had called him an unnatural parent. No one had touched their food. María Teresa had slammed the front door of her father's house and disappeared. Raúl had written to her about *Don* Hernán's stroke a few years later. No answer. He had asked if he could be of help with her investments. No answer. Yes, Ángeles had shown her the postcard from India. Perhaps María Teresa was still there. Perhaps she'd found peace. Sonia shrugs her shoulders.

The two women sit silently for a minute. "You've no idea what happened to Evelyn's brother?" asks Alma.

"I always thought that my sister-in-law was involved with someone who worked at the ranch. She was so naive about..." the woman thinks for a minute. Alma expects that she'll say "sex," but no, she says, "social class." Then she continues. "For instance, she begged us to let Ángeles and her brother sit with us at Sunday dinner. Can you imagine?"

"You must have an e-mail address for Tere. Could you give it to me?"

Sonia writes the address out for her but adds, "She won't answer. She never does."

As she gets up to leave, the woman turns to Alma. "Please tell Evelyn that she would be most welcome in our home. She has a cousin, after all, the same age."

Alma nods her head but thinks, why has this couple had such a change of heart in the space of less than twenty-four hours? She dials Sandra's phone. "I've got some news," she tells her friend. "I'll be around to talk in an hour or so, but for reasons I'll explain, it would be better if Evelyn didn't answer the phone to anyone but me or go out unaccompanied."

Alma next checks her phone, but there's still no message from Gabriel. She dials his office. Maru, his assistant, answers. Trying to sound casual, Alma asks if Maru knows on what flight Gabriel is returning.

"He's staying in Austin until Saturday or Sunday," the woman says.

"Is he having trouble with the deposition?" asks Alma.

"No, that got done last Friday. He's taking a week or so of vacation. Things are quiet right now in the office."

"Do you have Rosalia's number? I guess he's staying with her."

"No, he's at a Holiday Inn near the U. Do you want his

95

U.S. cell?"

Alma copies the number into her phone. She sits for a quarter of an hour in the empty restaurant staring off into space.

CHAPTER 6

*A*lma loses track of time as she wanders aimlessly around the mall. Every time she tries to rehash what Sonia has told her about María Teresa's teenage years, Gabriel pops back into her mind. Why hasn't he called her? Why is he staying on in Austin?

When her phone rings, she quickly fishes it out of her purse. She tries to hide her disappointment when she sees it's a local number.

"Evelyn, what's up?"

"Sandra said you were coming by in an hour. It's almost three o'clock. Where are you? Why can't I answer the phone or go out by myself?"

"Sorry, I'll be there in half an hour."

Evelyn and Sandra are waiting for her in the family room. "Sandra says you found out something in San Miguel de Allende," the girl's excitement is palpable.

"Yes," Alma thinks about measuring her words. She

doesn't want to get the girl's hopes up. After all, she is far from finding her brother, but she can't lose her trust either. She smiles, "I found the name of your birth mother. I managed to contact her old nanny, and her brother and sister-in-law. Your birth mother is María Teresa Gómez y Velasco Aragón. She's from an old distinguished family that dates back to the seventeenth century. They also appear to be a religious family, very involved with the Catholic Church. Apparently, your mother is a wealthy woman. She seems to have had a lonely childhood. Her mother died in childbirth, and her father was older. Some people told me he paid little attention to Tere, someone else said that he spoiled her. Both could be true. Your uncle and aunt seem to have very different attitudes to meeting you. But more important, the people I spoke to all told me that your mother is totally estranged from her family. No one has seen her the last ten years. The only contact has been a postcard she sent her old nanny from India many years ago."

"Is she still alive?"

"She regularly withdraws money from a Swiss account, so I assume so."

"My grandfather?"

"Yes, he's alive but he's ill. He had a stroke several years ago."

"Why can't I get in touch with my uncle and aunt?"

There seems to be so much conflict in the family, Alma tells Evelyn, that she's afraid the girl will be walking into a hornet's nest. Better to wait until Alma has more information about who these people really are. The reason she wants

Evelyn to keep a low profile is that she is concerned about the strange Mariachi e-mails. Someone intends for Evelyn to open old wounds in the Gómez y Velasco family, to stir up scandal. Or perhaps Evelyn was enticed to Mexico for some other reason. The girl needs to be careful and patient.

"Being careful and patient never gets you anywhere," says the girl. "You sound like my father, always talking about the bad things that could happen. I don't understand why you want to make things so complicated. My aunt and uncle could be great people."

Alma raises an eyebrow and turns to Sandra to back her up. "Evelyn, Alma knows the country and this situation better than any of us. I think we'd better listen to her." The girl shrugs her shoulders. She's not convinced, Alma sees.

Before leaving she asks if Evelyn needs anything: books or a game. The girl smiles, says she's playing big sister to Max and Kurt. She's enjoying the role. They follow her around like puppies. They bring her little gifts. They're adorable, make her laugh.

*   *   *

"I'm starving," are the first words out of her son's mouth when he jumps into her car a little after seven p.m. Alma has totally forgotten she had promised Kurt at breakfast that they would go out to his favorite restaurant for supper.

"Pizza?" she says as she starts the car.

"No, *tacos al pastor*, they're quicker and the restaurant is right around the corner from Gabriel's house."

Alma keeps her voice steady, even indifferent. Gabriel is away, she explains, probably for a week or so. Will he be back for the big game on Saturday? asks her son. She doesn't think so, but his grandfather will take him to the game. Will Gabriel be able to see the game on television or hear it on the radio? "I know him, Mom. He wouldn't miss the big game," Kurt informs his silent mother.

Sighing happily after he has finished off four *tacos al pastor* and several lemonades, Kurt leans back in his chair. He agrees to taste her *ensalada de nopal* although he finds cactus paddles slimy and tasteless, even when mixed in a salad.

"How was school today?" asks his mother. He shrugs his shoulders. Then he sits up in his chair and wide-eyed, asks her if she is really going to find Evelyn's lost brother. Alma groans, who'd told him about the investigation? Why of course, it was Evelyn. "She's so beautiful, Mom. I've never met a girl like her."

"I can't talk about the investigation, Kurt. It's confidential." She stares at her son. Isn't nine a little young to be thinking about girls? What happened to Lego and Action Man?

As they leave the restaurant, Kurt asks if they are going to check Gabriel's apartment because his grandfather always checks their house when Kurt and his mother are away.

"It's in a secure building, so I'm sure it's fine. Besides there aren't break-ins here like in our neighborhood; plus, I can't remember where I put the keys."

"They're in the basket next to the back door," he says. Not much gets past her son, she thinks, as she ruffles his shaggy brown hair.

*   *   *

Despite her distracted state of mind, Alma has promised herself that before the evening is over, she will draft an e-mail to María Teresa. But what to say, or more to the point how to say it? If she has any hope of getting an answer, she can't moralize or use legalistic language or play too much on the woman's heart strings. A straightforward approach is probably best, but she definitely needs to pique the woman's interest.

Did Tere, after all this time, have any attachment to the twins? Or for that matter had she ever had any attachment? They might be for her nothing more than an emotional scar that had marred her young life. Can you bond with children who had been yanked away from you after less than twenty-four hours? But those nine months in the womb surely had to count for something, didn't they?

She writes the e-mail several times before she's finally satisfied.

Dear María Teresa: I am writing on behalf on your daughter, Evelyn Hammond. Evelyn arrived in Ávila a few days ago. The purpose of her visit is to locate her brother. She does not have any siblings in her adoptive family, so she is very anxious to find her twin. I talked with Ángeles and with your brother, Raúl. Everyone agrees that you are the only person who can help us locate the boy.

In trying to locate you, I have seen how difficult it is for everyone who knows you to relive that painful time fifteen years ago. I can only imagine in the smallest way what a shock this e-mail must be for you, but can you see your way to helping Evelyn? It would mean so much to her. Any information you give us will be handled with total discretion.

Alma Jaramillo

Alma taps the send button at the bottom of the e-mail. She feels like the mythical sailor on a deserted island casting out to sea the bottle with the note that could save his life. He knows that there's only a million in one chance someone will find it. The odds of an answer from Tere, she thinks, are about the same.

"*Flaca*," says Elena when Alma answers her phone a little before ten-thirty that evening. "Have you gotten hold of Gabriel?"

"I don't know what to think. Maru in his office said he finished the deposition on Friday but was staying on in Austin for a vacation. Why hasn't he called me?"

There's a long pause on the other end of the line. "Alma, I hate telling you this but if I don't, you'll hate me even more. Go on line. There's a post from his ex, Linda. Call me back."

Alma sits looking at her computer for a good fifteen minutes before logging onto Facebook. Most of her being doesn't want to know what Linda has posted. She wants to hear Gabriel's laugh when he calls her later. She wants to hear that Rosalia and her family have absorbed him for the last few days. That he's working at the University of Texas library on some obscure point of extradition law. That his new phone isn't working properly. That he will be home in a few days. That he loves her and is missing her terribly.

When she sees the post, tears run down her cheeks. It is happening all over again, she thinks panicking, just as it had happened with Kenny. She's letting Gabriel get away just as she had let Kurt's father slip away. She reads the post for a second time.

Ran into my first and only real love on Saturday.
He's back in my life and this time it's for good.
Gabriel is such a takeover guy. It's wonderful.

There's a stupid emoji with hearts for eyes after the post. In the photograph, Linda's beautiful face glows with happiness.

*　　　*　　　*

"Are you okay?" asks Ana when Alma walks into the office Tuesday morning.

"I think I'm coming down with a *gripa*," Alma answers, realizing that the sunglasses and makeup aren't really covering up her bloodshot eyes, red nose, and blotchy skin. "I'll be better in a few days," she lies.

"Did you get my e-mail?" says Ana, moving on from Alma's hangdog appearance.

"But how did you ever find Lucero Sánchez's address? That's amazing work. Thank you!"

"I found an article on the social page about her wedding five years ago here in Ávila. It said that she'd studied Interior Design somewhere in New York City. So I started asking around, and Paulina on the business desk said she'd just opened a shop in Santa Teresa."

The traffic is light that morning. When Alma arrives in Santa Teresa at ten minutes to eleven, Lucero Sánchez's shop is still closed. She gazes for a few minutes at the square in front of the church, reliving the night more than a year ago when the then governor, Humberto García, was gunned down. The awfulness of that night makes her feel nauseous. It also makes her remember that that week was the beginning of her love affair with Gabriel Ruiz. She had asked him then and had been reassured that his marriage to Linda Wilcox was long over. His ex-wife had seemed no more than distant memory, a difficult but transitory episode in his past life. This last year she and Gabriel had been so happy. Had she misjudged his attachment to Linda? Had he? Is Linda one of those women who has to have a man in her life to lean on? She seems to fall in and out of love in a nanosecond.

Her thoughts are interrupted by a copper-haired woman about her own age who appears in front of Casa Sánchez: Interiores de Prestigio. The woman turns as Alma steps out of her car.

"Well, finally, I thought I'd have to actually go the newspaper to get you over here," she says. "Come in, come in. Let me put some coffee on. Why didn't you let me know you were coming this morning? I don't see a photographer, but he can come another day, of course."

Before Alma can speak, the woman opens the shop door and marches off toward the back of the store. Returning a minute later she resumes speaking.

"I'm glad you decided that my new store was newsworthy. You aren't going to bill me for the story, I hope. I know newspapers need to make money, but I had no idea that all the so-called local news except of course for crimes and political stuff had to be paid for. Shame on you people. Sorry,

I'm, of course, Lucero Sánchez and you must be Paulina or her assistant."

Before Alma can clarify the situation, the woman turns and walks again to the back of the store. She returns with a tray on which she's placed mugs of coffee, sugar, and a plate of cookies. "I have a client coming at eleven-thirty, but she can wait. This interview about the shop is just too important."

Finally, after Lucero ushers her to a chair and sets a cup in front of her, Alma gets a chance to speak. "I'm terribly sorry, but I'm not here about your shop."

"But it says PRESS on that sign stuck in the windshield of your car, and I've been calling the newspaper for weeks."

"I'm a reporter but I don't deal with business news. If you like I can put in a good word for you with Paulina. I do know that the paper does charge a fee for printing most social and business news. It doesn't seem very ethical, does it?"

"Why are you here then?" the woman's face brightens. "I know," she says laughing now, "you're redecorating your home!"

Alma frowns. "Sorry again. I'm here because I'm trying to locate María Teresa Gómez y Velasco. You were schoolmates many years ago, and I thought perhaps you might know where she is."

Lucero's hand goes up to her mouth. "Oh, my God, Tere! I haven't thought about her in years. Why are you looking for her? Is she in trouble?"

Keep it vague, Alma tells herself. "A relative wants to locate her and has asked me to help. She's not in trouble with the law or anything like that."

"Is it her clueless father who's looking for her? Or her brother? As I remember, they both looked down their noses at everyone. Tere Gómez! I had totally forgotten her, and we were best friends back then. We were inseparable." Lucero crosses her middle and index fingers and holds them up. "We were like that," she says.

"Why do you say *Don* Hernán is clueless?"

"Every summer from the time we were eight until we were fourteen, he took Tere and me to a fancy beach resort. I mean really high-end places, hotels my family could never have afforded. We would go for a week or ten days. We went to Los Cabos in Baja California one year, Puerto Vallarta another, then Huatulco and Zihuatanejo a couple of times. *Don* Hernán was trying his best, but he had no idea how to talk to kids and less so to girls. I remember dinner was a particular agony. We had to dress up and explain in detail what we'd done that day. But both of us loved the ocean so those dinners were a small price to pay. I guess he was trying to be a good dad. He was generous, but so uptight."

"When was the last time you saw Tere?"

Lucero sits back in her chair and takes a long sip of her coffee. Alma admires her lime green fingernails and the way her linen sheath fits her slim body perfectly. The bronze eye shadow and red-brown lipstick she has applied go well with her copper hair. *Why can't I get myself together like that?* thinks Alma. She raises her hand to fluff up her now rather disheveled new haircut.

"It must have been at the end of November of our

sophomore year at El Colegio del Reino de Dios," begins the woman.

Tere had been away for the whole summer at a ranch somewhere outside of Ávila. In fact, she'd had her *quinceaños* party at the ranch. It had been an unusual party to say the least. When Tere returned to classes in September she was different, very quiet, distracted. She didn't want to hang out after school. Then, poof, she disappeared. She'd left school one day to the next. Lucero had gone to her house, but Ángeles, the *nana*, wouldn't say where she was. A year later, someone had told Lucero that Tere was in Spain in a convent.

"I was very hurt," Lucero says. "I suspected she had problems, but why didn't she confide in me?" The woman's eyes cloud over and the corners of her mouth droop.

"Why was her fifteenth birthday party so unusual?" asks Alma.

"*Ay, ay, ay*, well, let me tell you," says Lucero, refilling their coffee cups.

Girls at the school that she and Tere had attended were from conservative Catholic families. Baptisms, First Communions, weddings and *quinceaños* celebrations had almost the same format that they'd had for generations. The music and dresses might change with fashion, but tradition was preserved in everything else. Tere didn't have a mother or even an aunt to plan the party. *Don* Hernán had given his daughter a large check and counted on the fact that she and the couple who ran the ranch would have the sense to plan a traditional day of celebration with the good taste for which the Gómez y Velasco family was famous.

Lucero begins to laugh. "Instead he got the party from hell."

The event was scheduled for a Saturday toward the end of July. *Don* Hernán had invited two hundred people or so from San Miguel, Ávila, and the surrounding area. Tere had invited the girls from her school and their parents.

"It was a very top-drawer crowd," Lucero says, "*la crema y nata* of our provincial society."

The first thing that should have alerted her father to trouble ahead was Tere's party dress. It had obviously been bought at the market in Ávila. It was bright blue satin and had layers of tulle and puffy sleeves.

"She looked like the Disney version of Snow White. What's more she'd fixed her hair in the fussy way that village girls sometimes do."

At that point, her father had just looked confused. Next came the Mass which was held in the ranch's dusty corral. The sun was brutal. Sweat began to roll down the faces and necks of the guests. Their designer clothes began to wilt. But it was the priest and his sermon that infuriated her father. For two months, Tere had been volunteering at a migrant hostel not far from the ranch. Its controversial founder, Father Frances Xavier, was the priest she had asked to officiate at her Mass.

"You mean *Padre* Francisco? The priest who was murdered?" asks Alma.

"Yes, that's the one."

His sermon was a rant against sanctimonious churchgoers

who hold the Church's rituals above the needs of the poor and unfortunate. Tere had sat in the front row of the ceremony with her six *chambelanes*. They were young boys from the migrant center dressed in blue tee shirts that matched Tere's dress.

But it had been the lunch which was the final straw for *Don* Hernán. It was served under a rather battered tent which was open on all sides. The food, as the crowd entered, stood ready on a long buffet table. No effort had been made to present the lunch with any kind of style: no flowers or decoration of any kind. The iron pots in which the food had been cooked had simply been plunked on the table. The plates and utensils were of thin plastic.

"Mole and rice soon began to drip down people's chins or spill onto their laps," says Lucero, now laughing so hard that she interrupts her story. "However, the plentiful supply of tequila and beer soon made people forget their now ruined party clothes."

Just as a giant layer cake decorated with blue confectionery roses was being brought into the tent, the thunder and lightning began. Lucero had been sitting near the head table where Tere, *Don* Hernán, *Padre* Francisco, and the six little boys were sitting. *Don* Hernán had not eaten a thing or spoken a word during the meal. *Padre* Francisco and Tere were the ones who had gone from table to table greeting the guests and thanking them for the presents they'd brought.

"All gifts and most of my father's check for the party are going to *Padre* Francisco's shelter for the migrants," Tere had confided to the bewildered guests.

Before Tere could cut the cake, a mariachi band dressed in elegant black *charro* outfits had entered the tent. They struck up the song "Guadalajara" and almost to the second, the downpour began. Waterfalls of rain soon began to cascade off the roof of the tent splashing the guests near the sides of the venue. Streams of muddy water poured over people's shoes. With the ensuing confusion, the little *chambelanes* began to cry.

"There was a mass exit from the tent and toward the cars as the musicians began playing "*Solamente una vez*." It was the perfect song, as at that point, most people were hoping that they'd never be invited to a Gómez y Velasco party again. However, the afternoon didn't end there because the cars were parked in a field that had turned into a sea of mud.

"I never heard my father use that sort of language before or after Tere's *fiesta*. He struggled for an hour trying to get our SUV out of the field," says Lucero swallowing the last dregs of her coffee.

Both women are silent for a moment. Alma speaks first. "What was Tere like as a teenager?"

"We were both boy crazy. We used to get Chucho to drive us around San Miguel, and when we spotted an attractive guy, we would blow him a kiss. It was silly, innocent kid stuff."

"Did Tere have a boyfriend that summer at the ranch?"

When Lucero and her parents had arrived for Tere's *quinceaños* party, the two girls had only had a few minutes alone. Tere had told her with great excitement that she was in love. It was the real thing, not kid stuff anymore, she'd said. The guy was older and crazy about her. She couldn't tell

Lucero his name because it was a big secret. Next year his life was going to change completely, and the two of them were going to get married. She said that they were going to dedicate their lives to the poor. When she came into her inheritance, they were going to build shelters for migrants and start schools for indigenous children.

"Even as a kid I thought it sounded like a pipe dream."

"Do you have any photographs of Tere from that time? And do you remember where the ranch was?" asks Alma.

"I just scanned all my old photos and put them online. I have some of the party. I'll send them to you. But the ranch? No, I didn't pay attention to where we were going. It was called after a tree or a plant is all I can remember."

Alma asks Lucero if she had any idea where Tere might be living. The woman thinks for a minute and then shakes her head. "Tere was a homebody. Somehow I don't think she's living on the other side of the world but who knows."

"I met Tere's brother Raúl and his wife a few days ago. Sonia said Raúl and Tere were close, that he adored his sister. You were at the house a lot. Is that true?"

"Raúl and Tere close? Where'd she get that idea? He was away at school some of the time but when he was home, she'd spend all the time she could at my house. He teased her unmercifully. It was mean teasing; more like tormenting. When no one was home, he'd lock her in the dark basement. He made fun of her in front of people, called her a *patita fea*. I hated him."

"Thank you for your help and your discretion, Lucero. I wish I could tell you more but it's not my story to tell."

"San Miguel de Allende is a small place. We all guessed what was going on with Tere. She got herself in trouble. She didn't have a mom, and it wasn't Ángeles, who brought her up, who was going to tell her the facts of life, or that clueless father. If you find her, tell her I'd love to be in touch again."

*   *   *

When at two o'clock Alma returns to the newspaper office, she finds a small pile of articles and ads from several newspapers on her desk. There are four or five articles about the organization Los Militantes de Jesús, in which Hernán Gómez y Velasco is mentioned both in his role as one of the officers of the organization and for his fundraising work. Who are Los Militantes de Jesús? she writes down in her notebook.

There are also twenty-five *esquelas* from March 1987. These are quarter, half, and even some full-page ads paid for by different family members, friends, businesses, and organizations lamenting the untimely death of Leonor Aragón de Gómez y Velasco. There are ten *esquelas*, five years later, marking the anniversary of her death, then one ten years later. Leonor had been buried at the Panteón San Juan de Dios in San Miguel. Should she check out the cemetery on her next visit to San Miguel? Maybe.

"More to come," says Ana, approaching her desk with a few more pages of paper.

"Since you are so efficient, can I also include a search for info on Father Frances Xavier or *Padre* Francisco as most everyone called him? He was a priest who ran a migrant hostel here. He was shot ten years ago."

Ana, whose good works had begun at an early age, says that she knows exactly where the migrant hostel founded by *Padre* Francisco is because she'd delivered blankets, water, and used clothing there as a teenager. "The members of my church admired him too," says Ana.

Alma looks at the pile of articles still to be edited on her desk and says, "How would you like, Ana, to delve a little deeper into the history of the mysterious woman I'm trying to track down?"

It takes Ana a little less than five minutes to get her things and meet Alma at her car. "María Teresa Gomez y Velasco, whom I'm searching for," explains Alma as she drives off, "spent a summer at a horse ranch named after a tree or a plant. The ranch should be quite close to the hostel for migrants because she went there often on her own."

The hostel, it turns out, is on the far side of the airport not far from the railway tracks that head north. Beyond the railway tracks are ranches and small farms.

"Look," says Ana after they have driven aimlessly around for a half hour, "how about some lunch? Do you fancy some *tacos de barbacoa?*"

The restaurant is full. "Barbacoa from the Foot of the Oven" is the slogan over the front door. Waiters crisscross the large space with plates of succulent mutton. Baskets of fresh handmade tortillas and spicy red sauce accompany the patters.

"*Refrescos o cerveza,*" asks the harried waitress.

"Ice cold Cokes" answer the women in unison.

"Are you sure you are all right?" Ana asks Alma looking at

her practically untouched food when she herself has made short work of her three large *tacos*.

"It's just a flu." says Alma, checking the messages on her phone for the second time since they'd sat down to lunch.

Before leaving the restaurant, Alma asks the manager if he knows of any ranches in the neighborhood named after a tree or a plant. The man looks intently out the window, and then snaps his fingers. Yes, he remembers now. There is a place called Rancho Los Encinos about a half a mile from the railway tracks. "The owner likes his *cheves*," he says. He folds under the three middle fingers of his right hand and then raises his thumb toward his mouth. The women laugh. "Fond of his beer, is he?" asks Ana.

As they drive off from the restaurant, Ana says, "My church forbids us to drink alcohol or to smoke; so I always wondered what beer tasted like."

Alma turns toward the girl, "You're not a Catholic? I don't think I ever met anyone in Mexico who wasn't a Catholic."

"We're Evangélicos. There aren't too many of us here in Ávila."

"Has that ever been hard for you or your family? I heard that Protestants were getting a lot of flak a couple of years ago, even being forced out of their homes."

"I think that's more in the southern part of the country. In Ávila people just look on us as peculiar. It was my grandfather who converted. As a kid it didn't bother me being different because the community is very close-knit, but I hated going around the neighborhood with my grandmother, trying to convert people. Not that people weren't nice. They'd listen to us for hours and then go off to Mass." Ana laughs. "Our only problem now is with the guy who owns the corner store in our neighborhood. He says that we're ruining his business because we don't buy beer, cigarettes, or junk food."

Alma smiles. "My mom would love you. She has her own private crusade against cigarettes and junk food." As the entrance to the ranch is just ahead, the women fall silent, but the picture Alma has had of Ana has shifted a bit.

Oak trees line the entrance to the ranch. The gate is open. As Alma's Jetta bumps its way up the rutted driveway, a man leading a horse walks toward them. What is most noticeable about him is his large black cowboy hat. It looks as if it might swallow his head whole. When he gets closer, she immediately notices the red bulbous nose, which has been broken more than once, and the purple, almost black circles under his eyes. A long mustache droops down the sides of his mouth. When Alma rolls down the window, the odor of stale beer drifts into the car.

"If you're looking to board a horse or for riding lessons, we don't do that anymore," says the man through the open window of the car. No preface of a *"buenas tardes"* or even an *"hola."* His sour breath makes Alma want to cover her nose.

"Oh no, we aren't looking for lessons, just a little information. I'm trying to trace a girl who I think stayed here for a summer many years ago. María Teresa Gómez y Velasco, do you remember the name?"

The man, despite his beaten-up face, isn't that old, maybe in his mid-fifties. He doesn't answer Alma's question immediately. Finally, he says, "If it's her crazy father who's looking for her then you can leave now."

"It's a relative that's trying to find her, but no one connected to her father. I was hoping you or your wife might be able to tell me about the boyfriend she had that summer."

The man snorts. "My wife! She's long gone. Tere's father accused me of screwing the girl. A fifteen-year-old who was staying in my house. *¡Qué pendejo!*"

"Do you remember any of the boys she hung out with?"

"Boys? No. There was that priest, *Padre* Francisco who came here once or twice."

"Was she sleeping with him?" shouts Ana.

Alma jabs the girl in the ribs with her elbow. The man looks thoughtful for a moment, as if he is contemplating something very weighty. He turns and spits. "You're asking me if the priest knocked her up." He shrugs his shoulders.

"Do you know where I can reach your ex-wife?" asks Alma.

The man gives a harsh laugh. "Last I heard she was somewhere in Patagonia with my ex-horse trainer. But my son works at the General Hospital in Nuevo Progreso, Doctor Aurelio Pérez Santín. He's a little younger than Tere. Maybe he knows more about what went on here that summer."

He tips his hat, mounts his horse and rides off.

"You know," says Ana as Alma backs the car out of the driveway, "the migrant center is just down the road. Shouldn't we check it out? I hear that the place went downhill after *Padre* Francisco died, but who knows, they might have records on the volunteers."

Alma's head is pounding. She wants to look at her phone to see if any e-mails have come in but doesn't want Ana to start asking her again if she's all right or to start recommending herbal cures for the flu.

When they pull up behind the building, Alma sees that half of the windows are cracked; a few panes are missing entirely. Some of the stucco on the outside of the two-story building has fallen off. The paint on the exterior is faded. The two women walk around to the front of the building. There are several older men sitting on a wooden bench next to the front door. A girl of about twelve chases four smaller children around the bare, dusty front yard. The wooden sign over the front door is no longer horizontal but hangs perilously by a single nail. The letters say, "El Refugio" and underneath "La Fundación Fray Peti Juan."

The door to the building is open; the two women walk in. Someone has a radio tuned to a station that is playing forlorn ballads about lost love. The air smells of tortillas frying in rancid oil. A few steps down the hall is a door marked "Office." They knock. They can hear the sounds of someone banging away on a manual typewriter. They knock again. "Door's open," shouts a woman's voice.

The woman looks up when the two women enter. She stands and tucks a stray strand of gray hair behind her ear. She's enormous. Alma notices first the folds of flesh that ripple around her neck like a collar. Her arms are as thick as the trunk of a pomegranate tree. She is dressed in a flowing white *huipil* that reaches down almost to her ankles. Her face hasn't a single wrinkle. She gazes at her visitors, "Yes? You are?"

Alma flashes her press badge. "We're from the newspaper, El Diario de Ávila."

As the woman begins to sit back down on a rather fragile looking desk chair, Ana rushes over to hold the chair in place. The woman says, "thank you" but looks more annoyed than grateful.

"Whatever you want to know, I can't help you," the woman says. Her eyes shift from the reporters to the office door. "I'm only a volunteer here. I come once a week to check the accounts."

"Is there a manager?" asks Ana.

"Yes, but he's gone to town to buy supplies."

"What's the Fray Peti Juan Foundation?" asks Alma.

The woman's eyes roll up in her head. Alma has to smile. She looks like the illustrations of saints in her old childhood catechism. Is she, like those good women, praying for God's divine guidance? Ana, who is not given to fanciful speculation, follows the woman's eyes to the ceiling. "Is the building safe?" she asks no one in particular. "That ceiling is covered in mold."

The woman ignores her and returns to Alma's question. "You've never heard of the foundation? It's quite large. It looks after women and children in need; finds them good homes, jobs, that sort of thing. I understand it does excellent work." She pronounces the word ex—cel—lent, drawing out each syllable for maximum effect.

"Well," says Ana, "I wouldn't call anything about this

place excellent. It looks like it's falling apart. Also, what happened to all the migrants? People used to be lining up here to stay. Now you don't seem to have almost anyone."

The woman is indignant. "Times change, young lady."

"Where are the headquarters of the foundation?" Alma asks.

"Querétaro," says the woman. Alma can see that she's done answering their questions.

"We're trying to trace a young woman who volunteered here fifteen years ago."

"Good luck," the woman stifles a laugh. "Records, if you can call them that, are only kept for five years."

"*Padre* Francisco, what do you know about his murder?" demands Ana.

"How rude of us," says Alma ignoring Ana's question. "I'm Alma Jaramillo and my friend is Ana Flores." She extends her hand. The woman barely brushes it. She ignores Ana's entirely.

"Mercedes Sierra," says the woman. "I'm sorry, but I have to finish these receipts I'm typing. Do you want to wait for José? He's only been here a year."

"Thank you, I think we'll be moving along," says Alma thinking that she can probably get more information from the foundation's Internet page than from Mercedes. As they leave the building, Ana walks over to the elderly men sitting on the wooden bench. She asks where all the residents have got to. "They don't come here anymore," is the answer.

"But why?" asks Ana.

"Word gets around," says a second man. Then both men

get up and walk away.

On the way back to Ávila, Alma thinks of talking to Ana about how she might improve her interviewing skills, but she feels too tired. Maybe she'll broach the subject another day.

*　　　*　　　*

After Kurt is in bed that evening, Alma contemplates turning off her cell phone. She's exhausted. She can't bear one more thought about what Gabriel has been up to in Austin. She doesn't want Elena's pity either. But when the doorbell rings, her heart stops for a second. It can only be Gabriel at this hour of the night. What will he say about the trip? Is he coming by to tell her that he's back with his ex-wife?

But it isn't Gabriel and her face shows the disappointment.

"*Ay, Flaquita,*" says Elena. "Why didn't you call me back?"

"I, I—," Alma can't continue. The tears that she thought she had under control start to roll down her cheeks. Elena leads her into the small sitting room and closes the door so as not to wake Kurt. She takes both of Alma's hands in hers. "That post is Linda's side of the story. You don't know what Gabriel is feeling."

"Let me go," says Alma. "I have to blow my nose." When she's finished she says, "I don't know what he's feeling because he hasn't told me. He could have called me to explain why he was staying. Obviously, Linda's second marriage is on the rocks, so she's decided that she needs Gabriel's shoulder to cry on. I get that. What I don't get is how quickly he fell back under her spell. He hasn't called because he wants to break it off with me in person when he gets back."

"*Caray*, Alma, you really can jump to some crazy conclusions. Linda sounds like a little manipulator to me. You don't know what's happening. Why don't you call him?"

"No, never, I'm not chasing him. If he wants to wreck his life again, then let him. I don't want him."

"But you love him, *Flaca*, and on the weekend you said you were happy."

After Elena has left, Alma tosses and turns in bed for what seems like most of the night. Her dreams come in waves toward dawn. She finds herself back at her own fifteen-year-old birthday party. The VFW hall is decorated with pink balloons and streamers. Her cousins and school friends are all there. She's wearing a purple dress full of ruffles and bows. Her chamberlains are not her high-school classmates but Gabriel and Héctor. They refuse to dance with her. She holds out her arms, but they are impossible to reach. The scenes in the dream are fuzzy but her feeling of being abandoned, discarded, is so painful that she wakes with a start. A thick layer of sweat coats the back of her neck and shoulders.

CHAPTER 7

*A*lma stands under the shower, cold water pouring over her head. It's six-thirty in the morning and she can't get the dream out of her head. The sudden pounding on the bathroom door, however, brings her back to reality. "Mom, Mom—it's Evelyn. She needs to talk to you, it's urgent," yells Kurt.

"I'll call her back in ten minutes," she says trying to get her head around the day to come.

When she enters the kitchen, Kurt is pouring corn flakes into a bowl. "Evelyn's dad is coming to get her tonight," he says. He looks frightened. What a little schemer Evelyn is, Alma thinks. How quickly she's managed to get Kurt caught up in her drama.

Despite the early hour, Alma calls Sandra's house. Evelyn picks up immediately. She's crying. "Why did Sandra have to tell my mom I was here? She got hold of my dad; he's cut short his trip to Africa. He called a half an hour ago. He'll be here this evening. He says I have to go back to San Diego with him."

"Evelyn, of course Sandra had to contact her. You're a minor. Look, we'll talk to him. I'm sure we can work something out. You can come back in the summer, and meanwhile, I'll continue to search for your brother."

"I knew you'd be on his side, but you don't know what he's like. He'll never let me come back. He doesn't want me to find my birth family. He can't share anything or anyone. I hate him, and I'm not going back."

With that the line goes dead. Kurt looks at her. Pushing the bowl of cereal away, he says, "Evelyn's really upset."

"Hey, we need to get a move on. The school bus will be here in ten minutes," Alma says walking out of the room.

"But Mom, you have to help Evelyn."

"Sweetheart, it's her dad. She's a minor. There is nothing anyone can do."

"Mom, when is Gabriel getting back?" asks Kurt on the way to the bus stop. When there's no answer. He begins to tug on her sweater. "Mom, are you listening?"

"What?"

"I asked you when Gabriel is getting back."

"I don't know. Maybe on the weekend."

"So, if today is Wednesday he'll be back in three or four days?"

"Why do you need to know when he'll be back? I told you that Grandpa will take you to the game."

Just then the school bus appears. "I'm going to Max's house after school. Pick me up later," he calls over his shoulder.

As she walks back home she sees herself reflected in a shop window. I'm a wreck, she thinks. What happened to the new Alma of the make-over? Less than a week ago, she was reveling in her new image, now she looks like someone with a life-threatening disease. As she rounds the corner of her block, she sees a big black Mercedes with tinted windows parked in front of her house. Maybe Linda's rich father has given Gabriel a new car this time instead of a house, she thinks spitefully.

"*Señorita* Alma?" says the beefy driver removing an odd knitted cap which covers his thick black hair. "I'm Ángeles's brother, Chucho." Then pointing to the interior of the car, he says, "*Don* Hernán wants to talk to you."

"In the car?" He nods his head and opens the door to the back seat.

A hunched figure occupies a corner of the back seat. His lower body is covered by a plaid blanket. He wears a heavy wool jacket which looks as if it was bought for someone twice his size. The face is lean; his thin white hair is plastered down with sweet-smelling hair cream. Someone has shaved him but not carefully enough. There are whiskers sprouting on his chin. His dark amber eyes are red rimmed, moist. His skin is so thin she can see the blue veins in his forehead. There is a smell of mothballs in the car. Perhaps it comes from his wool jacket, perhaps from the old man himself.

"Come in, *Señorita* Jaramillo, sit down. *Mucho gusto,*" he says extending his gloved hand. His voice is high-pitched, scratchy.

Alma wonders how he found her, but of course she had given her card to his daughter-in-law, Sonia. Maybe Ángeles also told him about the search for María Teresa.

The old man clears his throat. He doesn't look directly at Alma but seems to be speaking to a point somewhere to the left of her right ear. "I have been told, *Señorita*, that you would like to locate my daughter, María Teresa. Also, that you want to expose a painful incident in the life of our family, an incident that I thought was long forgotten."

"*Don* Hernán, I think there's a misunderstanding here. I don't want to expose any incident, as you call it. Evelyn Hammond, whom I represent, is looking for her twin brother, who disappeared the day both children were born. She would like to know who her birth parents are if that were possible, but it's her brother she is really seeking."

As a newspaper woman, the old man says, Alma must see Satan at work daily. He utters the word Satan so casually that one would think he was speaking of a neighbor or a workmate. Fallen angels walk among us, he continues. This time he emphasizes the words "fallen" and "angels" to get the maximum dramatic effect. He pauses. She must believe in the devil. He turns and looks her in the eyes. Ah, he says when he sees she doesn't respond, perhaps she is like many modern young people. She doesn't believe that there is rampant evil in the world; evil provoked by the forces who challenge our Almighty Lord.

Alma sees the saliva which has accumulated around the corners of his mouth from such a long speech start to drip down his chin. He seems unaware that he is drooling as he picks up the thread of his rant once more.

But he, Hernán Gómez y Velasco Santiago, is an old man, he continues, and he has seen close up the work of the devil. The children to whom María Teresa gave birth are the work of Lucifer; and although they seem to be innocent, even normal, they are the product of an unspeakable act. He has thought long and hard about the birth of Tere's bastards and concluded that they were sent to test his faith. He has always believed that God held him particularly close. He is a man so devoted to Jesus Christ that perhaps one day he might even be elevated to sainthood. But God needed proof of Hernán's devotion, so as He had tested Abraham, God had sent Tere's bastards to test him. Through a messenger, the Holy Spirit told him that he must reject the twins; they are Lucifer's offspring. Never waver, the messenger had said. Sin must be stamped out wherever and whenever it raises its pernicious head.

The automobile is stuffy, too warm, but Alma feels a chill run down her spine. She tries to open a window but as the engine is turned off, it won't budge. She starts to open the car door. The old man clamps his hand around her wrist. You're hurting me, she says. Ignoring her, he continues. Perhaps she doesn't understand. If the children were to find one another, it would be like spitting in God's eye. There would be no retribution for their parents' sins, no punishment for breaking the Lord's commandments. She must understand that. She must promise to give up this blasphemous search.

Alma wrenches her arm free and opens the car door. "I respect your religious beliefs; but I do not share them," she says, stepping out of the car. "I believe that the children need a chance to know one another if that's what they decide; so I will continue to help Evelyn find her brother."

As she sprints toward her front door, she hears Hernán shout. "You'll be sorry. I have friends, important friends. Friends who will squash you underfoot like—." He thinks for a few seconds. "Like we squash scorpions or snakes."

Alma leans against the inside of her front door until she hears the big car pull away. She sits down at the kitchen table and begins to eat Kurt's soggy corn flakes. She makes herself a cup of Manzanilla tea to calm her nerves. She cannot get the smell of mothballs out of her nose or the sight of the old man's crazy amber eyes out of her mind.

She manages to throw on some clean clothes and a little makeup. As she opens the front door, she almost ploughs into a woman standing on the door step. The woman, who appears to be a more or less her age, is dressed in a red suit with a knee-length shirt clinging to her thighs and a tight little jacket baring an alluring amount of bosom. Her short black hair stands up in spikes on the top of her head. Alma can see the palest tope eye shadow highlighting her dark eyes. Her lips are painted the same deep red as her suit.

"Yes?" says Alma stepping back into the house. She's prepared to explain to the woman that she has the wrong house, even the wrong neighborhood. At the curb she notices a new white Nissan with a young man slouched in the driver's seat.

"Are you Alma Jaramillo?" says the woman, her icy stare sliding over Alma head to toe. "I'm *Licenciada* Julieta Vega

Guzmán. Can I speak with you for a few minutes?" she presses a business card into Alma's hand.

Alma examines the card. The lawyer is a senior partner with the firm Guzmán, Muñoz y Ortiz, S.C. located in Querétaro. Below the firm's name is the phrase *Derecho Penal y Civil*. A law firm specializing in criminal as well as family law Alma imagines. What can they want with her? For some reason, which she can't quite explain, Alma doesn't want this woman in her house, but neither does she want to talk to her practically on the sidewalk where passersby can listen to their conversation.

"Come around to the back patio," says Alma eyeing the woman's stiletto heels and the uneven terrain at the side of the house.

"One minute," says the *licenciada*, "I want to send the Uber driver to buy cigarettes."

Once on the small patio, Alma points the woman to one of the green plastic chairs around the green plastic picnic table. Before sitting down, the woman runs her hand over the seat and then examines her fingers for signs of dirt. She places a large Louis Vuitton handbag on the table, opens it and extracts an envelope.

"Well, Alma, I see you have created a serious problem for a client of mine," says the lawyer frowning. "I'll get right to the point as I have an hour's trip back to Querétaro, and clients to see in the afternoon." When the lawyer speaks, Alma notices that there's a gap between her two front teeth, which gives her speech a slight lisp. A strange imperfection, she thinks, when the rest of the woman's appearance is so faultless. "May I read you the letter my firm has written on behalf of our client?"

Alma knows that this isn't really a question. The *licenciada* will read the letter whether she agrees or not. So she listens. After a paragraph of what seems to be antiquated rigmarole, the letter comes abruptly to the point. Alma is to stop searching for Evelyn Hamilton's birth parents and her twin brother under threat of legal action. She can be fined, and even jailed if the party in question decides to prosecute.

"Prosecute? Prosecute for what?" says Alma beginning to laugh.

"Stalking, harassment," says the lawyer.

Alma immediately thinks that this woman must be an emissary from *Don* Hernán, but there is no way he could have organized the letter so quickly. Unless, of course, he had calculated that Alma wouldn't be easily persuaded by his fire and brimstone speech, but that doesn't make sense either. "I'm sorry that you had to waste several hours of your valuable time, but both you and I know that such an accusation would be laughed out of court. It's not a crime for a journalist to search for information."

"Well, then," says the lawyer smiling in relief as if now that they have the annoying part of the conversation out of the way, they can quickly move on to the real purpose of her visit. "My client would like to offer you a different incentive. How does twenty thousand dollars sound to you in exchange for dropping your inquiry? Think of everything you could do with the money." The lawyer stares at Alma's small neglected backyard and the cracked cement floor of the patio. "You could put a down payment on a new condo, buy a nice car, take a vacation. It's a generous offer."

Alma stares at the woman. "Can I ask who you represent?"

"You know I can't disclose that."

"And if I'm not interested in the money?"

The lawyer looks at her small jeweled watch. "If you think you can negotiate a better offer, forget it. My client was very precise about the amount. If you turn down the offer, I suppose we will try and make your life as miserable as possible. You and your family will receive threats; your light and phone will be mysteriously cut off; your car tires will be routinely slashed. We hire people who have a whole bag of exasperating tricks. They've had a lot of practice in intimation. You have my card. Think about the offer, *Señorita* Jaramillo."

The woman takes out her cell phone to summon her Uber driver. She then teeters back around the house to the street. Her three-inch stiletto heels pulling up weeds as she goes.

*   *   *

"Boss was looking for you," says Paulina, the editor of the business section when Alma finally arrives at her desk at noon. She turns on her computer, stows her bag and purse, and slowly make her way to Ricardo's office thinking, is this already horrendous day going to get even worse?

"*Ay, ay, ay,* Alma, you do keep me awake at night," says Ricardo smiling.

"What are you talking about?" says Alma still wrapped up in her miserable morning.

"An hour ago, a certain Hernán Gómez y Velasco called me to complain that you were harassing him and his family. In fact, he used the word blackmailing. He said you were using the cover of your press credentials to hound them. For a rather slight, seemingly law-abiding person, you do get yourself into some sticky situations. I see that I need to give you a job more absorbing than editing to keep you out of trouble."

Alma feels what is left of the energy in her body drain away. Her head begins to pound; she feels tears forming at the corners of her eyes.

"Hey, Alma, are you all right?" says Ricardo coming around to her side of the desk. "You don't look so good. Are you ill?"

Alma shakes her head.

"Are Kurt and your parents okay?"

Alma nods her head, but she feels that if she opens her mouth all that will come out will be senseless babble.

"Where's Gabriel?" She says nothing.

"Coffee is what you need. I'll be right back." He leaves her be for a good ten minutes which allows her to regain her composure.

"Now," he says handing her a hot cup of coffee with three heaping spoonfuls of sugar. "What's all this about?"

"I guess you could call it a pro bono investigation," says Alma smiling for the first time in the last forty-eight hours. She explains how she became involved with Evelyn. She relates what she knows of the girl's history. She tells him about her weekend in San Miguel and her discovery of

Evelyn's birth mother. She includes the visits to the Boston Clinic and the meetings with Sonia Bianchi, Tere's sister-in-law, and Lucero Sánchez. She mentions *Padre* Francisco and her trip to Rancho Los Encinos. Then today the creepy visits from *Don* Hernán and the lawyer offering her a bribe of twenty thousand dollars. She says nothing about Gabriel.

"*Don* Hernán and *Licenciada* Julieta appeared out of nowhere. I never mentioned the newspaper to either one. Although I have to admit that I did use the name of the newspaper to get Raúl Gómez's attention. That was wrong. I'm sorry."

"Let's get some lunch, and I'll tell you what I know about the Gómez y Velasco family and also about *Padre* Francisco."

As they settle themselves into the worn leather seats of the restaurant's tall benches, Alma gazes around La Hostería de San Pedro. The brass plaque at the entrance says that the restaurant was founded in 1900. Local folklore maintains that Porfirio Díaz had suggested the first menu. Photographs signed by the celebrities who have enjoyed a meal over the years cover the oak-paneled walls. Before they even begin to examine the extensive menu and wine list, a shout comes from across the crowded room. "*Don* Ricardo, *bienvenido*."

Ricardo rises from his seat and shouts back, "*Don* Isidro." He folds the maître d' in a snug *abrazo*. After a few hardy slaps on the back, the elderly head waiter says, "We have all your favorite dishes today. The *escamoles* arrived yesterday afternoon, and they are delicious. The chef has sautéed them in a little butter with *cilantro* and chili. With fresh *tortillas* and a little *guacamole*, you couldn't find a better first course anywhere in Mexico, and then how about a fish dish?"

"Do you have *huachinango?*" Ricardo asks.

"Yes, fresh Red Snapper from the Gulf prepared *a la veracruzana.* Just thinking about it makes me hungry," the maître d' says starting to chuckle. Turning to Alma, the man apologizes for not attending to her first. "The same order for you, *Señorita?*"

"I've never even tried *escamoles.* I've read it was a prized dish of the Aztecs, but I'm not feeling so well."

"*Caldo de pollo* with a little chicken and vegetables is just the thing for you," says *Don* Isidro collecting the menus. "Beer, wine, tequila?"

"Two tequilas," says Ricardo despite the frown on Alma's face.

"*¿Reposado?*" asks the maître d'.

"No, *blanco*, but the best you have."

Ricardo settles back against the cracked leather seat. "Now to your pro bono work, Alma." She looks at her boss. He's in much better spirits today. He looks rested too, not so worried. She sees some of the women from other tables cast a lingering glace in his direction. He never seems conscious of his good looks.

"It turns out that it isn't totally pro bono," begins Alma, "because *Padre* Francisco's name has come up more than a few times. His murder has never been solved so something in this mess might still turn out to be a story."

Ignoring her comment about *Padre* Francisco, Ricardo takes a sip of his tequila before saying that he's more interested in the old man, *Don* Hernán. He's run into him on several occasions and the only word to describe the guy is *un cabrón*. So María Teresa's troubles don't surprise him. He remembers being at a regional meeting of the Rotary Club where *Don* Hernán got up and walked out because the club was making a large donation to a clinic specializing in women's health. He gave a pompous speech about promoting immorality because the clinic had family-planning services. Ricardo says that the old man raises money for Catholic schools, but even his most Catholic friends can't stand him. The Bishop groans if his name is mentioned. There's something not quite right about him. He's too fanatic, too full of his own righteousness.

"Well," says Alma, "I'll attest to his not being right in the head, but what do you know about his work with Los Militantes de Jesús?"

"The Gómez y Velasco family goes way back. They were on the wrong side of the Mexican Revolution. Some of them might even have gone to Paris for a time with Porfirio Díaz for all I know. *Don* Hernán told me that his grandfather had been very active in the Cristero movement in the nineteen-thirties—."

"The Cristeros were mentioned in the family history that I found on the Internet. But who were the Cristeros?"

"*Ay*, Alma. Haven't you learned any Mexican history in the last six years?"

Tossing back her tequila, Alma smiles. "Well, since my boss is so knowledgeable, I haven't bothered."

Ricardo laughs and promises to be as brief as possible. The Cristeros were a reaction to the attempt in Mexico's 1917 constitution to limit the power of the Catholic Church. When the government began to prohibit religious education in the public schools, to suppress popular religious celebrations, and to forbid nuns and priests from wearing their religious garb in public, there was trouble. Fervent Catholics, particularly in the central part of the country, egged on by the clergy, took up arms. The fighting petered out in the early nineteen-thirties, but the animosity hung around for seventy years. Mexico didn't reestablish diplomatic relations with the Vatican until almost the end of the twentieth century. The friction between the Church and the Mexican government was even the inspiration for a famous novel. Surely, she'd read *The Power and the Glory* by Graham Green?

"So, you're saying that movements like Los Militantes de Jesús sprang up to support Catholic causes like religious education."

"I believe Los Militantes was founded around the time of the Second World War by a priest who believed he'd been chosen by God to draw Catholics back into a life of holiness. So yes, religious education plays a big part in the movement."

Alma thinks for moment and then says, "I understand that *Don* Hernán could have strong feelings about how the Church was treated after the Revolution, but it seems so cruel the way he treated his daughter and the babies."

"I guess that expression, *"Más papista que el Papa,"* fits him to a tee. It seems that his moral code for how women should behave is even stricter than the Pope's. Then there's the issue of the family name, which he feels he needs to protect." Ricardo stops talking and casts a hopeful glance toward the kitchen door.

"You'd think he would have wanted to keep María Teresa near because she's the one with the fortune. His pride seems to matter more than his bank account," comments Alma.

"It's Raúl who's money hungry," comments Ricardo, but spotting the arrival of the waiter, he loses all interest in the Gómez y Velasco family.

He rubs his hands together as the *escamoles* are placed in front of him. "Come on Alma, don't be such a *gringa*, try one little *taco*."

Her soup looks very inviting, but she agrees to taste one small *taco*. "Oh, it's good," she says, surprise showing on her face. The taste of the buttery, nut-like ant larvae mixed with the flavor of the hand-made tortilla and the spicy *guacamole* is delicious.

"Another *taco*?" asks Ricardo.

Alma shakes her head as she begins to sip the hot broth. "Now to the other side of the coin. Tell me about *Padre* Francisco."

"I remember my dad telling me about his interview with the priest when he opened the migrant center. I don't suppose *Padre* Francisco was much more than twenty-seven or twenty-eight. He was so enthusiastic. So sure, he could do great things in his little part of the world. My dad said he asked him if he was ever afraid that his work would cause a violent pushback from either the gangs who prey on the migrants or from those who thought that the Church shouldn't be involved in social missions. His answer was curious. He said that he didn't believe he'd live long enough to see his work attacked. During his stay in Brazil, a *curandero* had told him he would have a short but happy life. He knew that as a priest he shouldn't believe in witch doctors, but he always kept that prophecy in the back of his mind."

"Who shot him?" asks Alma.

Ricardo pushes the empty plate of his second course away. "Next time," he says, "order the fish here. It's very tasty." He thinks for a minute. "The federal police as well as the local police investigated his murder but as far as I know, despite constant pressure from Church authorities, they never arrested anyone or came close to solving the crime. Talk to your friend in the local police, Captain Ramírez. He might have new information on the killing. Dessert? Coffee?"

"No, that's it for me. But getting back to *Padre* Francisco, a couple of days ago César Davila made an off-the-cuff remark about La Casa de la Esperanza. He said that it had had a stink about it, but he couldn't remember why. I mentioned this to my parish priest, and he said that *Padre* Francisco was a man of integrity, but his friends weren't exactly in the same boat. What do you think? Is the remark worth following up?"

Ricardo raises his eyebrows. "I love César but he's pretty old now. He gets a lot of things confused. My dad seemed to think that *Padre* Francisco was a straight arrow."

"Do you have any clue about the priest's family? How could I go about locating them?"

"Why?"

"There is some talk that he might have been the father of the twins."

"¡*Caray*, Alma! This is turning into a real hornet's nest. My wife's cousin is the Bishop's private secretary. Let me see if he still has his information on file."

Alma hesitates a minute but then looks Ricardo in the eye. "How's Héctor's story on Beto García coming along?"

"It's *basura*, total nonsense. We'd be the laughing stock of the state if we published it. He could, I suppose, submit it to some gushing celebrity magazine, but I'm discouraging that idea."

"So, what are you going to do?"

"Tell him to rewrite it. I'm willing to give the guy another chance; I'm willing to help him too, but he needs to deliver a good piece of journalism."

As they leave the restaurant, Alma gives Ricardo a small kiss on the cheek. "Thank you, Richie, that lunch did a lot for my morale. Are you okay with me continuing my pro bono work?"

"No problem, but I'd be careful about getting too close to the Gómez y Velasco family. Hernán is off his head, as you know. He's unpredictable. I've also heard rumors for years that the son, Raúl, has been involved in some very dirty stuff. Apparently, he's hand and glove with some cartel. The business with the lawyer worries me, too. Whoever is behind it is offering big bucks to stop your investigation." He pauses for a few brief seconds. "Do you want me to talk some sense into that guy of yours?"

The smile on Alma's face fades. "Are my personal problems that obvious? Thanks, but no, I need to deal with what's going on with Gabriel myself."

"Up to you," Ricardo says with a shrug of his shoulders. "I'll let you know as soon as I hear anything about *Padre* Francisco's family. I get that you think there might still be story behind Francisco's murder. I'm the last one to say go easy on a potential exposé, but keep me informed about any developments and don't take risks. It's not worth it. Stories come and go but good reporters are hard to find."

Heading back to the office, Alma decides to put Gabriel out of her mind and try to make a dent in the pile of stories to be edited. But she finds Héctor once again sitting at her desk, talking a mile a minute with Ana. *Pinche cabrón*, she mutters under her breath.

"Héctor, *mi amorcito*, I see you've lost your bearings again. I believe your desk is in the far back corner of the newsroom."

"Ana was just filling me in on your latest project," he snickers.

"Right," says Ana, "I was telling *Licenciado* Valdés about the new water-resources law that we're investigating."

With that, Héctor walks off chuckling to himself.

"Look, Ana," says Alma opening Lucero Sánchez's e-mail with the photos from Tere's *quinceaños* party. "Here are some photos of Tere when she was fifteen."

Ana puts a photo of Evelyn next to the screen. "Yeah, they do look a lot alike. But people change. I wonder what Tere looks like now. You know her hair might be dyed blue for all we know; she might be fat."

"Meanwhile, let's print three or four of the best ones. They could be helpful."

On the way back from the printer, Irma, "*La Gordis*," pops

her head out of her smoke-filled office. "I hear you're interested in Leonor Aragón. I'm curious to know why. The woman has been dead for thirty years."

"Nothing too exciting," says Alma following Irma back into her cubbyhole. Irma is an institution at El Diario de Ávila. Rumor has it that she had been Ricardo's father's "special friend" for thirty years; a friendship kept alive by Irma's ability to tell amusing stories about the social elite of Ávila. There are photos of Irma from forty years ago plastered all over her office walls. She is shown with the then governors, moguls of industry, and the local gentry of Tepetlán and the surrounding states. Always with a cigarette between her fingers and a small hat on her head, for years she had been the editor of the paper's social page. Under her tutelage, the page had grown to a whole section of the newspaper and then into a Sunday magazine.

When the rigors of partying and the quantity of cigarettes, canapes, and cocktails she had to consume played havoc with her health and figure, Ricardo placed her in charge of obituaries. Since she knew everyone who was anyone in a three-state area, she had immediately tripled the number of *esquelas* that the paper ran. These black-edged death notices honoring the passing, or remembering the passing of prominent citizens, family members, or even a beloved pet are now a mainstay of the paper's finances.

Irma waves Alma to a chair in front of her desk. She lights up a fresh Marlboro and blows a smoke ring. "I smoked Delicados for years, but the docs finally make me give them up. These are *una mierda*." The woman thinks for a moment and continues. "Leonor was my best pal for many years. We had some great times together. Leonor's parties were legendary."

"How did you meet?" asks Alma.

Leonor had arrived in San Miguel de Allende toward the end of the sixties, the fiancée of Hernán Gómez y Velasco. She was barely twenty; Irma, just nineteen. One afternoon, Leonor had turned up at the newspaper asking for the editor of the social page. There was none, there was only Irma, who wrote up the weddings and baptisms after a brief telephone conversation with the interested parties. Leonor had a different idea. She wanted the paper to cover her engagement party to Hernán Gómez y Velasco. Not some little note stuck on the back page, but a full page with photos of the *novios* and their influential guests. It mustn't look like an ad either. It had to look like a genuine story.

"I told her it would cost her," said Irma. "But she didn't care."

Ricardo's father had said that the Gómez y Velasco family was not going to be happy; they hated that kind of publicity. However, the fortune that Leonor was bringing to the family made them, at least initially, gloss over any faux pas the future bride might commit. The wedding a year later was spread across three pages of the Sunday paper. It was mostly photos of the bride and her entourage. The story was picked up by the Mexico City dailies.

"She was going to be the social mover and shaker of our part of the country or die trying," says Irma. "She knew that her own pedigree would never propel her to the top of the social ladder, but since her daddy had bought her the Gómez y Velasco name, it was full steam ahead." Irma smiles. She takes a photograph of Leonor out of her desk drawer. The woman is stunning. The dark hair, almond shaped eyes, and white skin look familiar.

"She was beautiful," says Alma. "What was her family background?"

Irma says that that's an interesting question. Leonor's father, Bernardo, had been a very minor official in the Sinaloa state government when World War Two broke out. He didn't have much of an education, but he did speak English. When the Americans came calling, looking for opium to make morphine because the usual supply routes had been cut off by the Japanese, Bernardo became the guy to see. As soon as the war was over, he married a local beauty queen, gathered the small fortune he had made from the war, and headed to Mexico City where he joined the postwar business free-for-all.

"Bernardo got an early start in many lucrative land deals," says Irma. "Leonor said he had the Midas touch."

"What attracted Leonor to Hernán in the first place, besides his illustrious name?" Alma asks.

Irma lights a new cigarette, pulls the smoke deep into her lungs and says that she had never quite figured that out. The couple had met at a weekend party at someone's *hacienda*. Hernán had been in his mid-thirties. He was good-looking. Tall and slim, he had a military bearing; he would have looked terrific in a uniform. His education was good; his manners pleasant enough. Not someone with whom you'd want to share a joke or go bar-hopping with, however. He didn't have much of a career. He'd been undersecretary of something or other and an adviser to a few ministers in the state government, but he had never fulfilled either his family's or his own expectations. "He thought he should be leading the parade, not marching behind some politician whose people were nobodies. So he threw in the towel when the jobs got tedious."

Was Hernán socially ambitious like Leonor? asks Alma. In the beginning, he indulged his pretty bride as long as she also organized dinners for his conservative friends and for the bishops and the then cardinal of the region. However, after Raúl was born, he had expected Leonor to more or less disappear into the woodwork. She had other ideas. She'd redoubled her efforts for the local charities. She became active in sponsoring music and art festivals. She invited writers, artists, and academics to dinner. Her parties became more lavish; she filled them with people who interested her, which by and large were not Hernán's friends.

He hated the constant socializing. He'd show up late for her dinners, if he showed up at all. He began to ridicule her in public. Her daddy finally intervened, and a truce was declared. Hernán kept his mouth shut, and Leonor continued to entertain the clergy and to prop up the family's finances.

"Why did she die in childbirth? Surely she could have had the best care in the world."

Irma stubs out her cigarette and lights another. She blows more smoke rings before answering. "The doctors told her after Raúl was born that there could be no more babies. She was in her late thirties when she became pregnant with Tere. The doctors said she had to abort, but she wouldn't do it. She told me that this baby was the key to a new life. She was sure that she could beat the odds."

"Was it a religious conviction?" asks Alma. "I know that some women feel so strongly about their unborn children that they're willing to sacrifice their own lives."

Irma doesn't answer. She starts to gather up the papers on her desk. "Got to move along," she says.

Alma doesn't move. After a while she says, "I bet Tere is intelligent enough to have figured out what I think you're telling me. I wonder if she's had a DNA test done. What do you think?"

"I never knew Tere. I tried, but Hernán didn't want me around. However, if she's at all like her mother, she's smart and curious."

"Do you know who the lover was?"

"No, and even if I did, I wouldn't tell you. Some things are nobody's business."

"Do you think Hernán knows?"

"Maybe, but how could anyone tell? He's such an odd bird."

"Can I look at the clippings you have of Leonor when she was a young bride?"

Irma opens a file drawer and takes out a battered folder full of yellow newspaper pages. "Turn out the lights when you leave," she says.

Alma continues to sit staring at the photos of Leonor long after Irma has packed her bag and left; that is, until she hears the ring of her cell phone.

CHAPTER 8

*A*s she picks up her cell phone, Alma looks at the time. It's almost seven o'clock. She should have picked Kurt up an hour ago.

"Sandra, I'm so sorry. I'll be right over."

"No, that's not why I'm calling. Evelyn's gone, run away again. Oh, my God, Alma, Nick is going to be here in a few hours. He's going to be furious with us when he finds she's gone."

"I don't see why. You took her in, but she was a runaway in the first place. You told him she was in Mexico."

Yes, Sandra replies, but Alma doesn't know the man. He's explosive; he's got a thing about Mexico and how insecure it is. Alma asks what was going on hours earlier when Evelyn took off. Sandra had gone out leaving the two boys with Evelyn. The maid went to buy a few groceries and was gone less than fifteen minutes. The cook was taking a nap. The boys say that they went off to Max's room to play some video game. Evelyn, when last seen, was in the library. When they looked for her a half an hour later, she was nowhere to be found. The maid called Sandra. The girl had at least left a note in her room.

"I'll be right there," says Alma.

As soon as Alma arrives she asks the boys if Evelyn mentioned anything about running away again. They seem disinterested, look down at their feet, say they don't know anything. She was there one minute and gone the next. They scamper out of the room. Sandra shows Alma the note the girl left, a quickly scribbled message written in pencil on a piece of notebook paper.

DON'T WORRY. I'VE GONE TO A SAFE PLACE. I'LL BE BACK AS SOON AS MY DAD LEAVES. HE NEEDS TO UNDERSTAND THAT I HAVE TO STAY IN MEXICO UNTIL I FIND MY BROTHER.
EVELYN

"What's she talking about? A safe place," says Sandra. "The girl doesn't know anyone but us in Mexico. God, do you think she's found some predator on line? This is just awful. Maybe she's got in touch with María Teresa's family? We should never have started the investigation. Nick and June are going to blame me for this." Sandra starts to pace the room. What should they do? Should they call the police?

"I think we all need to calm down and wait for her father to arrive," says Alma glancing at the time.

"We don't know if the family has other friends in Mexico. If anyone is to blame for this, it's her parents. Call me when you have any news."

Supper with Kurt is a silent affair. Both of them seem to be in their own worlds. "Don't worry too much about Evelyn," Alma says later, kissing her son goodnight. "She's probably found another friend of the family nearby." He turns over and closes his eyes. Alma tiptoes out of the room. Her words might have sounded reassuring, but in truth, she is not only concerned but angry. The girl is spoiled, headstrong, and inconsiderate. From what Sandra has said she seems a lot like her adoptive father, Nick.

Alma doesn't even want to contemplate the trouble that a pretty fifteen-year-old can get into on the streets of Ávila. She feels like Sandra. Why had she gotten involved? Yes, she had felt sorry for the girl, but it was her insatiable curiosity about a story that as usual had landed her in the middle of the mess.

She slips behind her computer and checks her e-mails. There's a short e-mail from Ricardo with the name and address of *Padre* Francisco's nearest relative, a sister named Inés Rabasa León. She lives in Nuevo Progreso, the same small city where Alma's father grew up. Nothing from Gabriel but then she didn't expect anything. Tomorrow will be a week since he left. Something is very wrong between them. She had promised herself, no she'd vowed, not to look at anymore of Linda's posts, but she knows that she can no more stop herself from reading the posts than a ghoul can resist looking at a car crash.

It's, of course, the first post that comes up on her Facebook page. The look on Gabriel's face makes her recoil against the back of her chair. She studies the close-up. He's got a half smile on his lips. His isn't looking directly at the camera but at something happening off to his right. The purple smudges under his eyes are more pronounced than usual. He's clean shaven but looks pale. His hair is slicked down with more care than usual.

Under the photograph, Linda has written four euphoric hash tags: #happyme, #lovehimtodeath, #togetheragain, #it'sforreal. Then there's a line of red hearts and another of smiling emoji. Weird, thinks Alma, how old is this woman? She turns off the laptop and slams down the lid. But she knows tomorrow night she'll go back to the website, subjecting herself to the same torture.

In her dreams that night she is back in Los Angeles. She and her ex-boyfriend, Kenny, Kurt's father, are babysitting someone's twins. But it's never clear if it's Kenny or Gabriel who is with her. The faces keep changing. The number of babies keeps changing too. One of the babies starts to cry and then to choke. But when she looks, it's Gabriel's ex-wife, Linda, who is choking. She screams to the man in the room to call nine-one-one, but he can't find the phone. She's still screaming in her dream when the alarm goes off at six-fifteen.

At eight o'clock she calls Sandra. She's gone out, says the maid and yes, Mr. Hammond has arrived, but he's gone out too, and no, she doesn't think there's any news about Evelyn. Alma phones her Aunt Isabel in Nuevo Progreso. Can she come for a late breakfast? Of course, her aunt says. It's been too long since they'd had a chat.

She is unlocking her car door when a white BMW pulls up in front of her. A large middle-aged man steps out of the car. His hair is still wet from the shower. His suit, although wrinkled, looks high-end Italian.

"Alma Jaramillo?" he says.

"Yes," she answers looking up into his dark eyes. She can smell the expensive aftershave, which wafts off his chin and neck.

"Where is she? My daughter, Evelyn, where is she? Is she in your house or have you hidden her somewhere else?"

"What are you talking about? Are you Nick Hammond?"

Suddenly the man grabs her by the shoulders and starts shaking her. He's shouting now. "Why did you tell her about María Teresa? Don't you know how crazy those people are, how dangerous? What kind of an irresponsible person are you?"

"Stop it," cries Alma. "I haven't got any idea where your daughter is. Let me go."

"*Déjala cabrón*," says one of the two men with lead pipes who appear at her side.

Nick Hammond steps back, dropping Alma's arms.

"I think you'd better be on your way, *Señor*," says her neighbor, Luis. His brother, Jaime, lifts the thick pipe he's holding and moves a half step closer to Nick.

"I'll be back, Miss Jaramillo, and I won't come alone next time. You know where Evelyn is. You've struck some kind of deal with Raúl."

"Are you all right?" asks Jaime when Nick's car has pulled away. "Maybe you and Kurt had better stay with your parents for a few days. That guy looks like trouble."

*   *   *

It takes more than a half-an-hour for Alma's nerves to

quiet down and for Nick Hammond's hand prints to disappear from her shoulders. Driving helps; so does the tranquility of the countryside. She can't square the picture that Gabriel had painted of Nick Hammond with the reality she experienced today. According to Gabriel, the man is a big international lawyer; what she just saw was a hysterical father. Evelyn had said he was temperamental, but assaulting a journalist! He couldn't have been thinking straight. Why did he think that the Gómez y Velasco family presented a danger to Evelyn? The girl had never told her father about the mariachi e-mails? He spoke as if he knew Raúl Gómez, more mysteries within mysteries.

She's on the new toll road to Nuevo Progreso. She's been to her father's hometown dozens of times since arriving back from Los Angeles six years ago. When her father had left in the early eighties to go to technical school in Ávila, the town was still a sleepy provincial backwater. The dam on the Río Ciénega, which was built to produce electricity for Ávila's new industries, had changed everything. It had created a lake ten miles outside of Nuevo Progreso. Hotels and restaurants, boat clubs, and a golf club had sprung up around the area. Jesús, Alma's father, could only say after each visit, "¡Caray! What a change! Thirty years ago, this town was going nowhere."

Thirty years ago, Alma thinks, Mexico didn't have a four-lane toll road between Ávila and Nuevo Progreso either. The highway had turned a three-hour stop-and-go ramble through the congested streets of small villages into an easy hour-and-a-half straight shoot. The scenery has changed too. There are now huge chicken hatcheries and vast greenhouses growing flowers for export. In some places, irrigated farmland has replaced arid fields. But for many small farmers, life is as precarious as ever. A scarce water supply and a primitive wooden plow produce only a mean life. Imported corn has wiped out the livelihood of many. Alma sighs and looks at the road ahead. The stately Sierra Madre Mountains loom up in the distance. She relaxes at last.

A visit to Nuevo Progreso has to include a stop at her Aunt Isabel's home. Isabel is three years older than Alma's father, Jesús. She, her two sisters, and their mother had worked to put their brother through school. Alfredo, her husband of more than thirty years, is a mechanic. Owner of a small automobile repair shop on a corner near downtown Nuevo Progreso, he does most of the work of banging out dented fenders and painting scratched car doors on the street in front of his shop. Their two daughters, an accountant and a pediatric nurse, both live in Ávila despite their mother's constant pleas that they get married and move back home.

Breakfast is on the table when she enters her aunt's kitchen. "I could smell the *huevos rancheros* as soon as I turned the corner," she says. Lingering over a glass of freshly squeezed orange juice after polishing off the eggs, Alma sighs. "This is the best breakfast I've had in a very long time. Uncle Alfredo? Is he around?"

"Working," says Isabel. "You know he can't leave his repair shop alone for more than a few hours. He might lose a customer or miss some neighborhood gossip."

Sitting down at the table with Alma, her aunt wants to

know to what she owes the pleasure of a visit on a weekday morning. Normally her niece arrives with the whole family on the weekend to picnic and to swim in the lake. Alma explains that she wants to interview a doctor at the Social Security hospital and to talk to Inés, *Padre* Francisco's sister. Does her aunt remember the priest who was murdered ten years ago?

"*Ay, ay, ay*, Alma, you're always in the thick of things. I don't think you look for trouble, but it does seem to look for you. You want some company today?" says Isabel standing up to remove her apron and to grab a shawl off the back of a chair.

Alma's eyes light up. "Oh, yes, please. I'd love that."

They park several blocks down the street from the large Social Security hospital but getting to the hospital entrance proves to be nearly as daunting as finding a parking place. The sidewalk in front of the hospital is only about two yards wide but it accommodates in the length of a block and a half no less than forty small *puestos*. There are stalls selling: *pan dulce* and *atole*; *tacos* made from *frijoles*, rice, head cheese, tripe or *chorizo*; *dulces de camote* from Puebla; newspapers, comics and girlie magazines; cold pancakes in plastic wrap; *tamales* both green and red; *tortas* in little plastic boxes; sodas and *aguas de sabor*. For those with problems greater than an empty stomach, an old woman sells medicinal *peyote* that promises to cure whatever ails you.

The hospital building is enclosed by a fence with a wide stone base providing a convenient bench for the street market's customers. Some of the more elaborate stands have small stools and serve their *tacos* on pieces of brown paper placed carefully on pink plastic plates. A blind man with a tin cup and white cane threads his way up and down the sidewalk, chanting *"Jesús me salva, Jesús me bendice."* Isabel drops a few coins in his cup.

When the women finally get to the head of the line at the hospital's information booth, the receptionist sends them to the second floor. A nurse tells them to take a seat on one of the orange plastic chairs that line the hallway while she goes to look for Doctor Aurelio Pérez Santín. "How do you know this doctor?" asks Isabel. Alma tells her about the visit to Rancho Los Encinos and her encounter with the cowboy in the tall black hat.

Twenty minutes later, what appears to be a teenager wearing a white coat walks up to them. His name tag says Doctor Pérez Santín, Internal Medicine. When Alma hands him her business card and explains who she is and the information she is after, he looks around the crowded hallway. "It's almost my lunch hour," he says. "Let's grab something to eat."

He leads the two women across the street to a small restaurant advertising an inexpensive *comida corrida*. The set menu consists of a soup or a plate of rice, a main dish—in this case *enchiladas*—and a dessert. Today, lime green gelatin, Alma's favorite, is the sweet. Seating themselves at a metal card table with the Coca Cola logo emblazoned across the top, they order lunch. Only when the waiter disappears into the kitchen does Doctor Pérez begin to speak. Close up, Alma can see that the doctor isn't really a teenager, but neither can he be much more than twenty-six or twenty-seven.

"It's been years since I've thought about the summer Tere spent with us. It was the best and worst summer of my young life. I was thirteen, and I couldn't believe that anyone so beautiful had walked into my life. Of course, she didn't pay much attention to me, a skinny kid who moped around after her, but I adored her. My parents accepted her for the summer because they needed the money. I'm not exaggerating when I say they hardly knew we lived there; they were so busy fighting their private war. My mother was getting involved with that horse trainer she eventually ran off with, and my dad spent his time with a six-pack of beer."

Alma asks if he knew that Tere had gotten pregnant during that summer. The doctor puts down his soup spoon and shakes his head. He looks stunned. He'd gone to live with his grandparents in Nuevo Progreso in September of that year. He'd visited his father from time to time, but they'd never talked about Tere. His mother had decamped to Argentina a few months later and her letters were few and far between. "Did Tere and her boyfriend get married?" asks Doctor Aurelio.

"No," says Alma, "do you know who the boyfriend was?"

The doctor pushes away the rest of his *enchiladas* and smiles. "I was so jealous of Andrés. He was everything I wasn't. He was eighteen, handsome, confident, and, of course, he could sing and play the guitar. She used to sneak out to meet him late at night. We had some empty cabins out behind the barn. They'd sit on the porch of one of the cabins and sing that popular song, '*Si nos dejan*.' Tere had this pure soprano voice. I thought that if angels could sing, that's what they'd sound like."

"Your father told me that Tere's father had accused him of getting her pregnant."

"He accused my dad of seducing Tere? That's crazy. Even after downing a six-pack he isn't that kind of guy."

"Did you know *Padre* Francisco? Someone said that he might have been the father of the babies."

Aunt Isabel suddenly comes to life. "Alma, what a way to talk! I can't believe you said that."

"Wait a minute," says the doctor. "There was more than one child?"

"Tere had twins. One child was adopted and taken off to California. The other was abducted from the clinic the day of the birth."

"So, where's Tere?"

"That's what her family and I would like to know."

"People think that the priest was fooling around with her? He came by our place a couple of times. Tere was in awe of him. She talked with him a lot about changing the world, doing good works, but it was Andrés she was hanging out with, seemed to be in love with."

"Andrés, Andrés who?"

"Sorry, Alma, I used to see them together at night, but I don't know who he was. Maybe he was a volunteer at the migrant center? There were a bunch of kids there that summer."

Alma reaches in her purse and pulls out the copies of the photographs that Lucero sent of Tere's *quinceaños* party. She passes them to the doctor. "Do you see him among the guests?"

He studies each photograph carefully. When he comes to the makeshift altar in the corral, he stops and points to a tall young man who appears to be assisting the priest with communion. "Maybe, that's Andrés," he says. "But I can't be sure."

When they are back in the car, Aunt Isabel says, "Alma, do you really think *Padre* Francisco was involved with that young girl? You know he was from around here. Everyone loved him. We always went to church when he came here to say Mass."

"I don't know, *Tía*. People revered him but—. Anyway, you need to get us to this address. It's *Padre* Francisco's sister's home. I want to know more about the man."

As they are parking in front of the address that Alma has been given, her aunt says that she will take a walk around the neighborhood. "See that small shop on the opposite corner, *Tía*? Could you chat up the owner about the families in the neighborhood? Pretend you might be moving here. See if they'll tell you anything about Inés Rabasa León, the priest's sister, and her family."

"So, you're turning me into your *achichincle*," says Isabel laughing.

Looking around the neighborhood before she rings the bell, Alma notices that the houses are on the whole rather plain. Some have two stories; a few have maid's rooms and laundry areas stuck on the roof. There's a park across the street with trees that need trimming and garbage cans that need emptying. Inés's family home has an open area in front of the house enclosed by an eight-foot wire mesh fence. It must have originally been a parking area but now seems to be a basketball court. Bicycles and a doll's carriage clutter the rest of the patio. The house is painted a light bottle green, which contrasts with its red tiled roof. The windows upstairs are open, and Alma can hear children's laughter drifting out to the street.

She presses the buzzer and waits. She can see her Aunt Isabel entering the store at the corner. Suddenly the front door of the house flies opens, and a child of perhaps of six or seven runs up to the metal gate. She is dressed in what looks like a hand-me-down party dress. The pink ribbons in her hair are several shades brighter than the much-laundered pink dress.

"*Buenas tardes*," says the little girl politely. "My mother says if you are selling something to please go away." The girl turns around and shoots back into the house closing the door. Alma doesn't want to annoy her busy mother, but she has after all come some distance to see the woman. She rings the bell again. An older girl appears this time. She looks to be thirteen or fourteen. Her message is that if Alma is selling something or from the government, she should come back another time.

Alma smiles. "I've come all the way from Ávila to speak to your mother about your uncle, *Padre* Francisco." She hands the girl one of her business cards. The small child comes back in two or three minutes and leads Alma into the front parlor. The house smells wonderful. A pork roast, potatoes, perhaps a cake too, are baking in the oven.

The small girl directs Alma to a much sat-upon, but still attractive, sofa. The rest of the solid wooden chairs and small tables in the room look as if they have come from someone's grandmother's house.

"I'm Clara," says the small girl. "What's your name?"

"I'm Alma. Who are all the people in the pictures over there?"

Clara looks at the photographs lined up on the bookcase. Pointing to the first large ornately framed photo, she says, "That's my mom's wedding. She keeps her dress in a box in her closet; sometimes we get to take it down and look at it."

Alma thinks that the bride and groom look serious, as if they had just received a sermon on the obligations of married life.

"I see a lot of babies in the rest of the pictures," says Alma smiling. "Who are they, Clara?"

"They're pictures of us when we got baptized," says the girl jumping up. She brings over what looks like the most recent photo. "This is me," says Clara proudly. The parents holding the baby still look serious. The obligations of married life or maybe their consequences having turned out to be all too true. The priest standing in the middle seems to be quite young.

"So, I count six of you. Is that right Clara?"

"Roberto and Álvaro, they're the oldest; they're twins. Then, there's Ana Paola, Manuel, Pedro, and me," she says counting out the names on the fingers of both hands. Suddenly there is a loud crash from overhead that shakes the plaster on the ceiling.

"They're jumping off the top bunk to see who can jump the farthest. Álvaro always wins because he's taller than Roberto," she adds lowering her voice. "The girls at school all want to be Álvaro's girlfriend."

"How come?"

The question hangs in the air. At that moment a robust woman in her forties comes into the room and shooing Clara out, closes the door. A few buttons on her blouse are still open and her lipstick has been applied without the benefit of a mirror. Alma has obviously caught her at an inconvenient time.

After introducing herself, the woman looks apologetic. "Sorry about all the chaos. We have a birthday today. Roberto, my husband, has gone to pick up his mother; I was trying to get lunch together. You've come to ask about my brother, *Padre* Francisco? Are they reopening the case?"

Alma feels slightly squeamish as she always does when she has wormed her way into someone's home without being completely forthright. "Your oldest son is named after his father," says Alma trying to score a friendly point with Inés.

"There is no oldest son," says Inés. "Our oldest children are twins. Roberto and Álvaro are twins." The woman says nothing more but the expression in her eyes shows irritation. She doesn't want me barging into her family life, Alma thinks.

"Yes, hopefully reopening the case of your brother's murder might be one of the outcomes of our investigation," says Alma switching back to a more professional mode. "I understand that your brother started a migrant center in

Ávila. It seems that he was returning from an appointment or from visiting someone when he was killed. Can you tell me anything about that night, or perhaps anything about his life which you think might help our investigation?"

Inés knits her bushy dark eyebrows together so that they almost form a narrow path across her forehead. She thinks for a moment. "He had dozens of projects: the migrants' center, the home for the girls. He spoke often about social justice around the region. It was too much for me to keep track of. They said he was sitting in his car when someone walked up to the driver's side and shot him. He wasn't found for an hour or so. There were no witnesses; the police believed at the time that he was the victim of gang violence. The murder might have been intentional or perhaps it was a case of mistaken identity. Everybody loved him or almost everyone," Inés says tossing up her hands and shaking her head as if to validate the senselessness of the death. She looks at a small watch on her wrist. "I'm so sorry. I need— "

"Just one more question. One summer fifteen years ago a girl named María Teresa Gómez y Velasco was a volunteer at the migrant center. Your brother officiated Mass at her *quinceaños* celebration. Later that year she was one of the single mothers at La Casa de la Esperanza. I know it was a long time ago, but did he ever mention her?"

The woman sits back in her chair and crosses her arms across her chest. Alma thinks that she sees a look of confusion come over Inés's face but at that exact moment, there is a still more thunderous crash overhead. All six children doubtlessly have jumped off the top bunk together.

Alma wonders if the whole tribe will fall through the ceiling. Their mother jumps up, opens the sitting-room door and shouts, "That's enough! All of you out to the park immediately and mind Clara crossing the street."

The house shakes as many feet pound down the stairs and repeatedly slam the front door. When Inés returns to the sofa, her face is perfectly composed. "Sorry, what were we speaking about?"

"A girl your brother helped, María Teresa Gómez y Velasco. Did he ever mention her?"

"No, I don't remember that name and anyway, what does some privileged fifteen-year-old have to do with a murder that happened five years later?" she says rising again getting ready to show Alma out; her irritation with the reporter's visit becoming quite obvious.

"Do you have other siblings that I might talk with?" Alma asks on her way to the door ignoring Inés's question about the fifteen-year-old girl.

"We have a sister who's a nurse. She's been in Dallas for many years, and a brother. He lives abroad too. They wouldn't know anything; they're hardly ever in Mexico. Sorry I couldn't be more helpful."

"Where's your family from?" asks Alma stepping out into the patio.

"From here, my parents were school teachers."

Aunt Isabel is sitting in the passenger seat when Alma gets behind the wheel. "Learn anything useful?" she asks.

"No," says Alma flatly. "Big waste of time. How about you?"

"Not really. The family has lived here a long time. Inés's parents moved in first. She cared for them as they got older. When they died, she married Roberto. They started having kids right away. The twins were a surprise to the couple and to the neighbors, but then twins often are. The rest of the kids arrived at regular intervals. The family is well-liked; they're respectable people. Good neighbors."

*   *   *

"Are you sure you want to take the old road back?" asks Aunt Isabel. "It's deserted in places and full of potholes."

"But it's pretty," says Alma. "And I haven't been that way for years. I'll be careful."

What Alma loves about the old highway is the first stretch of the road that winds through the foothills of the Sierra Madre Mountains, up and down goes the road around steep curves and over small bridges. She opens one of the car windows. The smell of pine trees and the sound of water rushing over the rapids as the road doubles back over the Río Ciénega begin to lift her spirits. She drives more slowly, enjoying the cool breeze, the sunshine, and the sparse traffic. She can feel the stress of the past week evaporate.

The high point of the trip, she admits, was breakfast with Aunt Isabel because the interviews, which she doesn't think she handled that well, were not particularly productive. The one nugget seems to be the name of Tere's boyfriend that summer, Andrés. But who is Andrés? She knows that the migrant center doesn't keep records. Where else could she look for traces of the boy? Her conversation with Inés really didn't go well. Alma tries to recall something the woman said which struck her as odd. Yes, she had spoken of a privileged fifteen-year-old. Alma had never mentioned that the fifteen-year-old was in any way special. Most of the young volunteers at the migrant center had been middle-class at best and La Casa de la Esperanza certainly wasn't for women of means. She needs to call Irma, *La Gordis*, first thing in the morning to see what information she has on *Padre* Francisco. She needs a photograph of the priest, too.

She suddenly realizes that she hasn't thought about Gabriel all day. Ah, she smiles to herself, the curative effects of a change of scene. It's a week since he left and not a single word except of course for Linda's posts on Facebook. Maybe he thinks that e-mail and the telephone are inadequate tools for complicated explanations. Alma had never thought that Gabriel's ties to Linda were deep. They had been married less than three years, no kids. They'd been separated for part of that time. What had he said that went wrong with the relationship? She couldn't adjust to Mexico. Her life in Texas had been filled with friends, university classes, shopping with her mom. In Ávila she only had her horses and Gabriel. She had complained that they had no couple friends. Gabriel's friends, when they came over to the house, would start out speaking English for Linda's sake but rapidly switch to Spanish. He explained that for them, English was like wearing a tuxedo: stiff, unfamiliar. Spanish was like jeans and a tee shirt; they could relax, tell jokes, use nicknames that meant nothing in English, reminisce about old times, swear a bit. Familiar slang rolled off their tongues.

When the couple visited Linda's new friends who were the

managers of the foreign companies in Ávila, the men talked about golf and American football, none of which interested Gabriel. Or they put on serious faces and talked about how they were helping his country pull out of poverty by teaching poor Mexican children English. Gabriel had commented mildly that the road out of poverty would be much quicker if their factories paid their workers better wages. The invitations weren't repeated.

So, if Gabriel and Linda's lives had been incompatible, why had he become involved with her again? The marriage seemed to have ended by mutual consent. She couldn't live in Ávila, and he thought he couldn't live in the U.S. Each one wanted their own familiar, cozy home. They wore an invisible sign that said: No sacrifice considered here. It seems to Alma a relationship with shallow roots, but as she is discovering, perhaps the same could be said about her relationship with Gabriel. She leans back in her seat and thinks that's enough soul-searching for today. Now a little music is called for. She slips an old Ricky Martin CD into the disc player.

She has been so absorbed in her thoughts and the music that she hasn't noticed the black pick-up looming up on her tail. She slows down to let it pass, putting on her signal light to show that the road ahead is clear. It moves closer. What is the driver's problem? She lowers her window and waves him on. Instead he bumps her, gently at first and then harder. She looks in the rearview mirror. The driver seems to be the sole occupant of the truck. What is he playing at? She begins to get angry. Is he some kind of lunatic who bothers women for kicks on lonely roads? Her heart lurches as he slams her fender again. Is he going to assault her? She's heard of robberies, some violent, on this road, but the police said they had gotten the gang. She starts to honk the car horn and flash her headlights in case someone appears coming from the opposite direction, but she and the pick-up are all alone on the curvy road.

He pulls out and moves closer and closer to her car. The windows of the truck are tinted so she can't see her assailant, but she assumes it's a man. He begins to bang the front of her car forcing her off the macadam and on to the gravel shoulder of the road. She grabs the steering wheel as tightly as she can, but begins to panic. She applies the brake before she hits the side railing but as her car slows, the driver of the pick-up continues to force her closer and closer to the edge. The terrain beyond the barrier drops off precipitously. If she crashes through the barrier, her car will roll hundreds of feet down the hill tumbling over rocks, bushes, and trees as it picks up speed. Just as she is calculating the chances of surviving such an accident, the truck speeds off. She breaks violently; her car comes to a full stop inches from the metal railing. She looks in her rearview mirror and sees a taxi pull up behind her.

The cabby jumps out of his taxi and runs up to the driver's side of Alma's car. "Are you okay?" he shouts through the window. Alma is shaking; her heart is racing. She puts her head down on the steering wheel. Her mouth tastes of bile. She feels as if she's going to vomit. The taxi driver stands next to her car looking up and down the highway. Slowly her head clears; she rolls down the window. The man is older.

His eyes are wide with fright.

"What just happened? Did that truck try to force you off the road?"

"Yes, I think that's what it was doing. Did you scare him off? If so, thank you and thank you for stopping."

"Why would someone do something like that?" asks the man.

"I don't know," she says but then she holds up her press badge. "It might be an investigation I'm working on."

"Are you on the way to Ávila? I'll follow you until you get safely to where you're going."

The kindness of strangers, thinks Alma, tears of rage and relief running down her cheeks.

*   *   *

When she parks in front of her house, the taxi driver stops for a moment. "You've gone out of your way," she says. "I'd like to compensate you for your trouble."

The man smiles. "Getting pretty girls safely home is no trouble but take the pay road from now on. I'd take it too if I had the money."

Before confronting her father and Kurt, whom she can see in the front room, she phones Ricardo. "Things have gotten complicated," she says when he picks up. She keeps her voice well under control; he doesn't need to know how frightened she is.

"What's up?"

"This morning Evelyn's father, Nick Hammond, came by to see me. He was hysterical. If my neighbors hadn't stepped in, I might have ended up with a black eye. He seems to think that I'm hiding Evelyn. That she's in some imminent danger; that I'm in league with the Gómez y Velasco family."

"Is it Nick Hammond, the lawyer who's always in the news? I've heard he's a bully. Did something else happen?"

"Someone tried to force me off the road on the way back from Nuevo Progreso. It could have been a random robbery attempt or someone trying to scare me. It could or could not have something to do with the Gómez y Velasco investigation."

"They tried to force you off the Interstate? How's that even possible?"

"No, I was on the old road."

"What the hell were you doing on the old road? Everyone knows how dangerous that road is."

"But it's so pretty and peaceful."

"*Por Dios*, Alma, you're making me feel like I should get you a therapist along with police protection. I'm calling Captain Ramírez right now."

"But this isn't a work-related problem, Richie, and my mom is going to give me so much flak. You remember the last time I had to have bodyguards. She's barely gotten over that. Couldn't I just call Pedro when I feel it's necessary? I don't need twenty-four-hour protection."

"Listen, Alma, police protection isn't like a *rebozo* you can wrap around you when it gets chilly. This is serious stuff."

"I know it's serious. You don't have to talk to me like I'm a child."

"Well, then act like an adult," he snaps. "A squad car will be around in the next couple of hours."

When she enters the living room, her father and Kurt are sitting behind an enormous bouquet of yellow roses. Is Gabriel back she wonders? She hopes he doesn't come around this evening. She cannot bear even five minutes more of stress.

"Who's Dan Sullivan?" asks Kurt. "Why is he sending you flowers and asking you out to dinner."

"He's an old friend from high school. You remember Dan, don't you, Pa?"

"What's he doing in Mexico?" asks her father.

"He works in San Miguel."

"Why doesn't Gabriel send you flowers?" asks Kurt.

"Don't you have homework, Kurt?" her father says.

"You want to talk about secret stuff," shouts Kurt as he climbs the stairs to his room.

Her father closes the living room door. "What's going on?" he whispers.

"What do you mean?" asks Alma. Then a second later she adds, "Has Elena been talking to you and Ma?"

"Elena? No. Your neighbor, Luis, pulled me aside while Jaime took Kurt off to look at his new motorbike. He said that some *gringo* had roughed you up outside the house this morning. He said maybe I should think of staying over for a few days. But where's Gabriel? Shouldn't he be here?"

Alma sits down on the sofa next to Jesús. "Gabriel's in Texas for a week or so."

"You don't look good, Alma, and Kurt told me that you were acting funny. Why is Gabriel in Texas? Has something gone wrong between the two of you? Kurt said he wasn't going to the big game on Saturday. He's a bigger fan than we are. What's happening?"

"I don't know what's going on. He's in Austin for the week. He ran into his ex-wife, and she posted on Facebook that they were back together. He was supposed to call me when he arrived. I haven't heard from him. What would you think?"

"I don't know Alma. I like Gabriel; he seems like a good guy. Maybe it's not what you think. Sometimes people do things, you know, out of character, but then they snap back. Why don't you call his friend Sergio? The guy he goes to all the games with. He's your friend too. He might have heard from Gabriel."

She doesn't say anything for a minute. "Don't tell Ma. She'll say it's because we aren't married," says Alma lowering her gaze.

"Your mother won't say that; she'll say what I'm going to say. If he leaves you, he's the biggest *pendejo* in Mexico, and he has a lot of competition for that title. Speaking of that kind of person, who's the guy who roughed you up this morning?"

Alma explains about Evelyn Hammond and her investigation. "Nick Hammond was upset this morning, but he's not coming back, Pa, believe me. He's a big-shot lawyer, and even if he thinks I know something about his runaway daughter, he's not going to risk getting his name in the papers for assaulting a reporter. You don't need to stay."

As he's leaving, Jesús gives Alma a hug. "Dry your eyes and put on some lipstick. We Jaramillos are fighters. You're not going to let some *Tejana* steal your boyfriend. And you and Kurt go out to dinner with Dan Sullivan. Give Gabriel a little run for his money," he says winking.

She has just taken off her shoes and put her feet up on the sofa when she hears a knock on the front door. Dan Sullivan, she groans. Before she can come up with an excuse to avoid dinner, Kurt is opening the front door. She can hear her son saying that certainly his mom is home and that she's expecting him.

Dan crosses the front room in three long strides, lifts her up and wraps her in bear hug. Then holding her at arm's length, she sees a look of concern come over his face. "Are you sick? You looked terrific last weekend. What's happened?"

Alma mumbles something about a lot of work and being too tired for dinner.

"Pizza, that's what you need. Come on Kurt. You can show me where the best pizza place is in town."

While they're gone, Alma examines her face in the bathroom mirror. She does look awful. There are bags under her eyes, her skin looks sallow, her hair is limp and lifeless. She showers quickly, applies a little eye makeup, lipstick and puts on one of her new summer dresses. It isn't an instant transformation, but at least she looks presentable and smells good.

Kurt excuses himself as soon as he's wolfed down two slices of pizza. In his new monosyllabic way of speaking, he says, "Homework" and goes to his bedroom.

"Is he always so quiet?" asks Dan opening a second beer. "You want some? It'll help you sleep."

"No to both questions. Kurt seems to have gone from nine to fifteen overnight. He's going to a big soccer game on Saturday with his grandpa. That will probably cure whatever it is that ails him."

Dan leans back in his chair. "So why are you so stressed out? What happened today?"

Alma closes the kitchen door. Kids, she explains, are the nosiest people on earth. "I'm working on an investigation. It's not strictly for my newspaper, more of a favor for a friend. It seems like more than few people would like it stopped, like your friends, the Gómez y Velascos. It's confidential so I can't tell you all the details.

"Yesterday I was offered twenty thousand dollars to back away from the investigation. Then this morning another interested party, an American lawyer, appeared at my door and started roughing me up. Plus, a colleague at work is trying to steal my job." Among her litany of woes, she purposely avoids mentioning Gabriel or the incident on the Nuevo Progreso highway. She definitely does not want Dan Sullivan taking on the role of protector and camping out in her living room for the night.

"Yeah, I wondered why you were so interested in the Gómez y Velascos. I first met Raúl and—. What's his wife's name?"

"Sonia."

"Yeah, I first met them when they came to the hotel looking for a venue for Verónica's *quinceaños* party."

He had met with Raúl three or four times afterward, Dan says. In the beginning he liked him, maybe because his

English was good, and he knew something about American football. Raúl liked to chat. He was certainly more relaxed when his wife wasn't around. He'd reminisce about how San Miguel used to be; how it had become a go-to place for Americans. It all started in the early nineteen-forties with a Peruvian painter named Felipe Cossío del Pomar and the American Stirling Dickinson. They founded an art institute and Belles Artes, a center for the performing artists. American G.I.s came after World War Two looking for a congenial place to paint; then in the sixties, hippies started to appear. Foreign retirees started arriving in droves in the seventies. "Sun, charming architecture, beautiful homes, interesting people, domestic help, cheap booze," Raúl had said. "Who could ask for anything more?"

Dan sits back in his chair. "But Raúl let me know right off," he continues, "who was top dog. He'd say stuff like 'You are so lucky that you don't have to spend hours in Mexico City getting your car serviced.' Because of course, he has a fancy imported car, and I have an ordinary company car. Or 'Hey, the prints that the decorator chose for the hotel aren't bad but come over to the house if you want to see real art.'"

When he started giving Dan advice on how to get San Miguel's big spenders interested in holding events in the hotel, it became less amusing. "You've got to join groups like Los Militantes de Jesús where you'll meet people with real money." Dan had told him that as a regular churchgoer perhaps he'd meet some of the Catholic business men there. "Meet them at Mass? No, that's only for old women and peasants. The people I'm talking about know how to make religion work not only for the Church but also for them personally."

However, his real disenchantment had been dealing with the wife, Sonia. She bargained endlessly and tirelessly about everything. She wanted discounts or freebees on every bottle of wine, hors d'oeuvre, or dessert. She kept saying that she and Raúl were doing the hotel a favor by holding the party on its premises. After all, wasn't their event with its prestigious guest list providing thousands of dollars of free advertising for the hotel? She'd laugh after saying it, but Dan knew she believed it.

"It was disagreeable. My staff got so they'd hide when they saw her coming. She was a dime tipper too. If your investigation has anything to do with money, be careful. The bank called me two days ago to say that Raúl Gómez's check for the party had bounced. When I phoned him, he made up some excuse about a mix-up with one of his accounts. Said he'd be around today with a new check, but my assistant says he never showed up."

Dan takes another swallow of his beer. "But where's that boyfriend of yours? Why isn't he around watching out for you?"

"He's in the States at the moment and," she said smiling "I'm not sure that it's his job to watch out for me. I realized a long time ago that being a journalist can be uncomfortable."

"You're one cool lady. Couldn't you at least sleep at your parent's house for a few days?"

"Speaking of sleep," she says, smiling. "I really appreciate the visit and the pizza, Dan—."

"Okay, I get it. Anyway, it's time for me to head back to San Miguel," he says, putting on his jacket and heading toward the door. "But I'm going to be checking up on you. Why don't you come to San Miguel this weekend? Bring Kurt, bring what's his name too if you have to. You've got a room at the Lakewood Resort any time you like."

"Thanks so much for the generous offer." She kisses him on the cheek. "I just might turn up one of these days."

As she watches Dan's tail lights disappear down the street, she thinks about her father's advice. Maybe she should speak to Sergio. She's a reporter after all, a gatherer of facts. So far, she's imagined the worst and has only heard Linda's side of the story. It's only nine o'clock; she punches in Sergio's number.

"Alma, *que milagro*, what's up?"

"I need to talk to you. Are you busy? Could you come over? I can't leave Kurt alone."

"Right now? Tonight?"

"Yes."

Sergio, kind but quizzical, is sitting in her living room twenty minutes later drinking a beer. "So?" he says.

She explains that Gabriel left a week ago to depose a witness in Austin. He had said he would be back in a few days, but she's heard nothing from him: no call, no text, no e-mail. His ex-wife, Linda, posted on Facebook that she and Gabriel had met up in Austin and were now back together. She was euphoric. Alma doesn't understand what's going on. She thought that she and Gabriel were a couple, but now she doesn't know what to think.

Sergio runs his fingers through his hair and looks off into space for a minute or two. "Here's the thing, Alma," he says. "I don't think Gabriel ever got Linda quite out of his head and, maybe, his heart. First loves are tough to erase. Both of them are complicated people but for different reasons. Do you want to hear a little of Gabriel's romantic history?"

She nods her head.

"Gabriel and I hung out together all through university. I fell in love at the beginning of every semester with a different girl. Gabriel dated a lot, but he never seemed to be in love. So I was surprised when he came back from his studies in Austin that first Christmas and could talk of nothing except Linda. She was the smartest, most beautiful, most accomplished girl he'd ever met, and she was fascinated with Mexico. That first summer she came for a visit, I guess we expected Linda would be Scarlett Johansson's twin sister, he'd given her such a build-up. Yes, she was pretty and seemed in love with Gabo, but I never got why he was so crazy about her. Maybe it's because she's so moody. You never knew if she'd greet you with a big smile or cut you dead.

"I'm sure you've noticed that Gabriel is stubborn but usually in a good way. He never gives up on anybody. He has clients who have been in jail for ten years, and he's still trying to prove that they're innocent. He's like a dog with a bone when he thinks someone needs him. The first year they were married, things seemed to go well. Linda was fixing up that ridiculous house, riding her horses, learning Spanish, making friends. She was on a real high. Gabriel was teaching and setting up his law office. But as time went by she seemed to deflate. She lost interest in the house, the horses, her classes. He told me she spent most of the day in bed. I could tell he was worried, maybe frantic is a better word.

"Then one day to the next she was gone. He went up to Houston like every other weekend for a while. She wanted him to come up there to live. He put her off. He started going less frequently because he had a lot of work. One day about eight or nine months after she left, he called me; he was crushed. Linda had met someone and wanted a divorce. He said he knew the guy, a lawyer named Lopez who worked in her father's firm. The guy was real *cabrón*. Gabriel was beside himself. He felt he was responsible for the failed marriage and the divorce. I'm not sure he was so in love with Linda anymore, but he felt he had failed her. He was in pretty bad shape for a while."

Sergio stops talking and looks at Alma. "Then he met me," she says.

"His friends were so happy for him. He seemed to be himself again."

"But he's still the dog with a bone. The man who has to save the world, protect the vulnerable; be the knight in shining armor."

Sergio sighs. "It seems so," he says.

When she opens the door to say good night to her guest, Alma sees that the patrol car that Ricardo has requested is parked down the street. She sleeps soundly that night, no dreams.

CHAPTER 9

"Mom," Kurt says shaking her shoulder, "there's a police car in front of the house." Alma groans.

"Do you think they're looking for someone?" He moves to the window peeking out between the slates of the blinds.

"Looking for someone? No, Ricardo thinks that—." She stops. "It's best if we don't mention the police car to *Abuelita*. Ricardo thinks that Evelyn's father is very excitable. He thinks he might bother me."

"But you're trying to help Evelyn. Why would he do that? Evelyn said she hates him."

"He's a frightened father, Kurt. It's cruel what Evelyn did, running away."

The boy starts to walk out of the room. "She'll be back soon. Where can she go?"

After breakfast, carrying his cereal bowl to the sink, he says, "There's a class trip today. I need some extra money, and I need to take some food."

"Sure, what do you need?"

"Two hundred pesos, a loaf of bread and that jar of peanut butter," he says pointing to the shelf on the far wall.

"Two hundred pesos! Where are you going? That's a lot of money for a school excursion. Is it for a donation to a park or something?"

"Yeah," says Kurt as he picks up his backpack. "It's for a good cause."

*   *   *

Alma finally gets hold of Sandra around nine a.m. There's no news about Evelyn. She's vanished. Nick hired three detectives, who arrived from Mexico City yesterday. They checked all the bus stations, taxi stands, and hotels. No one answering Evelyn's description has been seen. "Where could the girl be?" asks Sandra. Nick, she says, told her that they were his only real friends in Mexico.

Alma breaks into the conversation. Nick, she says, came to her house yesterday morning. He was like a wild man. He'd accused her of conspiring in some obscure way with María Teresa's brother, Raúl. She had never mentioned to Sandra or to Evelyn Tere's brother's name. Nick knows more about Evelyn's birth family than he's letting on.

"What a mess. I wish they'd all go home," says Sandra ending the conversation.

Alma has barely hung up when the phone rings. "*Licenciada* Julieta," says the caller unnecessarily, her lisp being her calling card. "My client is anxious to know if you've come to a decision. We need to know today where to deliver the money."

"*Vete al diablo*," says Alma cutting off the conversation. She feels just as exasperated as Sandra. She wishes the whole lot of them—Evelyn, Nick Hammond, the Gómez y Velasco family, and *Padre* Francisco—would disappear from her life. Gabriel too. She needs a vacation. Maybe she will take up Danny Sullivan's offer. A weekend at the Lakewood Resort could be just the thing.

*   *   *

Parking her car in front of El Diario de Ávila she runs into Irma. "Do you have any *esquelas* for *Padre* Francisco? You know, that priest who ran the migrant center out beyond the railway tracks?"

"Yes, pages and pages, I'll send you over the file. What's that cop doing? It looks like he's trying to get your attention. See, he's calling your name. Oh, oh, Alma, are you in trouble again?" says the woman, laughing loudly as she walks into the building.

"What's up?" she asks the cop. "We're going to get breakfast. Be back in an hour so don't disappear on us." They've read my mind, she thinks, as she gets into the elevator.

She bumps into Ricardo as she steps into the newsroom. "Anything new?" he says.

"No news about Evelyn, but that lawyer called me again."

"And?"

"I wasn't very nice."

"Come on, we're going to pay a visit to Guzmán, Muñoz y Ortiz. Just let me make a few phone calls first."

Alma sits down at her desk. Irma has left a file with the

death notices for *Padre* Francisco. There are several from the archdioceses, one from his fellow priests at the seminary. A few from Catholic associations and charities in the city. Several big *esquelas* from wealthy patrons, even a few from businesses in the area. As she closes the folder and stands up to take it back to Irma, a small piece of paper which had been stuck to the back of the folder floats toward the floor. Alma grabs the paper and starts to shove it back into the folder. It's a small death notice from the Rabasa León family thanking all those who expressed condolences for their brother's death. As her eyes skim over the text, she stops short. The ad is signed by *Padre* Francisco's nearest relatives: María Esther, who she assumes is the nurse in Dallas, Inés, Andrés, his brother-in-law Roberto, and his then four nieces and nephews. She reads the names of Francisco's siblings again. María Esther, Inés, and Andrés. Her heart begins to beat faster. She rushes to her computer, opens Goggle and types in Andrés Rabasa León. There are three young men who pop up but none from Mexico, none the right age. Could it be? Could the mysterious Andrés be *Padre* Francisco's brother?

She calls Ana over to her desk. She relates her trip to Nuevo Progreso, then shows her *Padre* Francisco's *esquela*.

"The doctor we talked to at the General Hospital in Nuevo Progreso said that Tere's boyfriend was named Andrés. Inés, Francisco's sister, told me that the family was from Nuevo Progreso. It may be a long shot, but shouldn't we check out the birth certificates registered in Nuevo Progreso for the time around the birth of the twins?"

"I'll take the bus," says Ana. "My car is too old for

highway driving. But will the state registry office give out that kind of information to just anyone?" Alma opens her purse and hands the woman several bills. Ana sighs but doubles the bills and shoves them into her pocket. "It's a good thing there's no confession in my church because my pastor is always on about corruption. I hate getting information this way. It's wrong. We object when we hear about politicians or the cops taking bribes, but we're no different. We perpetuate the system without even thinking twice."

Alma hands her two more bills. "Take a first-class bus. They're faster and more comfortable."

*   *   *

"Which of the law partners did your father know?" she asks Ricardo as they pick up the highway to Querétaro.

"Arturo Guzmán. He was the lawyer to go to if you had an expensive divorce on your hands or you were rich and in trouble with the law. He must be over seventy now. Maybe he turned the practice over to a less scrupulous relative."

"Perhaps he's got a son like your protégé, Héctor."

"That was nasty, Alma. No, *Licenciado* Guzmán never married. He's a big patron of the arts. I think he's trying to get Ávila or perhaps it's San Miguel de Allende to build a museum for his collection of folk art. My father also said he was honest even though he kept some very dicey people out of jail. Who do you think is behind the bribe?"

"Of course, my first thought was Hernán Gómez y Velasco since he told me to stop the investigation. He said he had important friends who would squash me like a scorpion or a venomous snake." Alma giggles in spite of herself. "But

Ángeles, his cook, said that money was tight. Nick Hammond? Paying me off would be better for his image than beating me up. Raúl and Sonia? My sources tell me that they have money troubles too."

Ricardo locates Guzmán, Muñoz y Ortiz S.C. in a fifteen-story glass tower on the outskirts of Querétaro. It takes a good ten minutes and the arrival of the *Licenciado's* personal assistant before they're allowed up to the penthouse.

When they enter his office, Arturo Guzmán takes Alma's hand and gives it the lightest possible kiss. He wraps Ricardo in a firm hug, patting rather than pounding his back. "I miss your father," he says, which launches the two men into a series of reminiscences about long-dead second cousins and half-remembered baptisms and weddings. Left out and bored, Alma turns her attention to the office. The dark wood chairs, desks, and tables come from a different space and era. They are obviously of good quality but belong in one of the seventeenth-century houses downtown.

Horses, sculptured, painted, and photographed, dominate the walls and bookcases of the office. She wanders over to the far wall. There are twenty or thirty photographs of a vigorous Arturo Guzmán in jodhpurs and helmet seated on sleek chestnut horses proudly flashing trophies or blue ribbons for the camera. As she begins to look more closely at a group of people at a party with cocktail glasses raised, the lawyer calls her back to the long table. Did one of the women in the photo look familiar? She thinks so but momentarily puts the image out of her head.

"Arturo," says her boss in the most conciliatory tone,

"Alma has had a rather," he pauses for moment, "unexpected," is the word he settles on, "visit from one of your associates, Julieta Vega Guzmán. It had to do with an investigation Alma's working on, privately, not for the paper. *Licenciada* Vega offered her twenty thousand dollars to drop the project. When Alma asked about the consequences of not accepting the twenty thousand dollars, the lawyer said she would be harassed until she did so. I can't say it was exactly *plata o plomo*, but it was nasty nonetheless."

The lawyer's expression is one of surprise. He looks at Alma and says he cannot imagine what could have prompted Julieta to act in such an unethical way. She's the daughter of one of his sisters and an exceptionally well-trained lawyer. She attended an excellent university in Mexico City and has an advanced degree from an Ivy League school in the States. The old lawyer's eyes cloud over. "You work too hard, you young people," he says. He's sure Ricardo and Alma are the same: work, work, work. His life had been different. Of course he worked hard, but he enjoyed himself too. He had his horses and his collection. "You need a hobby," he smiles now at Alma.

"Well," says Alma dryly, "horses and art are a little out of my price range at the moment, but if Ricardo were to raise our salaries, perhaps I would buy a horse or two." She feels a kick on her ankle from her boss's sharp leather boot.

Ricardo breaks into the conversation before Alma can get in another unsuitable dig. He asks Arturo if he would be so kind as to speak with Julieta's client about backing off. He says he has a good idea who the client is, and the person, he believes, will be reasonable.

The lawyer looks from one to the other of his guests. "How could you possibly know who our client is?" he asks. "Did Julieta mention a name?"

Not exactly, says Ricardo, but it wasn't hard to guess. The woman, says Ricardo, values her privacy. The lawyer looks alarmed now. He pushes back the long strands of gray hair which have fallen over his eyes. He starts to rise from his chair. He'll speak with Julieta. Of course, no one wants Alma to be harassed, particularly since he might meet her one day on the race course; his irony neatly matching her own. The lawyer, signaling the end of the meeting, kisses Alma's hand once more and wraps Ricardo in another firm *abrazo*.

"Do you still have that house in San Miguel?" asks Ricardo. "My father took me there once. You had the most wonderful collection of handmade toys. I was enthralled. The house was just behind the Cathedral. I remember a green door and a brass knocker in the shape of a lion's head."

"My boy, what a memory you have. Yes, it's where I keep my collection. The pieces are very old and quite unique. They deserve to be in a museum."

The assistant accompanies them to the lobby where they retrieve their driver's licenses. Ricardo tells the assistant that he was happy to see *Don* Arturo so fit. He had missed seeing him at the equestrian events in San Miguel. The woman sighs. It's a shame, she says, that her boss has lost interest in San Miguel. At one time he'd had such an active social life there.

"Whatever made you say that you knew his client was a woman?" asks Alma as they pull out of the parking garage.

To see his reaction, says Ricardo. The lawyer could be a good poker player, but he's almost sure now that the client is a woman. Who's the most likely candidate, he asks, glancing at Alma? Before she can answer he says, no one other than María Teresa Gómez y Velasco. So, the e-mail that Alma had sent did have an effect; Tere Gómez was coming after her.

"Could we make another stop in Querétaro?" asks Alma. She explains that a few days ago she visited El Refugio, a migrant hostel on the outskirts of Ávila. "You know the one. It's where your father interviewed *Padre* Francisco years ago. Well, this woman volunteer told me that the place is run by La Fundación Fray Peti Juan. She said that it's really well-known, but on the Internet, there's just a single page with the briefest description of the work they do."

"What do they do?"

"They help women and children who are in need or who are threatened with violence, mostly migrants from Central America. Do you remember your father mentioning that foundation?"

"Not that I can recall. Does it say who Fray Peti Juan was?"

"The website refers you to yet another page, but the page doesn't exist. I looked him up. He was a Spanish priest who came to Mexico in the seventeen hundreds to bring souls to the Church. Unfortunately," here Alma begins to laugh, "his funding came from the Inquisition; information the foundation probably doesn't want spread around."

When they locate the address, the foundation's office is shut tight. There's mail pushed partway under the door. Alma pulls two or three letters and leaflets out. They are all junk mail. She leaves Ricardo and looks into the offices up and down the hallway. She disappears into one of them; a good ten minutes go by. Ricardo pulls out his phone, goes to the stairs, sits down on the top step and calls the office.

When Alma finally emerges, she is smiling. "The plot thickens," she says, her eyes bright with amusement. "The president of the foundation is an Italian woman, the dentist said. He once did an estimate to replace an old crown that she'd broken. He looked up her name for me, and it is none other than Sonia Bianchi. The receptionist said that her husband, Raúl, works with her, but that she hasn't seen either one of them for a couple of weeks."

As they leave the building, Alma spots Mercedes, the volunteer from the migrant center, heading toward them. She is wearing another voluminous white garment. The wind is behind her. "My God," says Ricardo, "she looks like a sixteenth-century Spanish Galleon in full sail." The woman nods to Alma but says nothing as she enters the building.

*   *   *

"Love letter?" says Héctor as he passes Alma's desk. She has just picked up an envelope which must have been hand delivered as it has no stamp and no return address. She looks at the man, trying to focus on what he's saying.

"But it must be a new guy because a little bird told me that your boyfriend flew the coop. Must not like ball busters." He starts whistling as he walks off. She's tempted to say something rude, but then reflects on how open warfare with Héctor would only feed the office gossip mill. She wouldn't be surprised if half the office hasn't already rooted out her interest in the Gómez y Velasco family as well as her personal problems.

She opens the envelope carefully and extracts several sheets of thick cream-colored vellum stationery. The pages are covered in a fine spidery handwriting; the ink, dark blue.

Señorita Jaramillo,

I feel I owe you an apology. I now realize you came to see me in good faith with a sincere desire to help a young person. But that period of my life is still painful for me to recall, and truthfully, I still don't understand much of what went on.

Before joining Las Hermanas de Santa Margarita, I had been trained as a midwife. When Padre Francisco came to speak at our convent about his work, he mentioned that he was starting a home for single mothers. I told him I was a midwife and within a few months I was the director of La Casa de la Esperanza.

I loved my work there. We didn't have many girls, perhaps 10 or 12 a year. They were mostly poor women with families far away.

When I delivered the first baby I asked Padre Francisco what plans he had for the child as the mother did not want to keep the baby. He said that an agency which was run by a friend of his would place the child and find the girl a job. How wonderful, I thought, and so it went for a couple of years.

Then a fifteen-year-old was placed in our care. She was left at the door by a chauffeur. Obviously, she was different from our other girls. She spent most of her time alone in her room, wouldn't talk to anyone, wouldn't see a doctor.

A week or so after she arrived, Padre Francisco paid us a visit. The girl greeted him like an old friend. The next day she asked me how she could go about putting the baby up for adoption as she had decided not to keep the child. I told her about the agency. No, she said that wouldn't do. I remembered an American who had come to see us. I called him and although the girl wouldn't meet him, she agreed to his adopting her baby. He offered to move the girl to a real hospital for the birth, but events overtook us; she went into labor ahead of time. It was a long, difficult labor, and I realized that we couldn't handle the birth. I called the American. He appeared immediately with a doctor who said, "she's carrying twins." The American looked stunned when he realized he would be taking home two babies,

That night I was on duty. I remember glancing at my watch--- ten o'clock, time to check on the handful of new mothers in my care. To make a long story short, when I entered the last room and neared the girl's cot, I could hear her sobbing. I glanced at the cradles; my heart leaped. The cradle which should have held the boy was empty. I remember throwing off the sheet covering the girl, but the baby wasn't in the mother's bed either.

I rushed to the door of the room, I glanced down the corridor. Two men both dressed in black appeared in the shadows near the front door. As they stepped onto the sidewalk, the street light shone on the shorter man's face. He raised the index finger to his lips. I recognized him immediately. It was Padre Francisco.

I wanted to tell this story for years. I hope some good will come of so much confusion and distress. I continue to pray for the mothers and the babies.

Qué Dios te bendiga,

Hermana Fernanda

P.S. The girl was right in not handing her baby over to the agency. It was called La Fundación Fray Peti Juan. Padre Francisco learned a few years later that they were selling the babies and turning the mothers into prostitutes. It broke his heart.

She starts to read the letter for a second time, arranging in her mind the new information with what she already knows. María Teresa doesn't appear to have met Nick Hammond or June, but Nick knows her brother's name. How did Nick find out about La Casa de la Esperanza? There's no doubt that *Padre* Francisco had aided his brother Andrés in removing the baby boy from the home. She's almost sure now that Andrés is the father of the twins. Why didn't Tere keep the children, marry, or go to live with Andrés and his family? In a few years she would have come into a large inheritance. She puts the letter down.

Alma calls Ricardo. "I've been thinking," she says, "about that foundation that Raúl and Sonia run. I'm sure it was as deeply involved in La Casa de la Esperanza as it is in the migrant hostel. I keep thinking about César's comment that the home had a stink. Don't you have a contact in the federal police? If we've stumbled onto trafficking of minors, they probably have too."

"Actually," says Ricardo when he calls back, "it's the Attorney General's office in Mexico City that deals with that kind of trafficking. My contact tells me that five or six years ago they picked up some talk on the street about La Fundación Fray Peti Juan. They investigated but couldn't get anyone to testify against it. No one wanted to admit they had purchased a baby. He thinks that Raúl and Los Militantes de Jesús are probably the front men for one of the smaller regional cartels. Even more reason to keep Evelyn away from her aunt and uncle."

Alma thinks about her old colleague, César Davila. She must congratulate him when he next appears. He may have some facts in his head jumbled, but he was right about La Casa de la Esperanza. There was a stink buried under all the good intentions. Such a shame. Why did *Padre* Francisco trust Raúl and Sonia's Foundation so completely? She sighs. It seems that every answer in Evelyn's story is met with another question.

Ana breezes into the office a few minutes later. "That was quick," says Alma looking to see if she's carrying any documents. "Did you get to look at the records?"

"Well, it wasn't easy," says Ana flopping into a chair at the side of Alma's desk. "You must have had this same experience dozens of times. The clerk, the secretary, better let's just say the person who has access to the information you need, says that the rules don't permit just anyone the right to see confidential records. Besides, he is much too busy today or any other day to look up the information you want. He points to a pile of files on his desk and sighs. There's a sign nailed to the wall over their head which says, *GRATUITIES ARE PROHIBITED UNDER STATE LAW.*"

"So," says Alma, "you say the magic words. 'Isn't there some way you can help me out?'"

"Alma, I'm ashamed to say I deposited those two hundred pesos in his desk drawer."

"No doubt there were two or three other bills there, right?"

"More like five or six."

"And so, what did you find out?"

"There were no births registered to either Andrés or to María Teresa in 2002, but in June of that year, Andrés's sister and brother-in-law registered twins: Roberto and Álvaro. Their birthday is listed as the twenty-fifth of April. They were born at home and delivered by a midwife. The midwife's signature was simply an X. Her name wasn't legible. When I asked the clerk why the family had waited two months to register the babies, he said it was a common practice. Parents often wanted to make sure the infants would survive before they went to the trouble of filling out a lot of forms. What's Evelyn's date of birth?"

"May second."

Alma leans back in her chair. It seems like too big a coincidence that Inés would have had twins around the same time as Tere and Andrés, but perhaps twins ran in the Rabasa León family.

"But," says Ana, her eyes shining as she puts a leaflet in front of Alma, "I found something just as interesting as *Niño G*'s whereabouts. I found Andrés. Look, he's speaking this evening in Nuevo Progreso. Alma, he's a priest, a missionary. He's back here from Africa raising money for his mission."

Alma stares at the paper. "*Padre* Andrés. Director of Our Lady of Guadalupe Elementary and High School in Southern Kenya, will talk about his experience in this challenging part of the world." The meeting she sees is being held at a rather modest downtown hotel and is sponsored by Los amigos de nuestros misioneros. A small photograph of *Padre* Andrés wearing a wide-brimmed straw hat and surrounded by smiling

African children sits in the middle of the leaflet.

Alma gazes at the fuzzy image of the priest. She places the newspaper photo she has of *Padre* Francisco next to the brochure. Yes, they could be brothers, she thinks. Andrés is now tanned by the African sun, and thinner and taller than his brother ever was, but yes, she thinks she can see a family resemblance.

"Will you go to the meeting?" asks Ana.

"Wouldn't miss it for the world."

As Alma rises to begin packing up her papers, Ana tucks in the label of her friend's blouse and picks off a stray strand of hair which has fallen on Alma's shoulder. "There," says the woman looking Alma up and down to make sure everything is in order. "You're all set."

Time to get rolling, Alma thinks after Ana walks away. She calls her father, inquires after Kurt, and then asks if she can borrow her dad's truck. She has to go back to Nuevo Progreso, and his truck is much better for highway driving than her ten-year-old Jetta. Anyway, he and Kurt will be going to the game tomorrow with Elena's husband and three boys. "Stay the night with Aunt Isabel," advises Jesús. "Even the Interstate isn't that safe late at night," he adds. She agrees.

Next, she calls Captain Ramírez. "I think you can call off your guys. That nut case who came a little too close to me on the highway was some *macho* who gets his kicks out of scaring women on lonely roads. I can't see how it could be tied to anything I'm working on." This is such a downright lie, she almost blushes, but she does not want a car full of cops following her around Nuevo Progreso. She'll be safe with her aunt and uncle.

"Oh, it's the Teflon lady, *Señorita* Jaramillo, who never thinks she's in danger. How come your boss called us then?"

"Come on, Pedro, you know Ricardo. He's a worrier."

"Okay, but Alma, remember how last year you were sure that you were *Señorita* Nobody and then all hell broke loose. We're here if you need us."

CHAPTER 10

At seven-fifteen, Alma parks her father's precious truck in the Hotel Nuevo Progreso's parking lot. The highway trip was uneventful. Aunt Isabel is waiting at the door of the conference room where the talk that evening is to take place. She presses Alma's arm. "Is this part of your investigation?" she asks, her eyes darting around the room.

Alma smiles and puts a finger to her lips. Her aunt nods. There are perhaps fifty people assembled. It's a middle-class crowd: men in newish windbreakers or sports jackets; women in skirts, panty hose, and light coats. In Nuevo Progreso, the evenings in February are chilly. A table at the back of the room holds cups for coffee and tea; there are several large plates of cookies. "Do we need to give a donation?" Isabel whispers as they take a seat in the middle of the back row.

Alma shakes her head and looks around. She is nervous about running into Inés, whom she now knows is the sister of both priests. She would much rather catch *Padre* Andrés off guard, unawares that it is she who visited his sister. She breathes easier when she sees no sign of the woman.

There is a lectern on a small platform at the front of the room. Behind it is a figure dressed in black talking to two women. When the man turns she sees he's wearing a Roman collar. A cross hangs around his neck. The chain is carved from black cow horn, her aunt whispers; the cross looks to be old ivory. The woman who introduces the priest is the president of the local chapter of Los amigos de nuestros misioneros, an organization founded some years ago to help finance the work Catholic charities are doing in Africa and other parts of the world.

Padre Andrés's biography, she says, is an inspiration to us all. Called to the priesthood at an early age, he studied at the seminary in Puebla. After his ordination he went immediately to Africa, teaching in Kenya, Tanzania, and South Africa. *Padre* Andrés comes from an amazing family, a Nuevo Progreso family. No one will ever forget his saintly brother, *Padre* Francisco, God rest his soul. What's more, there is an older sister, a nurse who works among poor immigrants in Texas. And another sister, Inés, who is the mother of six wonderful children. Polite applause greets *Padre* Andrés as he approaches the lectern.

At first glance Alma feels let down. The trip is a waste of time. She's annoyed. This tall, thin man with slightly sloping shoulders and pleasant but quite ordinary features could not possibly be the charismatic Andrés of whom the young doctor spoke with such envy. The priest stands for a moment expressionless regarding the audience. Then the stadium lights go on. His lips curve upward, and a thousand-megawatt smile appears on his face. His eyes begin to sparkle. He greets the audience with a voice which is both melodious and forceful. Music critics would call it a perfect baritone. He tells a priestly joke about himself and smiles again. He has the audience in the palm of his hand. People sit up a little straighter. They listen as he describes his devotion to La Virgen de Guadalupe and his stewardship of Catholic schools in Eastern Kenya, but mostly he speaks about vocations. How important vocations are for the future of the Church; that is his life's work, he says, and should be the concern of all Catholics. He is humble. He is sincere. He knows how to laugh at himself. Alma looks over at her Aunt Isabel. The woman is enthralled. Now she can see this man sixteen years earlier strumming his guitar in the moonlight while a young woman intoxicated with romance, falls in love.

Half way through the talk, a slide projector appears; the lights are lowered. The photos of the villages, people, and natural landscapes of Africa are stunning. *Padre* Andrés, it appears, has an artistic streak. The applause is loud and enthusiastic at the end of the talk. People are drawn to him. Alma thinks, I like him. He's a take-charge type of guy. The kind of person you might tell your troubles to. A priest who wouldn't pass judgment but listen and give you advice.

As the lights come up, she gazes around the room; she sees a middle-aged man with two teenage boys standing near the back. The taller boy continues to stare at the screen, still wrapped up in the photos. The smaller boy heads toward the table with the cookies. Envelopes are passed out for contributions. Alma deposits one hundred pesos in hers. Her aunt does the same. "I'm so glad you invited me," Aunt Isabel says. "Such a wonderful priest, such a good speaker."

A crowd gathers around the priest. Mostly women, they seem to hang on his every word. He looks tired, Alma thinks, even a bit bored. She presses nearer and hears the middle-aged man say that he needs to get the boys home to bed. *Padre* Andrés nods. He'll get a taxi. She watches the boys walk out with their father. If they are Roberto and Inés's twins, they are very dissimilar. The taller boy is very handsome. What did Clara say? Yes, all the girls were in love with Álvaro.

As the crowd around him disperses, Alma walks up to the priest and says in a low voice. "Do you still sing '*Si nos dejan*,' *Padre*?" His face holds no expression but all the color drains away. "We need to talk. It won't take long. Meet me in the coffee shop," Alma says.

She tells Aunt Isabel that she'll be right back. She waits for the priest to say his good-byes; then follows him out of the room. They sit at the back of the deserted restaurant just off the lobby. He waves the waiter away. "What do you want? Are you the woman who contacted Inés the other day? Why are you ferreting around in our lives?"

Alma takes the photograph of Evelyn out of her purse. She places it in front of the priest. "I believe this is your daughter. Her mother is María Teresa Gómez y Velasco. Evelyn came to Mexico two weeks ago to find her twin brother. You probably know that she was adopted by Nick and June Hammond and has been living for the last fifteen years in California. The Hammonds have no other children.

Her parents are divorced and although, I believe, she has been treated well, she is determined to find her birth family. So much so that on hearing that her father, Nick Hammond, was arriving in Mexico to fetch her back to San Diego, she's run away. This is a dangerous country for a fifteen-year-old alone on the streets. We need to get her back as soon as possible, and the only way I can think of is to tell her I have a lead on her brother's whereabouts. By the way, Evelyn did not know she was adopted until a few months ago."

Andrés asks if Alma has contacted Tere. She's tried, she says, but hasn't had an answer. He starts to stand up, "I have no idea where the boy is. My brother took care of all that."

"Your daughter, *Padre* Andrés, is in danger. Someone tipped her off about her real identify. Someone wanted her to come to Mexico and open up all these old wounds or they wanted her here for another reason."

"I think that this is all your idea. The girl approached you, and you saw in her story some juicy article or even a book. Now because of some stupid adolescent mistake, my family and Tere's are going to be dragged through the mud. You people are so ruthless; you don't care whose lives you ruin."

Alma hears the priest's voice rising. The waiters at the far end of the coffee shop are beginning to stare. "Believe what you want about me, but I tell you the girl is persistent. She got all the way to Ávila on her own. I think both these children have a right to know where they come from. Your son can choose not to meet his sister, but one day he'll find out the truth. If it happens like it happened to your daughter, it will be far more destructive than facing up to it now."

The priest shakes his head. "Why haven't you asked me about Francisco's death? Surely that's going to be part of your article too."

"If there is an article, that would be the only thing of interest in this story. What happened that night? Do you know who killed him?"

The priest doesn't even look at her. He mutters, "*Santísima Madre de Dios*," and walks out of the restaurant into the night.

What was that all about? asks Aunt Isabel when Alma returns to the conference room. "Something complicated," she answers. "Let's go home. It's getting late."

*　　　*　　　*

The knocking on her bedroom door is not gentle. "Alma, wake up. Something's happened."

She looks at her phone. It's barely seven a.m. She throws a shawl around her shoulders. "What's happened?" she shouts as she rushes into the kitchen.

"It's okay, don't get scared. Nobody's hurt. It's your dad's truck."

"Someone banged into it?"

"No," says her uncle taking her by the hand and leading her to the front door, "Someone had a go at it with a can of spray paint."

The once impeccable white paint of her father's pride and joy is covered with obscene drawings. "*Puta*" is written on every door and on the top of the car, "*cabrona*" also.

Alma covers her mouth. She sits down on the front stoop of the house and starts to cry. "Almita, don't cry. You're lucky. Your Uncle Alfredo is the perfect guy to fix the truck.

That's what I do twenty-four-seven. Please don't cry. Your dad will never know what happened. I promise. I'll paint it today and drive it back tomorrow."

He takes her by the hand. "Get dressed. Your aunt is making *huevos rancheros* just the way you like them." But she can't stop crying. What did Pedro Ramírez call her, the Teflon lady, but he was wrong; she's the fly-paper lady. She doesn't have some magic coating that rejects misfortune; misfortune lately has been stalking her. Then she has to smile, you are turning into a drama queen, she tells herself. Buck up, the car will be repainted; we'll all live through this little episode. But she knows it's another message. The truck that tried to push her off the road wasn't an aberration; it was a warning. The vandalism to her father's truck is another warning. The sooner she gets back to Ávila the better.

Ten minutes before the first-class bus reaches the Ávila bus station, she gets a call from Ana Flores. She has trouble hearing the woman because there is a dubbed movie about trucks that turn into monsters being shown over the bus's loud TV. "Alma," Ana says, "something weird happened this morning."

It certainly did, says Alma, but how had Ana learned about the damage to Jesús's truck? There's a long silence on the other end of the line. Ana asks what happened to Jesús's beautiful white truck. Vandals painted obscene graffiti all over it. Ana wants to know if that happens often in Nuevo Progreso. "No, it's my bad luck," says Alma. "But what's the other weird thing that happened this morning?"

The dossier about Evelyn's case that Ana had written up

yesterday has disappeared off her desk. What dossier? asks Alma. Ana explains that she thought it would be a wonderful help to Alma if she wrote up all the details of the search for Evelyn's birth family. That is, all the details that Ana was privy to. She thought Alma might find the document useful if—. "If what?" asks Alma.

"If you want to write a story or a book about your investigation," says Ana.

"But who asked you to do that?" There is a long silence on the other end of the line. Little Miss Do-Gooder, Alma thinks. "Did you include anything about the forged birth certificate?" she asks.

"Of course," says Ana, as if her professional credentials were being questioned.

Alma groans. "Who else was in the office this morning?"

"Irma, *La Gordis*, and *El Chaparro*," Ana says, then after a slight pause adds, "and Héctor."

Alma groans again. She asks if Héctor is still in the office. He's gone of course. But why, Ana asks her, would Hector want the dossier? Exasperated, Alma would like to say, "Because, you idiot, he thinks we're working on an interesting story." Instead she carefully explains that Héctor might well try to sell the story of Evelyn's disappearance to a Mexico City tabloid or he could upload it on line. He might try and find a publication in the U.S.

"It isn't a huge news story," says Alma "but a teenager gone missing in Mexico with a father famous for defending drug lords and corrupt politicians might interest a few U.S. editors." Ana apologizes. She says she's going to speak to

Ricardo. But both women know the damage is done. The cat is out of the bag.

*　　　*　　　*

"Everybody gone off to the game?" Alma says when Elena picks up the phone. "Yes, it's quiet as a tomb here. You want to go shopping?" asks her cousin.

"No, I want to have a picnic. I want to sit on a blanket in the park and eat *tortas* like we did as kids." She needs to decompress, relax with comfort food and her best friend. She needs to make some sense of the last ten days.

She meets Elena in front of the McTorta stand on the far corner of Independence Park. It's hardly a secret that *Don René* in his small yellow *puesto* produces the best *tortas* in Ávila. Nothing even comes close to the deliciousness of these sandwiches, says Elena as the two women stand in line watching the stone-faced cook fabricate his signature *torta*: *La Tor-to-ta.* Elena whispers to Alma that this creation was more or less René's answer to the Big Mac.

First, he grills the meat—*cecina, chorizo,* and/or a hot dog—on an old iron grill, the electricity for which is free as it comes from a *diablito* fixed to the nearest lamp post. Next, the cook begins to build the sandwich. He opens a *telera*, a roll big enough to contain all the ingredients he has in mind. He spreads a thick layer of refried beans on the bottom of the roll, and adds the grilled meat, dribbling fried onions over it. The cheese comes next. You can choose Oaxaca, yellow American cheese, or *Manchego.* Sliced tomato, lettuce, avocado, and *jalapeño* chilies are piled on top of the cheese. The upper part of the roll is coated with mayonnaise and mustard. Placing the top layer of bread carefully on his invention, *Don* René cuts the sandwich in two and wraps it expertly in white paper.

Elena and Alma order simpler *tortas* that feature just one serving of meat. They choose *pierna* and watch while René cuts thick slices of ham. The rest of the ingredients for the sandwich are the same. Alma doesn't know why watching René make the *torta* and savoring the taste of the sandwich makes her feel that life isn't so bad after all, but it does. Normal and even boring tasks are reassuring, she thinks. The two women pay for their sandwiches and Cokes and walk into the park. Alma spreads out an old blanket under the nearest shady tree. Both women sit for a moment taking in the leafy smells of the park, the sounds of a distant radio, and shouts of children at play. "Anything new?" asks Elena diplomatically.

"Oh, my God, you are ten episodes behind in the Evelyn *telenovela*," says Alma. "But for the next half hour I only want to munch on my *torta* and listen to your news."

"It's that bad," says Elena as she launches into tales of her clients and her kids. When the last drops of soda have been drained and the sandwich paper deposited in a trash can, she says simply, "Shoot."

It takes a good twenty minutes for Alma to relate a blow-by-blow account of the last five days. It is an abridged as well as a carefully edited version of the events. No mention is made of the truck trying to push her off the road or of the visit from Nick Hammond. She half laughs off Hernán Gómez's crazy diatribe.

Elena says she sympathizes somewhat with Evelyn. She'd thought a lot about running away herself when she was fifteen before she went across L.A. to live with Alma. She didn't get along with her mother but being on the street seemed scarier than being wacked at regular intervals by the back of her mother's hand. Plus, it would have hurt her dad. Evelyn, she says, sounds like a kid who is used to clean sheets and three meals a day. She's holed up with someone she knows. "But she doesn't know anyone here," says Alma.

"So you thought," says Elena.

"What do you think of Ricardo's idea that it's María Teresa who's trying to bribe me?"

Could be, says her cousin. Elena thinks that there are several people whom Alma is looking for who might be hiding in plain sight. Tere, for instance; her friend Lucero had said that Tere's a homebody. Her experience in Spain and San Francisco weren't all that great. Maybe India had been better, but that country must take some getting used to. If you had all the money in the world wouldn't you live in the place you love best? Tere loves the ocean and the beaches she visited as a child. "Bet you anything María Teresa Gómez y Velasco is living in luxury on a beautiful Mexican beach."

Evelyn's twin brother? Of course, *Padre* Andrés knows where the kid is. He and Francisco took the boy from the hospital for a reason; otherwise they would have let him go with his sister to California. They had a plan for the boy.

Maybe it's Tere's real father, Leonor's mysterious lover, who is the one offering Alma the twenty thousand dollars. "He's like a fairy godfather," Elena says, "he goes around making Tere's wishes come true."

Alma says Elena should add fortune-telling to her list of services and since she's so proficient at it, could she please tell Alma where Gabriel is and why he hasn't called her?

If she were Alma, Elena says, she'd go off tomorrow, spend the day at the Lakewood Spa and get her new friend, Dan Sullivan, to take her to dinner. She'd send Gabriel Ruiz packing.

"Did you see Linda's last post?" Alma asks.

"Very over-the-top," says Elena. "She's desperate to have a guy in her life who she thinks will provide an anchor for her roller-coaster emotions. She doesn't care that Gabriel has a new life or that he's happy with someone else. Linda gets what Linda wants."

"My dad said to be patient but—," says Alma, her voice trailing off. She rolls over on her stomach. Elena's probably right about Linda, but it's too depressing to think about.

"What about work?" says Elena, glad to get Alma's mind off Gabriel. "How's your handsome boss?"

"Now there's someone who's patient. Héctor can do no wrong. He keeps getting second chances." She tells Elena about the missing dossier that Ana compiled on Evelyn.

"My head hurts, *Flaca*. Your life is way too complicated. You need a *limpia.*"

*　　*　　*

When Alma walks through the front door of her parents' home, she finds her mother napping on the sofa in the front room. Sofía gives a start when Alma turns off the TV. "I thought you'd be in the shop," Alma says.

"Everyone's watching the game, and I was sleepy."

"Are you feeling all right?"

"I'm worried. I'm worried about you, Alma. What's going on between you and Gabriel?"

Alma sits down and leans her head on her mother's shoulder. "Did Pa talk to you or did Elena?"

"No, but I've got two eyes, and Kurt said you'd been acting funny. Not that he hasn't been strange too. What's the matter with that boy? He used to be Mr. Talk Your Head Off and now is as silent as a ghost. But you're my girl, and it's you I'm most worried about."

Alma explains about Gabriel's trip to San Antonio. His total silence for more than a week. His decision to take a week of vacation. The posts from his ex-wife that they were back together.

"Marriage is tricky, Alma. Even when there's a divorce and the legal ties are gone, there could still be emotional ties, little bits of leftover attraction or guilt. He might think he owes her some kind of help if she's down."

"Well, what about his ties to me? Doesn't the last year mean anything to him? Do you think it's my fault because we never talked about getting married?"

"No, of course not. I think things happen for a reason. Maybe he isn't the guy you thought he was. Maybe—."

Alma's phone rings. She looks at the number, looks at her mother and pointing to the phone, walks out of the room.

"*Flaquita*," Gabriel says, his voice husky. "I'm so sorry I've been out of touch. My assistant said you called the office. I don't know what to say. The past week was so difficult, so chaotic." He waits but there's only silence at the other end of the line. "Alma, are you still there?"

"Gabriel, I don't want to talk about this over the phone. Let's get together tomorrow."

"Okay, I'd like to see you right now but if you're busy," he sounds offended, "then it will have to be tomorrow. But wait, did you put someone up in my apartment?"

Alma takes a deep breath. "Why?"

"There are boxes of pizza in the kitchen garbage that aren't mine. There's a jar of peanut butter and a half-eaten loaf of bread on the kitchen table, and your set of keys are there too. The door to the apartment was unlocked when I got home this morning. So, I figured you had a guest staying here, which is fine, no problem."

"I'm sorry, Gabriel, I can't explain now; we'll talk tomorrow."

When she reenters the front room, her mother looks up, expectantly, anxious for news. "You aren't going to believe what your grandson has done. I can't believe it myself. He's only nine."

When Kurt walks through the front door, his mother's face shatters his high spirits. She pulls him into the kitchen. "Do you have any idea of the harm you've caused? Why did you help her run away? Where is she now?"

The boy hangs his head. Tears start to roll down his cheeks. "She told me and Max that it would just be for a few days. She told me she would go back to Max's house on Friday even if her dad was still there. She was so sad, Mom. She said she was going to run away to Mexico City and live on the street. That would have been terrible."

"Gabriel called. She's not at his apartment anymore. Do you know where she's gone? I called Sandra; she hasn't gone back there."

"I'm sorry. I don't know. Look," he says pulling out his phone. "She sent me this text last night."

Alma reads the message out loud. "Thanks, *hermanito*." So the girl learned one word of Spanish. "They got in touch. They want to meet me. Should be back at Sandra's tomorrow evening."

"She lied to me," says Kurt. "She promised she wouldn't start looking for her real parents on her own."

"Well, she's in good company because you lied to me, to Sandra, to Evelyn's father, or rather you kept the truth from us, which is just the same as lying. You helped her run away. If you hadn't provided the place, she might still be safe at Sandra's house. Do you realize what you've done? Do you understand what it means to betray a trust? I trusted you, Sandra trusted you, Gabriel trusted you." She wants to go further because she is furious with the boy. She wants to say that by encouraging Evelyn's crazy plans, he might have put the girl's life in danger. She stops herself. Haven't her own actions contributed just as much to Evelyn's risky behavior? She should never have revealed her birth mother's name or where she was from.

"I have to see Nick Hammond now. I think you'd better go up to your room and try to remember if Evelyn told you anything about who she was in contact with. Anything at all, Kurt. We have to find her."

*   *   *

As she tugs on the Wearings' front door bell, she remembers that ten days ago when she had stood in this spot, she was worried about how she was dressed. How ridiculous! Her life then seems to her now to have been as innocent as the Garden of Eden before the snake, or in her case snakes, appeared. She imagines Nick Hammond's righteous indignation as she tells him about her son's complicity in his daughter's disappearance. She visualizes Sandra and Bob Wearing's disappointment. Will anyone even believe that she knew nothing about Evelyn's whereabouts? She wonders if Kurt will ever be welcome in Max's home again.

"We were just about to call you," says Bob Wearing as he opens the front door. "Kurt called Max a few minutes ago. Told him that the cat was out of the bag. He said you'd discovered where they'd hidden Evelyn. He also said you were one angry mother."

"Max knew?"

Of course he knew, Bob says as they stand in the hallway. According to Max, when Kurt mentioned that Gabriel was out of town, he was the one who suggested that Evelyn use his apartment to hide. Evelyn had used the same charm on both boys. Bob scoffs. She called them her *"hermanitos,"* and they rolled over like two little puppies. "Wish we'd never laid eyes on the girl," he whispers. "She's been nothing but trouble. You look like you need a tequila. Come on in to the family room. We're all having a drink."

Nick Hammond stands up when she enters the room. Sandra remains sitting. The woman looks as if she hasn't bothered to look in a mirror for days. Her hair is tied in a careless ponytail; her skin without makeup looks grayish. No one speaks for a moment; then Nick Hammond walks over to Alma. He holds out his hand. "I'm sorry about the other day. I wasn't thinking straight."

Alma briefly shakes his hand. He doesn't look too good either. She notices the carelessly shaved jowls and his red, irritated eyes. He looks as if he hasn't slept in days. "Well," says Bob, handing Alma what looks like a double shot of tequila, "what next?"

Nick says that two of his private detectives are at Gabriel's house right now, but he doesn't expect they'll find anything. Someone is also staking out Raúl Gómez y Velasco's house in San Miguel, but so far there's nothing to report.

"Mr. Hammond," says Alma, "perhaps we could get our heads around Evelyn's story and maybe her whereabouts if you were more open with us. I realized almost from the first that you knew the identity of Evelyn's birth mother and had information about the girl's family, but for your own reasons, you kept the information from Evelyn. Why?"

It's too warm in the room. There's a gas fireplace roaring away in one corner, and the windows are all closed. Nick Hammond removes his jacket; there are beads of sweat on his forehead. He swirls the ice around in his drink. He sits back on the sofa. Alma can tell he's preparing his story as if it were a jury in front of him instead of a group of friends. He wants his client, in this case, himself, to be presented in the best possible light.

"We couldn't have children, or rather June couldn't. We

put our name into countless adoption agencies, but since we traveled so much, we always seemed to end up on the bottom of the lists. As we got older, we were less attractive to the agencies, although financially they couldn't have found a better bet. June became desperate about not having children, sadder and sadder. Of course, I felt guilty. If my job hadn't taken us around the world, perhaps she would have developed a career or an interest that compensated for the lack of a family.

"After a few years of setting up deals for foreign companies in Mexico, I became bored. I was earning good money, but I wasn't getting rich by any means. It was obvious that the U.S. government wanted the Mexican drug lords and the money launderers extradited to the U.S. The jails here couldn't hold them. I realized that all these guys were going to need a good American lawyer; someone they could talk to who understood them.

"My first client was an ex-governor. He was a real piece of work. He'd embezzled millions of state funds, mostly money that should have been used for education. He'd also set up several chains of restaurants, laundering money for one of the more notorious cartels, but," Hammond smiles, "you couldn't help but like him. He was *simpático*. You know, a born politician, always trying to do favors for people whom he could tap for help later. His biggest concern was what would become of his family when he was extradited. He had two sons who were studying at Princeton. They'd need help. He asked me about my family, so I told him we'd been trying to adopt for years but hadn't had any luck.

"'*Amigo*,' he said, 'you've got the best place to adopt practically at your front door. It's called La Casa de la Esperanza. Ask the nuns to put you in touch with the agency that places the babies. It might cost you, but you can get a kid in a couple of months.' So, I did contact Sister Fernanda, but I didn't want to buy a baby. I found that repugnant. I asked her if there wasn't some way to adopt without going through the agency; she said that it wasn't her decision. They always went through the agency. I checked out the agency on the QT. It was registered to an organization called La Fundación Fray Peti Juan. I called a friend at the U.S. Embassy who was with the D.E.A. He said that the foundation was a front for Los Militantes de Jesús, a religious group that was very business-oriented, but that some of their businesses weren't entirely legal. He also suspected that some local cartel might be involved with the foundation.

"I went back to see the nun, took June with me. We begged. The nun said that there might be an opportunity. She had a fifteen-year-old from a good family who was due in a month or so and didn't want her baby placed with the agency. The girl's only condition was that the baby be taken out of the country immediately. I agreed. I knew that June and I were headed for a break-up, and this was the one thing I could do for her.

"It wasn't that hard to get a detective to check out the girl and her family. When they came back with the information that her brother and sister-in-law ran the agency which placed the babies from La Casa de la Esperanza, I could understand why she didn't want her kid sold like a carcass of baby goat, but I didn't get why she wanted the baby out of the country. I agreed to all her conditions. When the nun called that the birth had become difficult, I brought in an old friend, Doctor Geri. When he said that twins were on the way, I wondered what I had gotten us into. Then we got really frightened when the nun called to say that the boy had been removed from the clinic. I was sure that it was the agency that had taken him; I thought that they would be coming back next for the girl. We got Evelyn out of the country as soon as it was possible."

Nick takes a long swallow of his whiskey. "I have no excuse or explanation for the person I was fifteen years ago. I wasn't even that young a man. My life revolved around my work and only my work. I adopted the baby for June. As I said, I wanted out of the marriage. Evelyn was my parting gift, and honestly, the first couple of months I didn't pay much attention to the baby. But when she started to smile at me and to hold out her arms for me to pick her up, I was a goner. I had never felt such a fierce love for anything or anyone. I began to think about María Teresa's family. How they had treated her. She could have died giving birth. How could they not have wanted their beautiful grandchild? I hated them. I never wanted Evelyn to find out what despicable people she'd come from. I didn't want those bastards to reject her again."

There's a total silence in the room. No one speaks, no one moves. Finally, Nick gets up and serves himself another Scotch.

Alma speaks very softly. "I think more than ever we need to get Evelyn back as soon as possible. She needs to learn about the Gómez y Velasco family from you. She needs to know why you've been protecting her."

Hammond nods his head. "But she needs to find that brother too. I didn't get it. I didn't get how lonely she was. So, what have you found out, Alma? Now it's your turn to spill the beans."

Alma takes another small sip of her tequila. She's impressed by Nick's story and what appears to be his honesty about his failings. But where his daughter is concerned, he's ruled by his emotions. He might be a model of pure reason in a courtroom, but she can still feel his hands gripping her shoulders, shaking her as if she were a rag doll. He's capable of rushing off to Nuevo Progreso and barging in on Inés and her family, ruining everything.

"Do you know why Tere gave birth in La Casa de la Esperanza?"

"I assumed it was because of Raúl."

"No, I think she went because of a priest, *Padre* Francisco, to whom she was close during the summer of her fifteenth birthday. I think she found out later that Raúl had something to do with the home. I also believe that *Padre* Francisco was involved in many different projects and didn't realize until a few years later that the babies were being sold and the mothers pushed into prostitution."

"Didn't he get murdered?" says Sandra.

"Yes, about ten years ago. *Padre* Francisco had a younger brother named Andrés. He admitted to me that he's the father of the twins, but he's very antagonistic. He says he has no idea what happened to the boy. I don't believe him, but I need more time to investigate."

"I'll go to see this Andrés myself. Where is he?"

"That's a bad idea. Let's concentrate on getting Evelyn back," says Alma. "I believe she has to be in San Miguel. That's the only clue she has at the moment about her birth family. Do you know about the mariachi e-cards? She said she'd never told you."

"What mariachi e-cards?"

"She didn't just stumble on those papers in the safe. She received a series of e-cards from someone who questioned her identity. He or she was trying to lure her to Mexico."

"Jesus Christ," says Nick. "This gets worse by the minute."

CHAPTER 11

*A*s Alma stands up to say her good-byes, the Wearings' maid enters. She gives Bob a card. Sandra immediately takes it out of his hands. "Who's Héctor Valdés Robles, Alma? He's apparently with your newspaper? He's written here—'Need to interview you about Evelyn'."

"I'm so sorry. He is a reporter on the paper, but I've told him nothing about Evelyn. He's," she hesitates, "a pain in the neck. I'll take care of this; he won't bother you again."

Alma stands for a moment before opening the front door. When she steps out into the evening, she smiles at the young man who's waiting on the steps. "Héctor, how clever of you to pick up on this story. It has possibilities doesn't it? It might even get into the international press. Nick Hammond is well-known, even a bit of a celebrity."

He gazes at Alma uncertain for the moment. "You aren't angry that I'm here?"

"Surprised, but not angry. No, perhaps we should combine forces, compare notes. How did you find out about the missing girl?"

"Ana mentioned something."

Alma takes him by the arm and leads him away from the house. "Aren't you busy with the story on our new governor?" With that question he seems to recover his normal demeanor. He looks at her suspiciously. "Why are you being so friendly?"

"We're colleagues, aren't we? Ricardo has been telling me what great work you're doing. We can share information. Perhaps you have a different perspective on the girl's disappearance. I need to change and check up on my son, but how about we meet downtown for a drink around nine or nine-thirty? Have you been to that new bar around the corner from the mayor's mansion? I think it's called The Sword of Damocles." She gives him a light peck on the cheek and says, "See you later."

Walking to her car, the conversation that she will eventually have with Ricardo pops into her mind. Was it really necessary, Alma, Richie will say giving her a stern look, to send that poor man on a wild goose chase, to keep him waiting for you in a noisy bar until after midnight? Yes, she'll answer; he's a nuisance. He stole Ana's dossier. I was going to text him later to say I was sorry that I couldn't make it, but things got complicated.

As soon as she's driven a block, she texts Dan Sullivan. "Room for tonight still available? Arrive by eight p.m. Alma." She plans to pick up a few clothes before starting off for San

Miguel de Allende, but as she reaches the corner of her street, she sees a patrol car parked in front of her house. No doubt Ricardo has been told that she had asked Captain Ramírez to call off the protection and has requested that the cops keep an eye on her anyway. She turns the car around and heads toward San Miguel. She'll buy whatever she needs leaving town.

*   *   *

When she arrives at the Lakewood Resort, the receptionist tells her that yes, *Señor* Sullivan has reserved a lovely room for her on the second floor. She'll be facing the courtyard. Is that all right? Alma has never been in a hotel room this luxurious. First, she notices the size of the room. It's as big as the ground floor of her house. The king size bed only occupies about a quarter of the room. There is a desk, an upholstered armchair, and a foot stool. A large antique *ropero* opposite the bed smells of cedar. Inside the cabinet there's a mini-bar and a large TV. The room is painted a soft light gray-green. The lithographs on the walls are scenes, she imagines, of old San Miguel. The heavy drapes have the same delicate pattern as the bedspread; they blend with the color of the walls. The bathroom is all glass and chrome. She longs to take a bubble bath in the deep tub. Ten little bottles and jars of delicious smelling creams, bath gels, and shampoos are arranged on a tray near the sink. The towels—she puts her face into one of them. It's warm and smells of lavender; it is as thick and downy as the coat of a young lamb. On the bed, the hotel maid has spelled out *"Bienvenida"* using different colored bougainvillea leaves. There are two chocolate creams wrapped in pink cellophane on her pillow.

Near the window on a round table is a bowl of fresh fruit and a bottle of wine. There is also a large bouquet of flowers. "Let's have dinner, Dan" says the card. She opens the overnight bag she's acquired at the mall and takes out clean underwear, new black jeans, a black tee shirt and tennis shoes. She puts on one of Kurt's baseball caps which has lain forgotten in her car and slips on her jeans jacket. At the last minute she ties a long silk scarf around her neck; in part because it's chilly, in part to dress up her rather spooky outfit. She leaves a note at the front desk for Dan. "Had to go out. Breakfast at 8?"

It isn't nice what she's doing, leaving her friends and colleagues in the dark. They'll demand millions of explanations tomorrow. But she has work to do tonight. She has a feeling that if she doesn't find Evelyn soon, the girl may slip though their fingers altogether.

She decides first to try and see Ángeles, Tere's old nanny. At least she's a somewhat friendly face, and maybe she's picked up some family gossip. She enters the front gate of *Don* Hernán's home, but instead of ringing the bell, she decides to skirt around to the back of the house in hopes of finding the kitchen door. She does not want to run into *Don* Hernán. She raps on what seems like the back door. No answer. There's a garage off in one corner of the property. As she heads toward it, a voice says, "That's far enough."

"It's Alma Jaramillo, Chucho."

"I know who you are. What d'you want?"

She explains that Evelyn is missing. She's sure that

Ángeles has told her brother about her encounters with Alma. She guesses that the pair have puzzled over the photograph of Evelyn. "The girl was in Ávila until this morning, and now no one knows where she is," she tells Chucho. "I thought that perhaps you or Ángeles might have heard something. Has the girl tried to contact her grandfather?"

"You'd better talk to Ángeles," he says. When he turns to walk toward the house his jacket opens slightly. He has a gun tucked into his belt. Alma becomes uneasy. She wishes now she'd told someone where she was going.

They enter the kitchen. She sees a refrigerator that should be in a museum. It rattles as if it is dying but not without putting up a brave fight. The stove is also primitive and looks filthy. The room is poorly lit, but she can see the badly patched linoleum on the floor. Poor Ángeles, she thinks, cooped up here day after day.

"Where's your sister?" Alma asks as Chucho marches her through the dismal room. When she tries to hold back, he takes her by the arm and forces her on.

"You're hurting me," she complains, but he keeps pulling her along.

She can hear voices coming from the front of the house. It's Ángeles and also, Oh, God no, it's *Don* Hernán going on about something. "Please, Chucho, I don't want to see him. He scares me."

Chucho gives an ugly laugh. "He needs company. He's lonely. He'll be happy to see you." In a matter of seconds, the man has pushed her into the front room and practically into

Don Hernán's arms.

"Who's this woman, Chucho?" the old man asks. Alma can see Ángeles at the far side of the room arranging flowers on what appears to be an altar. "It's the nosy reporter from Ávila. The woman we went to see a few days ago." Alma sees Ángeles swing around and put her hand up to her mouth.

Don Hernán claps his hands. "Oh, this is wonderful. I thought I'd be saying Mass just for you, but now we have another guest." Alma notices that he is wearing the vestments of a priest. She feels she is sinking down a rabbit hole.

"Come in, sit down, *Señorita* Alma. You are in God's house. This is the center of my life. Let us begin." She can see that the old man is thrilled. She realizes that for him worship is part food for his soul, part theater. *Don* Hernán knows that too. He needs an audience. "Years ago," he says, "we had bishops and even a cardinal in this room. Every priest who could deliver even a half-way decent sermon stood at that pulpit. Don't worry, my chapel is sanctified. I saw to it. But my friends have stopped coming. Stopped years ago. So did the clergy. They snub me, avoid me. Of course, it has to do with money. When Leonor was around, they loved to come here. She said it was the post-Mass dinners that drew them, but it wasn't. It's the chapel: God's mysteries."

Alma avoids the old man's eyes. "Are you going to say Mass?" she asks.

"Of course, I was ordained you know. But like the apostles, I was ordained by *Jesús Cristo* himself." She'll hear the story if she wants to or not. "It was the night of Tere's birth. Births are sacred things, *Señorita* Alma. In my mind I see María Teresa's birth, and I see Christ's birth. I was like Saint Joseph; I wasn't the biological father of the child. Leonor hadn't even tried to pretend that I was. She mocked me for my celibacy, said she was leaving me and taking the child. But it was I who had the last word. When the doctor said I must choose whom to save, the mother or the child, I chose the infant. It wasn't vengeance; it was what God wanted. The child's soul was pure; Leonor's tainted. As a reward the Holy Spirit came to me in a dream, and said I was now an ordained priest. I had the power to transform bread and wine into the body and blood of Christ."

Although *Don* Hernán is still rambling on, Ángeles takes Alma by the arm and leads her to a pew. She gazes around what was at one time the parlor of this lovely old house. Now it's a chapel that can seat thirty people. *Don* Hernán has installed an eighteenth-century altar, no doubt bought at an auction with Leonor's money. It's beautiful: decorated with gold leaf and jolly fat cherubs. To one side of the altar is a terrifying statue of Christ on the cross; his suffering body painted in the most vivid colors. Blood runs down His face and off His hands and feet. He has welts and stab wounds all over His chest. The iron nails in His hands and feet are real. The crown of thorns is driven into His skull. His eyes—, but Alma looks away from the statue, the Mass has started.

It is a short ceremony. Ángeles lends Alma a short black mantilla to throw over her head. Chucho serves on the altar. Both women, afraid to refuse, receive communion from *Don* Hernán's hand. "Didn't your soul sing during the service?" the old man asks as he wheels himself away from the altar.

Alma nods. "Why don't your friends from the Militantes de Jesús come to your services?"

"Raúl says they're not as enlightened as they used to be. My father, you know, was one of the original members of the society. He was a close friend of the founder. Now, there was a dedicated priest," says Hernán smiling. "And practical; a great business man. He knew that if you were going to grow a movement you needed cash and lots of it." The old man rubs his thumb and index finger together. "They said he was corrupt, even said he was a pervert, but he wasn't. It was all politics. He became too powerful, so the do-gooders brought him down."

"You say Tere wasn't your daughter, *Don* Hernán but you took care of her until—," says Alma.

The old man's face becomes serious. "I am, *Señorita* Alma, a good Christian. I treated Tere as a daughter until she became involved with that *hijo de la chingada, Padre* Francisco. Why does the Church treat him like a hero? He was a devil."

"You believe he seduced Tere?"

"Who else? I saw them together at her *quinceaños* celebration; how he hung around her, like a bee to honey. I suppose he wanted her money. But he was taken care of. Got what was coming to him."

"Do you know who killed him?" Alma asks.

The old man gathers his vestments around his legs. "Time for bed, Chucho," he says.

Ángeles hurries Alma toward the front door.

"Have you seen the girl?" Alma asks.

"What girl?"

"Tere's daughter, Evelyn. She's run away. We think she may have come to San Miguel. I think María Teresa might be here too."

Ángeles opens the front door. She looks around. "Try the house with the green door. We used to take Tere there every Friday when she was little."

The house with the green door? Alma thinks as she steps into the street. Yes, of course, *Licenciado* Guzmán's toy museum. What had Ricardo said? It was behind the Cathedral. It had a brass lion's head for a knocker.

It's a bit late to be knocking on a stranger's door. Alma isn't sure anyone will answer. But still she takes the lion's head with its flowing mane in her hand and bangs it sharply three times. Is it her imagination or can she hear someone stirring on the other side of the door? She takes the knocker again and bangs it three more times. Suddenly the door opens; a woman steps out onto the sidewalk. Alma notices that her left arm is in a sling.

"You can only be the persistent Alma Jaramillo," the woman says. She smiles, and two dimples appear just below her cheek bones. A beautiful face thinks Alma, and so composed, apparently so serene.

"Ángeles warned me that you might be headed this way." The woman checks the hour on her cell phone. "We don't have much time, but I need to apologize to you. It was Julieta who suggested the bribe. She's my cousin, but I don't know her well. I knew nothing about the intimidation. I was horrified when Arturo told me. I am so sorry." The dimples disappear, and a frown crosses her face.

227

It's Alma's turn to smile. "I'm pleased to meet you at last, María Teresa."

"Please, call me Tere." The woman pauses for a moment, takes a deep breath and says, "I need your help. I can't drive," she raises slightly the arm with the sling. "I am supposed to be in Querétaro right now meeting Evelyn. Would you mind terribly driving? Plus, Evelyn knows you. Arturo says she seemed a little nervous when he picked her up this morning."

Arturo Guzmán picked up Evelyn? What is his part in the story? Alma takes a deep breath. This is going to be more trouble, she thinks. Driving around on deserted highways late at night is a bad idea. "Can't this wait until morning?" she asks.

"Something tells me that Evelyn needs to be with a friend tonight. Arturo has told her that's he's her grandfather but," says Tere.

Tere looks up and down the street. "I can explain everything in the car. I'd prefer not to stand around talking in front of the house. The wrong people could be watching. Please," she says holding out the car keys for Alma.

Alma thinks that this drive will probably go on her list of "things I should never have done," but turning Tere down doesn't seem to be option either. Angry as she is with Evelyn, she can imagine how fearful the girl must be, stranded for the night with a strange man who claims to be her grandfather.

As they walk around the corner, Tere says "It's that four-door pick-up on the corner."

"Looks sturdy," says Alma and thinks that at least it isn't the black truck with tinted windows that tried to push her off the road. She turns toward Tere and says, "Someone tried to push my Jetta off the road two days ago coming back from Nuevo Progreso. I wish I'd been in this tank."

"I swear, Alma, I had nothing to do with that. Neither did Andrés, at least not directly. Inés's husband, Roberto, is a hothead. His life revolves around those kids. They're the poster family for the parish, which is a small conservative community. I guess he saw a bomb about to be thrown into the middle of his picture-postcard life; you know what damage a newspaper story can do. The gossip, the people who suddenly don't speak to you anymore. He panicked, thought he could scare you away." She doesn't look Alma in the eye. "He decorated your truck too. I'm sorry. We'll reimburse you for the expense."

"It isn't just the expense, Tere. I was terrified. What is it with you people? You can't seem to let even the tiniest bit of light into your lives. I never intended to write a story about Evelyn's birth. El Diario de Ávila isn't even interested in that kind of news."

"I know. What can I say? But it isn't a tiny bit of light you were letting into our lives, Alma. You were about to shine a search light on all of us."

"Okay, you're right. Your family secrets were not safe with me. So, where to?" Alma asks as she climbs into the driver's seat.

"Querétaro, Arturo Guzmán's office. You know the lawyer you visited the other day."

As they head out of town, Alma takes a few quick glances at the woman she's been pursuing for the last ten days. She hasn't changed much since those photos taken at her *quinceaños* party sixteen years ago. Her figure is still slight, not an ounce of surplus fat. Her black hair is long and wavy, her white skin seemingly untouched by the sun. Her large eyes, yes, have a few tiny wrinkles at the corners, but in the glow of the street lights, the green irises sparkle.

"What happened to your arm?"

"Raúl paid me a visit yesterday. I don't know how he knew I was in town. He needs money as usual. He seems to think I should be paying for his daughter's *quinceaños* party. He said he had borrowed money from a drug cartel, and was in trouble. When I didn't answer right away, he got hysterical, started screaming about what a selfish bitch I was. I started to walk away. He grabbed me, and I want to think he was only trying to scare me, but I ended up with a broken arm. I guess that's the end of yoga for a few months."

Alma rolls down the car window just a touch. The evening is cool with a slight breeze. There are night smells in the air: pine from somewhere in the hills, the last embers of a charcoal fire. There are night sounds too. She can hear the roosters, who have no built-in clock, crowing. Why in rural Mexico do dogs bark all through the night? she asks Tere. Because they are plagued by cats, rats, *cacomixtles* and *tlacuaches*, creatures that were created to disturb a poor dog's slumber, she answers.

Alma waits until they hit the highway before she speaks again. "Would you mind answering a few questions? I just want to get a few things straight in my mind."

"You're curious, of course. I would be too."

"How did you find out that Arturo Guzmán was your biological father? He seems like the soul of discretion."

"Yes, well, he is, but children are perceptive. If there ever was a child who wished she'd been adopted, it was me. No one ever mentioned my mother. I only had a name to hold on to, not even a photograph. I asked questions about her until I was maybe seven or eight; then I realized that for some reason my mother was *persona non grata* in the family. My father, Hernán, seemed to be a person respected in our small circle of friends and family, but he was totally unlike my school friends' fathers. They actually talked to their children. They weren't obsessed by saints and church history." Tere laughs. "I had this fantasy that my father took the wrong baby home from the hospital. My one consolation was the Friday visits to the toy museum where this nice man would greet me and ask me about myself. When I got too old for the toy museum, we'd run into the kindly man at the ice cream store or in the park. In the convent in Spain the nuns told me one day that a lawyer had come to speak to me about my inheritance." Tere stops for moment. She's wearing a down parka. "It's cold," she says wrapping with one hand a wool scarf more tightly around her neck.

"When I was shown into the living room of the convent, there he was, the man from the toy museum. Of course, I asked who he was. He said that he was my mother's lawyer, and that she had told him before she died that he must keep an eye on me. We talked for hours about her until the nuns finally shooed him away. He left me documents about my inheritance and a letter from my mother. The documents explained about the money. I was stunned. No one had ever told me that I would be so rich one day. The letter from my mother was very loving."

"Wait a minute," says Alma. "A letter from your mother? I thought she died giving birth."

"She did. Leonor was stubborn but not stupid. She knew that she might not survive the birth. Arturo suggested she leave a letter 'just in case.' Anyway, the letter was full of such regret about leaving me without a mother's love, of missing all the joys of my childhood."

Tere pauses. Alma can see her fingering the fringe on her scarf. She begins again. "The letter said everything I felt about abandoning my own children; all the grief I still feel when I think of them growing up without me. She begged me to stay close to Arturo Guzmán. She said he would always be my friend.

"I needed a friend when I came back from San Francisco. I was lost. At first, I turned to Hernán who seemed glad to see me, but I soon realized what he wanted was for me to admit that *Padre* Francisco was the father of the twins. He wanted to have that poor priest defrocked. What Raúl wanted was control of my investments. They hounded me day and night. When I wouldn't give in, there was a terrible scene. Hernán called me every foul name he could think of.

"I went to see Arturo. He sat me down, and I finally learned the truth. It wasn't that the wrong baby came home from the hospital; it was that the wrong father brought the baby to the wrong house. It wasn't Arturo's fault that Hernán brought me up. What could he have done? But the truth made me realize I had to rethink who I really was. I wasn't a Gómez y Velasco. I was María Teresa Guzmán Aragón, a person with a whole different ancestry and a different birth story too. It changes everything when you know you are part of a great love story."

Ah, thinks Alma. Is Tere finally ready to tell her own daughter that her birth was also part of a love story? Instead she says, "So, you went to India."

"Yes, but first Arturo persuaded me to see how my children were doing. I went to San Diego. When I saw Evelyn with June, I was so jealous. I wanted that little girl but not at the cost of ruining June's life and maybe Evelyn's too. My son was a happy twin in a growing family. I was barely twenty. Yes, I had all the money in the world, but I had no idea how to provide a home for them. So, I went to India to find myself. I learned yoga. I meditated. I found out what I want to do with my life."

Tere pauses again still fiddling with the fringe on her scarf. "Do you have children?"

"Yes, I have a son who's nine," says Alma.

"Then you know that there's hardly a day that goes by when I don't think about Evelyn and Álvaro. It's like there's a memory switch in my head that flicks on when I see the name Álvaro in the newspaper or there's a mention of twins on the radio or a thousand other little things. However hard I try, my mind flashes to that night in the clinic and those two tiny cots at the sides of my bed. Are they happy, I wonder? I try to imagine what they look like now."

The women's truck is practically alone on the highway.

Every once in a while, a large semi rolls by, or a long-distance bus, the occasional car. Neither woman speaks for some minutes. Tere blots her eyes with a Kleenex and blows her nose. "I don't talk about that time easily, Alma. I've been in therapy for years and perhaps it's helped a bit. Every time someone asks if I have children, I feel I want the earth to swallow me up. Instead I listen with a polite smile on my face while some well-meaning person tells me about the joys of motherhood."

"Is that why you tried to get me to drop the search?"

"When you wrote me that e-mail saying Evelyn was in Mexico I froze. What would I tell her? How could I face her and Álvaro? Would they ever understand how alone I was through the pregnancy? You know for years I resented my mother for abandoning me, and she had no choice. I could only imagine how my children would feel about a mother who abandoned them and who now has all the money in the world. A monster, I thought. That's what they'll see, an unfeeling, selfish monster."

"Wow," says Alma, "truthfully, I don't think anyone could be harder on you than you are on yourself. They're fifteen. I'm sure they can't imagine taking care of two babies. But again, I am curious how you ended up in La Casa de la Esperanza."

"I think a lot about who I was that summer sixteen years ago. Who was Andrés? They're questions that don't go away. For a long time, I thought that I was a pretty simple, romantic kid looking for someone to love and that Andrés was the one with all the conflicts. He had to contend with his family's expectations. What his mother called 'God's plan' for their family. That was creepy. When I fell for Andrés what was I looking for? Some kind of normalcy, probably. A romance between a girl and a boy like you read about in novels or see in the movies. That seemed a safe path out of my weird family life. I wanted Andrés to fall in love with me, but I also wanted to know how love changes you; how you could become a different person if someone loved you. I never imagined that love could crush you too. Sorry I'm talking the long way around to answer your question. Am I boring you?"

"Hardly," says Alma. "I've been trying to puzzle out this story for the last ten days."

"After I returned from the ranch, it finally dawned on Ángeles that something was wrong with me. I wouldn't see a doctor, so she talked to Sonia, who figured it out in half a second. She called a family conference. Raúl wanted to know who the boy was or was it a man? Had I been raped? I felt as if I had been thrown into a cage of starving hyenas. They wanted the guy's blood. I decided I'd rather die like a martyr than denounce Andrés, who surely was coming to rescue me any day."

Tere pauses for a moment. "It's funny when I think of it now," she says laughing, "but it wasn't then. I even went one Sunday to Puebla to try and see Andrés just before all hell broke loose at home. I stood in front of the gate of the seminary trying to get up enough courage to go in. Finally, a priest came out and told me to go away, that I was distracting the young men who were at prayer.

"It was Sonia who without consulting anyone made the decision to send me to a home for single mothers in Ávila. Ángeles and Chucho dropped me off. One day I saw *Padre* Francisco enter the clinic. I thought he had come to take me to Andrés. I ran up to him in the corridor of the clinic. When he saw me, the look that came over his face said it all. We sat not speaking for a very long time. Finally, he took my hand and said that Andrés would not be coming for me. Andrés's life was to be dedicated to God. He would have to purge his sin, of course. It would take years of penance, exile, but there was no other way.

"I wasn't to worry. They would find a suitable home for the baby. He hoped that it was a boy. They would dedicate his life to God. I must pray, he said. He and Andrés would pray for me too. He released my hand, bowed his head and left. I had felt lonely most of my life, but that afternoon I hit bottom. I actually began to plan how I could kill myself, but I was Catholic enough to know that I would be damned eternally. I would also be killing the baby. The child was the source of all my trouble, but I wanted the baby to live."

"Why did you want the Hammonds to take the baby?"

"I was furious with Andrés and his brother. Hypocrites, I thought. How could they leave me all alone? Soon afterward, I learned, through one of the other girls in the home, that La Casa de la Esperanza's so-called agency that found parents for the babies was run by none other than Sonia and Raúl. That explained why Sonia had brought me to that awful place. I didn't know then what happened to the babies and to the young mothers, but I didn't want my brother to have the baby. The Hammonds were Americans. Americans were good people. Hadn't I seen all those good *gringos* in the movies? They would surely let me have the baby back one day when I was older and could take care of it. How naive was that?"

Tere glances out the window. "Aren't we on the outskirts of Querétaro?" she asks. "I need to meditate for a few minutes; what's ahead is going to be tough." She pulls her scarf over her head and closes her eyes.

So many secrets in Tere's life, Alma thinks, powerful secrets, secrets which guided the entire course of her life. Then she thinks of her father and the secret which changed his life. She looks out at the silent city and thinks of the millions of secrets people everywhere must hold locked up in their troubled hearts.

CHAPTER 12

*I*t's after eleven o'clock when they enter the lobby of the law offices. The only other visitor is, of all people, Mercedes. Alma does a double take. The woman is wrapped in an enormous shawl; she's knitting a small sweater. What's she doing here at this time of night? What's she doing here at any time at all, Alma thinks?

"Mercedes, we meet again. Our paths seem to cross like ships in the night."

Mercedes seems to be unimpressed by Alma's poetic imagery. "I'm here to pick up my daughter. She works for those lawyers on the top floor."

Those lawyers indeed, thinks Alma, as if the woman hasn't been spying on Arturo Guzmán for years. She whispers to Tere that she knows how Raúl has been keeping track of her movements.

María Teresa has some kind of magic card which takes them immediately to the top floor. As the elevator door opens into Arturo's office, Tere steps back as if she wants to get off at a different floor: a floor, Alma muses, where there is no Evelyn to contend with.

As Alma walks into the heart of the office, Evelyn jumps up and runs to her. She throws her arms around her. When the girl finally lets her go, she clings to Alma's arm. María Teresa meanwhile is standing very silently behind Alma. Arturo walks over to the three women. "Evelyn," he says taking Tere by the arm and pulling her in front of the girl, "this is María Teresa." Alma is relieved that he doesn't say "your mother."

Tears are streaming down Tere's cheeks. She can't seem to move out of Arturo's grasp. She stares at Evelyn, taking in every inch of her face, her hair, her figure. It is finally Evelyn who breaks the spell. She extends her hand and says "*Mucho gusto.*" She blushes when the three adults laugh.

"Did I say something wrong?" she asks.

"No, of course not," says Tere wiping her tears away with the back of her hand. She steps forward and pulls the girl toward her. She hugs her and says, "It was exactly the right thing to say, and you pronounced it perfectly. I'm pleased to meet you too. I've been waiting for this moment for such a long time. I'm so glad you came looking for us."

Alma studies the mother and daughter. They certainly aren't clones. Evelyn is on the short side but taller and sturdier than her mother. Her walk is different. But apart from their skin tone and almond shaped eyes, which are the obvious similarities, both women have small pointed chins and the same light laugh.

Evelyn reaches again for Alma's arm. No one can think of anything to say until Arturo blurts out, "It late. We should be heading back to San Miguel."

"You're coming with us?" asks Tere.

"Yes, it's too late for you women to be out on the highway alone, but I won't be going to Nuevo Progreso with you tomorrow. It would be too many people for the boy."

"You'll take me back to my dad in the evening, right?" Alma can't see Evelyn's face, but she can hear the pleading tone in her voice. The past four or five days have taken their toll; the girl now longs for the familiar. Finding her brother has lost some of its allure.

"Do you mind driving?" Arturo says to Alma when they reach the car. "I don't see that well at night."

María Teresa and Evelyn climb in the back seat. Arturo sits next to Alma. As he fiddles with the seatbelt, she studies his face. Thirty years ago, she thinks he must have been quite a catch, but not because he is or was handsome. No, his nose is too big; his eyes too closely set. Still he is a fine figure of a man: tall, broad-shouldered with a booming voice, an old lion of a man. The kind of man that flicks his little finger and your troubles disappear. She imagines what an impressive figure he must have cut on a Chestnut Bay, not to mention in a lady's bed. "Off we go," he says.

For the first ten minutes of the trip, María Teresa and Evelyn engage in casual chit-chat. The kind of conversation one hears from seatmates on an airplane. What were Evelyn's first impressions of Mexico, did she like the food? Evelyn asks Tere where she lives. "Zihuatanejo, near the sea. I have a yoga studio connected to a small boutique hotel, La Casa que Canta. For me it is one of the most beautiful places on earth. Maybe you'll come visit one day." That is as personal as the dialogue gets, but it's a start, a good start. Yawns and talk of sleep follow, next the soft sound of shallow breathing. Arturo looks over his shoulder. "Dead to the world," he says.

As they pick up the highway to San Miguel, Arturo says, "Dark night, no moon." He's silent for a few minutes, then continues. "I used to love driving around the countryside at night with Leonor. When it's pitch-dark, the known world changes; it can be transformed into something strange, even sinister, or become magical: shooting stars flying across the sky, bats and owls looking for prey." He laughs, "I sound like the poet I used to be."

"When did you write poetry?"

"When I was teenager. It was shockingly bad stuff." He chuckles. "Good thing for literature that I became a lawyer."

"What poets did you like?"

"Anyone who wrote about love but particularly Pablo Neruda. My favorite line is: '*I love you as certain dark things are to be loved, in secret, between the shadow and the soul.*' Do you have a great love, Alma?

"I thought I did but now I'm not so sure."

"Is he or she married? That was my problem."

"Not technically. But I think he might still be tied to his ex."

"I sympathize. My love affair with Tere's mother can only be talked about in superlatives like the opening lines from *The Tale of Two Cities.* 'It was the best of times. It was the worst of times.'"

"How did you meet?"

"Before I tell you how we met, you have to understand who we were before that faithful spring evening. I was a very successful lawyer, never married, from a large, unexceptional Querétaro family. My father had been the manager of a branch bank. I was the oldest of seven children. I was the family success story. Leonor was— "

"I know quite a bit about Leonor. She gave our newspaper's social page some of its best copy."

"Yes, of course. Then you know about her rich daddy and her marriage to Hernán."

"Thanks to Irma."

"So, the old gossip is still alive."

"Very much so."

"Leonor and I met at a horse show, where else. It took me two days to be totally infatuated. I had had many girlfriends, many affairs, but I had never met a woman like Leonor. She had the sparkle of a glass of champagne. She was so alive, so passionate about everything. I had to have her. She was in her late thirties, but people still stopped and stared when she walked across a room. For a year and a half, we carried on the most thrilling affair. I had never been so happy nor had she. Life seemed to hold endless possibilities."

Arturo stops speaking for a moment. He considers his words as if he were arguing his case in a court of law.

"I wanted her to divorce Hernán immediately. She hesitated. It was her son, she said. She was afraid the scandal would hurt him. Leaving Raúl with Hernán was unthinkable.

Then she became pregnant. She was determined to have the child. She insisted that I would never be happy unless I had a child of my own. I knew a little of her medical history and was concerned, but it was impossible to dissuade her. I wanted her to leave Hernán and live with me until a divorce could be arranged, but she resisted. 'My son,' she would say, 'he has to be protected.' Finally, she and Hernán settled on a plan. She would stay with him until after the baby was born and Raúl was safely away at boarding school. After that, there would be a quiet divorce, and Hernán would let her leave with the new baby."

"Did you believe him? Did you think that he'd actually let her go?"

"What choice did I have? She felt that if she didn't do things his way, he would turn her son against her, and he might lay claim to our child. Of course, the ultimate irony is that by adhering to his rules, we let him kill her legally and keep our child."

"Do you think Hernán laid a trap for her?"

"Who knows. He had a chance at revenge, and he took it."

"Did he know that you were Tere's biological father?"

"He's not stupid. Leonor and I were certainly in each other's company enough. He did invite me to Tere's awful *quinceaños* celebration. I think he wanted the world to see how well he had done as a single father; instead he showed us what a hash he had made of Tere's upbringing." Arturo pauses for a minute. "To be honest, I should have said what a hash we all had made of Tere's childhood."

"But you did get to see Tere now and then."

"That's why I started my toy museum. I had an understanding with Ángeles. Leonor had left the woman money in her will. I offered to manage it and to contribute to a retirement fund if I could see Tere as often as possible. She also was to inform me about the girl's activities. The best I can say is that I kept tabs on my daughter."

Suddenly, out of nowhere, Alma sees headlights ahead. Headlights pointing in the wrong direction, five or six large trucks. She slows down. "It's an Army check point," she says.

"Don't stop," shouts Tere from the backseat. "They're going to assault us or worse."

"It's the Army," says Arturo. "Don't be ridiculous. They'll start shooting if we don't stop. Pull over, Alma. I'll take care of this."

A young Army officer approaches the car. Alma rolls down the window. "Out of the car," he says. "Everyone out of the car."

Arturo leans across Alma. *"Buenas noches, Oficial,"* he says in a voice which carries all the authority of his class and profession. He introduces himself, *Licenciado* Arturo Guzmán Rosas, he says, *su servidor.*

"Buenas noches, Señor," says the young sergeant lowering his rifle.

"I'm accompanying these young women to San Miguel. They're tired. Must we get out of the car? My granddaughter is asleep in the backseat."

"So sorry, *Señor.* Let me just have a quick look in the back of the truck."

He returns a few minutes later. "You can go on," he says

tipping his cap slightly.

"What's going on?" asks Arturo.

The young man looks around. "Shootout at a ranch nearby. Drug gangs. Don't tell anyone I told you."

As Alma pulls away from the road block, she sees an SUV stop behind her. The Army sergeant walks over to the car. The woman driving steps out of the car. It's Sonia. The man who emerges from the other side is not Raúl. He looks like a bodyguard, Alma thinks. Is Sonia following them? Why is she traveling with that thug? She keeps the information to herself, no need to alarm anyone in the car. It's probably just a coincidence but certainly an odd one.

The two women in the back seat fall back to sleep immediately. Alma concentrates on her driving. She's nervous about the shootout at the ranch. She tries the radio, but all stations have signed off for the night.

Arturo clears his throat. "I sent Evelyn those e-cards," he says.

"You did? Why?" Alma asks.

"Tere got so angry with me when I told her. I swear I never thought about Leonor's will when I was sending them. I know that's nonsensical because she dictated the will to me. I knew the will backward and forward. It was an old man's obsession. I had grandchildren I'd never seen, never known. I wanted to meet my grandchildren before I died. It never crossed my mind that I might be putting Evelyn in danger."

"But didn't you think about Tere? How she'd feel about suddenly being," Alma pauses, "outed."

"When I think about what Tere has gone through, I am

amazed how well she has put her life back together. They love her there in Zihuatanejo. She does so much for the community. She supports a small hospital and an alternative school for gifted village children. She buys instruments for the children's orchestra, but she has no family of her own. She never talks about the two children she bore, never talks about that summer. Maybe she talks about it to the therapist she's been seeing for years. She and I are close. I talk about Leonor all the time. I thought Tere needed to know her children, see them face-to-face in order to get on with her life. She's young enough to marry, to have a family. There's a doctor in Zihuatanejo she's started seeing. Maybe—?"

"Wow, you don't mess around," says Alma glancing at Arturo. "I'm surprised she's still talking to you. But what's so special about Leonor's will?"

"The will is pure Leonor: trying to control from the grave what she couldn't control while on earth. María Teresa is the sole beneficiary of eighty percent of the Aragón wealth. Raúl got stocks and a few mines, hotels. I understand he burned through that almost immediately. Tere's money is held in trust. She gets a monthly stipend which is very generous. If she wants a larger sum, she has to make a proposal to the trustees, but they're a soft touch. The kicker is what happens to the money on Tere's death. If she has a daughter or daughters, they take over the trust. If not, the trust goes to the nearest female blood relative which now would be Raúl's daughter, Verónica."

Alma sees in the distance the lights of San Miguel and a sense of relief floods over her. "I see why Tere might think it was foolish to bring Evelyn here. She'd be a sitting duck."

"Raúl is not going to do anything. It would be too obvious, and besides, the girl will be out of the country in a few days. I don't regret for a moment that I got to meet her. She's lovely."

As they walk around the corner toward the house, Tere stops short. "There's someone in front of the house. See the figure near the door."

"For God's sake, María Teresa, you're scaring the girl. Wait here. I'll go ahead to see who it is," says Arturo. "Women," he mutters as he walks away.

"Oh," says Tere as the two figures start walking toward them. "It's Andrés."

"Andrés, my real father? He," Evelyn points to Arturo, "told me that my real father became a priest."

When the two men reach the women, Arturo says, "Evelyn, this is *Padre* Andrés."

The priest's smile lights up his whole face. "We finally meet, Evelyn. The pleasure is all mine."

Arturo puts his arm around the girl. "It's chilly out here. Let's get into the house."

"Why are you here?" says María Teresa. "Did you talk to Álvaro? Are we still on for tomorrow?"

"Yes, we talked to Álvaro. We're still on for tomorrow, but the poor kid is in a state of shock. We told the rest of the children about Álvaro's adoption too. I stayed for lunch, but it was very uncomfortable. Only Clara spoke; she asked all the embarrassing questions that the other children wanted to ask, like: 'How could you get married, Uncle Andrés, you're a priest?' Álvaro looked like he wanted to drop through the floor; I would have gladly joined him. It was awful."

"Where are you staying?" asks Arturo.

"I guess on your sofa."

Alma says she's exhausted. She has a room at the Lakewood Resort.

"No, no, no," says Evelyn when they reach the house, "you have to stay overnight with us, Alma, doesn't she—?" She turns toward Arturo and María Teresa, but she can't think how to address them, so she avoids using any names. "She can share my room," Evelyn continues.

Alma thinks about the soft, warm towels and scented sheets at the Lakewood. The last half-hour of the drive she had been fantasizing about a luxurious bubble bath in the large tub.

"Yes, of course," says Arturo, "I'm not too sure about the supply of hot water or food for breakfast, but we'll manage."

As Alma is drifting off the sleep on a very hard mattress between rather scratchy sheets, she suddenly thinks about Gabriel, and how much he would enjoy meeting Arturo Guzmán. She imagines the two men laughing about some of the shady characters they've known. She's sure that Arturo would remind Gabriel of his father. Then her thoughts darken. Why, after the last ten days, does she assume she knows anything that's in Gabriel's head?

She wakes just before dawn. Evelyn is still sound asleep. She dresses and creeps out of the room. Maybe she can make a quick run to the Lakewood and enjoy a hot bath. She sees a light on in the kitchen. When she enters, Andrés stands up.

"*Señorita* Jaramillo," he says "coffee? That's about the only thing I can do in the kitchen."

"It's Alma," she says sitting down, the hot bath at the Lakewood receding from her current plans.

Padre Andrés doesn't speak for a moment. "I love the early morning," he says finally. "I love saying Mass at any time. I love my work in Africa with the children, but my favorite part of the day is still daybreak. It's the simplicity of those Masses just after dawn that makes me remember why I became a priest. It's when I feel very close to our Lord." He stops. "I'm sorry I got angry the other night. I was very afraid of what I knew was ahead, and I was right. It was terrible telling Álvaro the truth about his birth. With a few sentences we blew his world apart. He said nothing. He crept away to his room. Inés said he buried himself under the covers of his bed. If Roberto hadn't insisted on his coming to lunch, I think he'd still be there."

"I feel like a bull in a china shop," says Alma. "In the beginning I was on my high horse talking about the children's right to know their birth family. But if I'm honest, my reporter instinct took over. I was curious; I couldn't let go of the story. Now it all seems such a mess. My parish priest, *Padre* Rafael, told me I might be stirring up a hornet's nest. He said, *Agua que no has de beber, déjala correr.*"

Andrés laughs. "No, we all needed to drink the water you discovered, even if it comes from a poisoned well. Did you ever betray anyone, Alma? Serious betrayal, not kid stuff." Alma shakes her head.

"I didn't look on it as betrayal when I was eighteen," says

Andrés. "It was simply survival. All I had then was my family and a chance to enter a prestigious seminary, and that was thanks to my brother. I had no idea if I had a vocation. I was doing what was expected of me. What had always been expected of me. That summer with Tere was fun. I was living a fantasy that I knew had to come to an end. That song that she was so attached to, '*Si nos dejan*,' even if they had 'let us,' we wouldn't have survived. How could we? We were kids with no money, no jobs. We could hardly take care of ourselves. How were we going to live on a velvet cloud and take care of a baby?"

"But did it have to be so brutal? Did you have to split up the children? What were you thinking when you took Álvaro from the clinic?"

"Me? I wasn't thinking anything except 'get me out of this nightmare.' Francisco thought the boy should stay in Mexico, follow in the family tradition of entering the priesthood. He and Inés cooked up the idea. I'm not in any way excusing myself. It was only later, when I did become a priest, and I did realize that I had a vocation, that the guilt began. What had I done to those children? What had I done to Tere? It took years, many lonely years in Africa, for me to even begin to imagine that God might forgive me one day. I never expected that either Tere or the children would ever forgive me."

"Do you think your brother was murdered because someone thought he had seduced Tere? *Don* Hernán hinted as much to me..."

"Back to your role as the intrepid reporter, I see. Honestly,

I don't know. I don't want to accuse Raúl of anything, but my brother did find out that the agency that Raúl and his wife ran was mixed up in trafficking the babies from La Casa de la Esperanza. But then Francisco was also continually at odds with the drug gangs who were exploiting the migrants at El Refugio. They threatened him many times."

"Hey," says a sleepy-faced Evelyn entering the kitchen. "What's for breakfast?"

Alma leads the girl out of the kitchen. She hands her a cell phone and says, "You've got to call your dad. He's sick with worry." The girl punches in Sandra's number. When Bob Wearing picks up he says that June arrived last night, and that Evelyn's parents went to stay at a hotel. He'll call them immediately. Alma takes the phone. Tell them, she says, that Evelyn is fine and will be back in Ávila this afternoon. She is going to meet her brother. She'll be dropped off at the Wearings' house around four o'clock. Bob Wearing says "Hallelujah, this nightmare is finally coming to an end."

"My mom is here," says Evelyn and does a little pirouette. "I can't wait to see her."

Alma peeks into the room on her right. "Come see this, Evelyn. It's amazing." The four walls of the room are covered from floor to ceiling with shelves on which rest every handmade toy, children's game or book produced in Mexico for the last fifty or perhaps one hundred years. There are cloth dolls from Oaxaca dressed in frilly blouses and skirts with ribbons tied in their yarn hair. There are wooden tops, yo-yos and acrobats who dance on the end of wooden sticks. On the lower shelves are trains, cars and fire trucks also carved from wood. A fairground made out of tin takes up an entire shelf. There are xylophones, little violins and guitars. Displayed on other shelves are different games of Lotto and *Memoria* together with picture books illustrated by Mexico's finest artists. An orchestra of clay frogs dressed as mariachis march down another shelf. The room is a child's paradise.

"Did Grandpa Arturo do this for Tere?" asks Evelyn.

"It seems so," says Alma.

When Alma and Evelyn reenter the kitchen, Arturo and Tere are there. "I can make pancakes for everyone," Evelyn says. "Thank goodness," says Tere, "because no one else in this lot can even boil an egg."

"Have you looked out the window this morning?" asks Arturo scraping the last bits of butter, honey, and hotcake onto his fork. "Carnival starts today. In a few days it will be Ash Wednesday and Lent. Here the festivities are mostly for children. They'll be running through the streets smashing *cascarones* over their friends' heads; they and anyone else who's on the street will get covered in confetti and glitter. Sometimes there's a parade too. People dress up in costumes; wear comic masks. You'd better get started for Nuevo Progreso before the streets become so congested you can't move."

S.B. URQUIDI

CHAPTER 13

*A*lma says that she remembers almost second by second the ten minutes that led up to the moment that fractured her life. Tere, Evelyn, and *Padre* Andrés are ready to leave for Nuevo Progreso. Inés and family have been alerted. Alma remembers that she's forgotten her best scarf in the truck. She hurries down the street. Both the sidewalk and the road itself are packed with children and adults celebrating. Cars thread through crowds slowly. Some adults are wearing masks, most everyone is carrying a bag of *cascarones,* the colored eggshells filled with cornstarch, confetti, and glitter. Children and teenagers are laughing and running as they smash the eggs on any near-by head. She sees Chucho at the corner. She's glad she's not going with the group to Nuevo Progreso. She wants to get home. She greets Chucho with a brief *"Buenos días,"* he nods his head. She gets her scarf, and he walks alongside of her. He says he's happy to see his *"niña"* María Teresa back in San Miguel at last. He hopes she's happy; she deserves it after all she's been through. He looks forward to getting to know the *Señorita* Evelyn on the drive this morning. His jacket is zipped up; Alma wonders idly if he still has the gun tucked in his belt.

As she leaves him and walks back toward the house, she feels optimistic. She's happy that her part in Evelyn's odyssey is over, and that she will be able to get on with her own life. She'll call Gabriel as soon as she's on the road. Where should they meet today? What will he say? She's a short distance from the house when she notices Evelyn and Tere walk out the front door alone. Andrés must have forgotten something. Evelyn is smiling. She stops to observe the festivities. She asks Tere something. She's probably asking where she can get some *cascarones*.

A second later, two men break away from the crowd. They're wearing Guy Fawkes masks. How sinister they look, Alma thinks, so different from the rest of the people. The men stop directly in front of Tere and Evelyn. They grab the women by their arms and begin hustling them down the street away from the house. People move out of their way, but no one interferes. Alma can see a car with the doors open at the end of the street. Evelyn turns around. She begins to scream. She's terrified. Tere tries to pull away from the man who's clutching her good arm, but he has it wrapped around his and pressed tightly to his body. One of the men begins to shout that it's only a rehearsal for a TV show, but the crowd shrinks back, afraid. Alma begins to run. She feels as if she's in one of her recent weird dreams. She catches up to the two men and the women. She wraps the ends of her scarf around her clenched fists and throws it around the neck of the man holding Evelyn. He struggles; she presses her knee into the small of his back. As she pulls the man backward, she shouts to Evelyn, "Run back to the house!"

The man drops Evelyn's arm as he stumbles. At that moment the assailant holding Tere's arm spins around to see what's happening; Tere takes off running. The first man disentangles the scarf from his throat and throws Alma to the ground. She hears a gun shot. She sees that the assailant who was holding Tere has a pistol. He's looking around to see where the shot came from. Alma catches sight of Chucho running toward them. He has his gun in his hand. He stops and takes aim. The masked man whom Alma attacked spins around, sees the gun, and sprints toward the car at the end of street. Men, women, and children are running to get out of the way of the gunfire, everyone is screaming. People are hiding in doorways, crouching with their arms covering their heads.

The other gunman looks down at Alma, and this is the part she will play over and over in her head for years to come. He points his gun at her head. He's going to kill me, she thinks. She's furious. She can't die. She has too many things to do. She has a child to raise. She covers her face with her hands. She hears another shot. She peeks out at the street through her fingers. The assailant in front of her doubles over, but he can still lift his gun. His hand is shaking. She tries to curl into a fetal position. She hears the man say through the mask, "Bitch," and then he fires. The impact of the bullet jerks her head off the ground. Her shoulder seems to explode in dozens of pieces. Perhaps he's blown my arm off, she thinks, but after that the pain obliterates all thought. As everything goes black, she hears another explosion of gun fire.

Is it a minute or an hour later? She feels someone pressing a cloth to her shoulder and yelling. "Get an ambulance! She's bleeding to death." Someone else lifts her head up slightly. She sees a body a few feet away. The man's mask has been thrown to one side of his body. She can't see his face, but she hears someone say, Raúl Gómez y Velasco. Is it Raúl who shot the assailant? Or is it Raúl who shot her? She tries to ask but passes out again.

When her mind swims back into consciousness, she's surrounded by men and women in white. She's being lifted into an ambulance. Someone is holding her hand. Through a haze she sees the hand holding hers. It looks familiar. A voice says, "I'll follow in my car. We need to get her to Ávila as quickly as possible. The surgeon is waiting." It's Ricardo who's speaking. Why is he here? A needle is jabbed in her arm and all memory ceases.

*   *   *

Her mouth is dry; it feels like her tongue is paralyzed. There's something cold on her lips. Someone is rubbing an ice cube on them. She parts her lips slightly, so the moisture can seep into her mouth. She sees the hand holding the ice cube. Then she sees her mother. "She's waking up," her mother says leaning over her. She can hear her mother praying, thanking God that her daughter is alive. Her father passes a cold towel over her forehead.

"*Ay*, Alma, don't scare us like this again. We're too old," he says.

Kurt moves close to his grandmother. "The doctor told Grandpa that you're going to get well soon," he says. "I asked him if I could have the bullet they took out of your shoulder, but he said that he had to turn it over to the police. I thought we could put it in the cabinet where you keep all that stuff like my baby shoes and those old dried flowers."

She wants to ask what happened to her shoulder, where she is, who had operated, but a nurse appears to shoo her visitors away. She drifts back to sleep. When she wakes next, the room is barely light. Someone is holding her hand. "What time is it?" she asks.

"Almost dawn," says Gabriel.

"Have you been here long?" she asks trying to focus on the man she hasn't seen in ten days. He has deep shadows under his eyes and a stubbly beard which isn't very attractive.

"Since six o'clock last evening. You were restless around two-thirty. I got the nurse to give you a larger dose of pain killer. How do you feel now?"

"Well, I can speak, which I couldn't do yesterday. What day is it? What happened after I got shot?"

"It's Monday morning. Your dad told me that they brought you in around noon. Ricardo got the ambulance and arranged for the surgeon. You're still alive because the bullet missed any major artery, and it wasn't fired from a high caliber weapon. Still it did a lot of damage to the bones, nerves and tendons in your shoulder," he clutches her hand. "He could have killed you, Alma. What were you thinking when you attacked that man?"

"I was thinking about Evelyn; what might happen to her and to Tere. No one else was around. What was I supposed to do? But who shot me? Who were those men?"

"I think Ricardo is the best one to tell you about that. Thank God, he came on the scene a few minutes after it happened. Look," Gabriel says reaching over to the table behind him, "I bought you some roses, your favorite color, and also a huge apology for dropping off the radar screen for so many days."

Alma looks at him. His face is very serious. "First of all, nothing happened with Linda. I mean we didn't sleep together or anything like that. We ran into one another the second evening I was there. Okay, it was at a restaurant we used to go to in Austin, but I didn't even know she was in town. She was in a very bad way, Alma. That Lopez guy, the big lawyer she'd married, left her and the firm a year after they married. She was devastated. She knows that she has a problem with mood swings, but he kept accusing her of being seriously mentally ill, saying she was bipolar. Linda, bipolar! That's ridiculous. What an asshole he is. She doesn't like the meds the doctors put her on; she says that she's not herself. I told her that she had to give them time. I spoke with her mother yesterday; she said that I had come along at a very critical time. They were grateful that I'd been there for their daughter."

Alma emits a low pitched but audible moan. She isn't sure if it comes from the pain in her shoulder or the pain in her heart. She loves this man. She thought she knew him so well.

She thinks about how he likes to have the back of his neck rubbed when he's tired; how she has run her fingers along the deep scar on his left leg from some childhood accident. She has eaten hundreds of the delicious meals he cooks, laughed with him over his students' antics and slept in his bed more times than she can count. But suddenly she feels Gabriel's heart is a mystery to her. She remembers his affable father with his two households. Her conversation with Sergio comes roaring back. What did he say? Yes, that first loves are difficult to erase.

"Gabo, thanks so much for the flowers and watching over me. You are the guy to call when there's a damsel in distress. I'm glad you're back, but I think I need to sleep now." She closes her eyes as much to end the conversation as to give way to drowsiness.

He kisses her on the forehead and says that as soon as she's well they have to talk seriously about the future. She nods her head but cannot imagine her part in the conversation.

Blissfully, no one is at her bedside when she wakes up. The nurse brings breakfast, which consists of watery oatmeal and Jell-O. She eats a few spoonfuls of the Jell-O with her right hand and pushes away the unappetizing oatmeal. Thank God, she thinks, it was her left and not her right shoulder that was damaged. There's a dull ache on the whole left side of her body. The surgeon finally appears. "What's the prognosis?" she asks.

"You're lucky to be alive," he says flatly. "Ricardo Núñez, your boss apparently, the man who called the ambulance and who sent you here, saved your life. Your prognosis is good, but you're going to need lots of rehab and patience with the pain. You should have complete use of your left arm after the rehab, but your professional baseball career is at an end." The doctor smiles at his little joke, pats her good shoulder and hurries off.

She sees a head peek around the door. It's Ricardo himself. "I'm going to bill you for all the sleep I've lost lately. How are you feeling?"

"Not great," she says. "But I'm alive, which is more than I thought when that guy pointed the gun at me."

He pulls up a chair and puts a newspaper down on the tray table which extends over her bed. "You made the front page," he says but he's not smiling. "You want me to read the story? Ana did a pretty good job."

"Ana Flores, the intern who's been helping me?"

"Yes, the same Ana who most of us have been avoiding," he says as he lifts the newspaper and begins to read.

ÁVILA JOURNALIST SERIOUSLY WOUNDED IN SHOOTOUT

Ávila, Tep. Yesterday morning noted local journalist Alma Jaramillo Martínez was shot while trying to stop a kidnapping. Jaramillo was on assignment in San Miguel de Allende, Gto. for El Diario de Ávila when the incident occurred. According to witnesses, two masked men approached Ma. Teresa Gómez y Velasco and Evelyn Hammond as they were leaving home. The men grabbed the two women and began dragging them toward a getaway car parked down the street. Jaramillo, seeing the women in trouble, ran to their aid. A witness said that the journalist jumped on the back of one of the assailants seizing the man by the throat. In the ensuing chaos, the kidnappers loosened their grip on their victims allowing them to escape.

According to another witness, Jaramillo pulled out a gun and fired at the kidnappers. This account was disputed by Jesús Rivera, the Gómez y Velasco chauffeur. He said he was returning from checking the family car when he saw a scuffle going on in front of Arturo Guzmán's home. Seeing that one of the assailants was armed, Rivera fired at him. The second kidnapper ran away when the shooting started; the assassin with the pistol then shot Jaramillo. The chauffeur's second bullet killed the assailant. Rivera said, "I couldn't get to the *c*...... before he shot Alma, but I finished him off before he could do anymore damage."

At the time of publication, the identity of the dead assailant has not been confirmed. Jaramillo is expected to make a full recovery. Neither Ma. Teresa Gómez y Velasco nor Evelyn Hammond could be reached for comment.

"For God's sake, Richie, who shot me?"

"Raúl Gómez y Velasco, of course."

"Why haven't they released his name?"

"Because the family, meaning old Hernán, is trying to get the governor to cover up the whole thing. I talked to a source in the Guanajuato state police. He said messages are coming into the governor's office from the old man's influential friends, but they won't succeed. There are too many witnesses, and Tere and Arturo won't go along with it."

"Can we start from point A and you walk me through your part in Sunday's events? What were you doing there? What happened after I was shot?"

Ricardo looks at his watch. "My wife is here for some tests. She'll be through in twenty minutes so here's the abbreviated version of the last twenty-four hours. You aren't going to like this part of it, but if anyone saved your life it was probably your colleague, Héctor Valdés." He holds up his hand silencing any potential comments from Alma. He says that Héctor had called him at twelve-thirty Saturday night, or rather Sunday morning. He'd told Ricardo that Alma was supposed to have met him at some *antro* called The Sword of Damocles at nine o'clock, but that she'd never shown up.

"Héctor said you were working on some hot story and knowing your propensity for trouble, he thought I should know that you might have gone missing. I called Captain Ramírez to see if the security detail that I had requested once again had you in their sights, but he said you hadn't come home yet.

"I figured I'd get a few hours' sleep and see if you showed up at home during the night. When I spoke to Ramírez at six-thirty Sunday morning, he said that they'd checked your home, and that no one was there. I called Sandra Wearing, the woman who got you into this mess. She wasn't very happy to be woken up, but she told me about your son's assist to Evelyn and that the girl was on the run again. I suspected then that you must have gone to San Miguel. I called Ana Flores. She said you had a friend there, Dan Sullivan, who was the manager of the Lakewood Resort. She also said she was coming with me. We ran into Dan in the lobby of the hotel about nine o'clock. He said you'd checked in and left him a note about having breakfast but that you hadn't shown up. We checked your room, but you hadn't slept there.

"I suspected that you had probably gone to see old Hernán, and sure enough after an endless conversation about my misplaced trust in modern Catholicism, he told me you'd been there last night. As Ana and I were leaving I asked the housekeeper if she knew where you might have been heading. When she mentioned the house with the green door, I remembered our conversation with my lawyer friend, Arturo Guzmán.

"We were still a block away when we heard the screams and the shots. When we pushed our way through the crowd, a woman was bending over you trying to stop the bleeding. I saw a priest kneeling beside a body giving the man the Last Rites. Arturo spotted me. He said the dead man was Raúl Gómez y Velasco and the woman bending over you was Raúl's sister, María Teresa. I got onto a private ambulance service I've used and a surgeon I trust here in Ávila.

"Even though Ana kept telling me all morning that I needed a shave and suggested I might want to change my barber, I have to say she really jumped in there like an old pro. She found out who everyone was, and what they were doing when the shooting took place. *Padre* Andrés had gotten a last-minute phone call from his travel agent. That's why he didn't leave the house at the same time as the women. Arturo was just about to take a shower. Ana also tracked down

Evelyn's parents, June and Nick Hammond, in Ávila and waited with the girl until they showed up. Evelyn was pretty shaken up. She wouldn't let go of June's hand even for a minute.

"Ana said the meeting between the two sets of parents, the birth couple, *Padre* Andrés and Tere, and the adopted parents was very awkward. Arturo, ever the diplomat, smoothed things over. He told Evelyn that he would bring her brother, Álvaro, up to San Diego in the summer, so she could go home having almost completed her mission. Ana said the Hammond family left Mexico that night."

Ricardo stands up. "I've got to go. Elvia is not well. I'm worried. She needs more tests tomorrow. I'll stop in then. Oh, and by the way, your new best friend, Héctor, says he wants to move to the sports page. He thinks political reporting is boring which is fine because *El Chaparro* is retiring. So Beto García, our stellar new governor, is probably waiting impatiently for you to schedule an interview."

Alma lies back on her pillows. How random, how serendipitous life is, she thinks, and yet, it is and it isn't. The chain of events which led her from Sandra Wearing's family room ten days ago to this hospital bed today seems now to be almost predetermined; a slippery slope that once stepped onto, would inevitably bring her down. She sees each breakthrough in the investigation as a signpost on a long hiking trail. The trail had always been there, but the signs were often obscured by the jungle foliage.

Alma hears María Teresa outside her door pleading with the nurse on duty. She holds her finger on the bell until the nurse appears and agrees to let Tere visit for ten minutes. "Where's Arturo?" asks Alma. "He'll be up in a minute," answers Tere. "An old client buttonholed him in the lobby." She takes Alma's good hand. "I'm so sorry about everything," she says. "How are you doing?"

"It's going to take a while, but the shoulder will mend. How about you? What with Raúl's attempted kidnapping and then his death, you must feel pretty beaten up yourself."

Tere leans back in her chair. The beautiful face is no longer serene; she looks tired, haggard. "We were never close, too big a difference in our ages, and then there was the whole money thing. Our mother's will made him resent me and hate her. When I wasn't around him, I felt sorry for him. I don't think he had much of a childhood, either. Hernán was hopeless as a father, and Leonor? I think she was a good mother on paper. She had good intentions, but she mostly wasn't there: too busy being Lady Bountiful, pursuing her own interests. I'm sorry he had to die in such a miserable way, but," she pauses. "I can't say I'll miss him. He's hounded me for money for years, both he and Sonia, and now they're both gone."

"What do you mean, both gone? Did something happen to Sonia, your sister-in-law?" asks Alma.

"She and, her daughter, Verónica, disappeared a few hours after the shootout. I'm sure they're in Italy, probably trying to change their names. Sonia knew, even more than Raúl did, that the cartels never forgive or forget. They were going to collect on their debt in whatever way they could. She'd be killed, and Verónica kidnapped for some capo's bed. The girl would end up drugged and in a bordello somewhere, or if she was lucky, married off to some minor gangbanger." Tere shudders. "For once Sonia did the right thing getting the girl out of the country. If Verónica makes contact, I'll be happy to help her."

Arturo bursts into the room. He smiles at the nurse who follows at his heels and with a few words completely charms her. Settling himself in a chair next to Tere, he tells Alma that they have just returned from Nuevo Progreso and lunch with his new grandson, Álvaro. Alma studies the father and daughter sitting side by side. Although Tere resembles her mother more than anyone, expressions flit across her face which are purely Arturo. She could never have been Hernán's daughter, Alma thinks. There is not the slightest resemblance.

"How did it go?" asks Alma. "But before you answer that, was Roberto, Álvaro's dad, at all repentant about almost killing me on the old road from Nuevo Progreso and vandalizing my dad's truck?"

"I've been hearing my whole life," says Arturo, "that quote from the New Testament: 'And ye shall know the truth, and the truth shall make you free.' My experience as a lawyer says the opposite. Most of the time people are terrified of learning or telling the truth. They know instinctively that rather than setting them free, it's going to get them into a lot more trouble. Roberto was protecting his family. He didn't want his son's life and their family life torn apart. He thought in his misguided way that he could scare you off and be done with you."

"Well, he was almost done with me," says Alma. "So, how

was the lunch?"

"Uncomfortable is the best word for it," says Tere. "Poor kid, he'd had two days to get used to a new identity and to an entirely new set of relatives."

"We showed him pictures of Evelyn," says Arturo. "He said he looks a lot more like her than like Roberto, but he didn't say much else during lunch. Tere told Inés and Roberto about her yoga studio in Zihuatanejo, and I talked about my museum project. Roberto said that Álvaro loved photography, so I suggested he come over to San Miguel and take a few photos for the catalog we're bringing out."

Tere breaks into the conversation. "Álvaro walked us to the car when we were leaving. It was the first time he'd spoken more than a few words. He said he was glad to meet me, but he didn't know what to do because he already had a mother. I said I understood perfectly but hoped we could be friends. It was the same thing I'd told Evelyn. It's going to be like walking a tightrope, but I want to be part of their lives. They're beautiful children. Their adoptive parents have done a wonderful job," she pauses and takes Arturo's hand. "However, I think they started out with some pretty good genes, too."

A smile starts to spread across Tere's face. "Then the boy turned to Arturo. He said he was really excited to meet him because he didn't have a grandfather, and it would be cool to have one. Arturo said he didn't have a grandson, so he was delighted also. Álvaro hesitated for a moment after that, but asked if Arturo could do him a favor. Arturo looked a little taken aback, but said if it was something he could do, he would be happy to help in any way."

"What did he ask you?" says Alma, looking at Arturo who is smiling too.

"He asked me to tell his parents that he didn't want to become a priest. He would promise, he said, to remain a good Catholic, but he really liked girls, plus he wanted to be a photographer when he grew up."

The nurse comes in just when Alma tries to laugh, painful as it is. Her visitors depart under the woman's stern gaze.

Left alone, Alma closes her eyes for what seems like a few minutes. "Alma," a voice says, "the nurse said only two minutes, and that's because I'm a priest and might offer you some spiritual comfort after your ordeal."

"*Padre* Andrés," she says, "how nice of you to come. Are you heading back to Africa?"

"Yes, the black suit and roman collar sometimes help to get an upgrade," he says smiling. "But I've come to tell you that I know who killed my brother. I wanted you to know before it becomes public. I thought you deserved that much because you were right about the motive. Well, maybe we were both right. On Sunday morning, after the police had talked to all of us and had collected the weapons used in the shootings, Chucho, Don Hernán's chauffeur, asked if he could talk to me alone. We found a space in the back garden. He said he wanted to confess something to me. He wanted my forgiveness. Frankly, I had no idea what he was talking about. He knelt down and blessing himself said, 'Bless me Father for I have sinned.' Then he looked up at me and said, 'It was me. I killed your brother.' I pulled him up to his feet.

'Why?' I said.

"We sat down on a bench at the back of the garden; he said that he'd figured out soon afterward that he might have been used by Raúl, but that at the time, he'd believed him. It was right after Tere's disastrous visit when she'd come back from San Francisco and had had that big fight with Hernán. Raúl asked Chucho to come to his house. He said that Tere had confessed to him that *Padre* Francisco was the father of the twins. He had said that the priest had mistreated her, and abandoned her and the babies. He had laughed at her when she'd said that they should marry and keep the babies.

"Chucho always felt that if he wasn't Tere's real father, then he was her protector. After all, he and Ángeles were the ones who had really raised her, who had seen her through childhood illnesses, taken her to *Don* Arturo's toy museum every Friday, and done a million other things for the girl. Raúl had said that he knew how much Chucho loved Tere. He had given him a gun and said that it had to be Chucho who avenged the tragedy that the evil priest had caused. Tere was in India so he couldn't check anything out with her. He had finally understood why Tere had kept the name of the babies' father secret.

"When he had returned that night after shooting the priest, Raúl had said how proud he was of him. He had done a great service for Tere and for the whole family. He wanted him to keep the gun as a memento of his brave deed. When Chucho read about how much *Padre* Francisco was loved by ordinary people and what good things he'd done, he began to think that perhaps Raúl had been wrong, but it wasn't until

Tere had come back a few days ago that he learned who the real father of the twins was, and he saw how he had been used.

"He said that the police have the gun now, and they would do ballistic tests. It wouldn't take them long to figure out that it was same gun that had been used to kill *Padre* Francisco. The only thing that made him happy was that it was he who had killed Raúl. ¡*Qué cabrón*! He kept saying over and over again."

"Are you going to tell the police?" asks Alma.

"No, I don't feel bound by the secrecy of the confessional, but there's no need to go to the police, they'll figure it out sooner or later."

"Do you hate Raúl?"

"You know Raúl and my brother were old friends, long before Raúl started that foundation. They were in the same class at the seminary. For a short time, Raúl thought that he might become a priest. After he met Sonia in Rome, he changed his mind. I think it was his mother's will that ate away at him. He felt that she had betrayed him. He became cynical. He started to hate people like my brother who genuinely wanted to help those in need. Finally, he just became scared about losing everything."

Padre Andrés is silent for a few moments. "But I don't let myself off so easily either. If there is a Judas in the story, I fit the bill rather than Raúl. Over the years, I felt that even if I did betray Tere, I had done it for a greater good. That at least I was not betraying God and my vocation. I never thought that sweet summer would cause a tsunami in our small world.

My brother died for our sin, and that is something I have to live with."

Alma doesn't answer for minute. Then looking at Andrés's grave face she says, "I hate the word 'sin.' Hernán used it all the time about the birth of the twins. No God that I could ever imagine would damn two beautiful babies. I know you feel that you must honor your religion's beliefs, but wasn't what happened between you and Tere just two kids getting caught up in the thrill of the moment?"

"That's not an excuse," says Andrés, regaining his priestly demeanor. "What would happen to our souls, not to mention society, if we all acted on what our emotions dictated in the heat of the moment?" He picks up his bag. Alma wonders if that thousand-watt smile will ever reappear.

"You'll be happy to get back to Kenya," she says.

"Yes, things, at least for me, are a lot simpler there. Take care of yourself, Alma."

"You know too many people," says the nurse when she comes in to give Alma her evening medications and to fluff up her pillows.

"Yes, I'm very lucky." She is lucky. First of all, she's alive. She's got her family and a rewarding, if risky line of work. She's got good friends. She thinks about that moment ten days ago when she stood at the kitchen sink and thought about her life humming perfectly along. It certainly wasn't humming along now, but things could be worse. When Gabriel comes into her thoughts, she doesn't know what to think. He wants to talk about the future, but will it be a future with a clinging Linda lurking in the background or worse, hanging around in the foreground? Or if not Linda, will it be another pretty damsel in distress needing his attention?

Alma is almost asleep when the door inches open; a small figure slips into the room and slides into bed beside her. "This is the third time today I've been here, *Flaca*, but that dragon nurse wouldn't let me in. You always had other company. Look what I brought, our favorite." Elena places a container of ice cream on the tray table in front of Alma. "Pistachio chocolate chip and two spoons. Now," she says snuggling down next to Alma, "how did things go with Gabriel? I saw him here early this morning."

Alma sighs. "He wants to talk about the future when I'm better, but I can see part of his heart is still in Texas with Linda. He's a guy that needs to be needed. When I met Gabriel, I was the damsel in distress, and he was wonderful. Now it's Linda he's bent on rescuing. Perhaps, if I'm understanding, until she gets back on her feet—? But she's not dumb; she could stretch out her recovery for a decade. Although who knows, my injuries might keep him here in Ávila long enough for Linda to look for another Prince Galahad. What I'm feeling, I guess, is confused."

Elena opens the carton of ice cream and scrapes a spoonful off the top. Alma pops it into her mouth and purrs audibly. Elena takes a bite next. "Enough of this soul searching," she says. "We have to talk about something really important, your dress for my wedding. I think something knee-length would be good and how about pink? Or maybe dark rose is more your color. What do you think?"

The soft murmur of their voices can be heard in the hall outside the room, but the young nurse on duty just rolls her eyes and goes on about her work.

THE END

S.B. URQUIDI

Glossary

A la veracruzana: a sauce named for the state of Veracruz whose long coastline borders the Gulf of Mexico. Made from red tomatoes, garlic, onions, green olives, capers, *jalapeño* chili and oregano, it is usually served over fish.

Abrazo: a hug. With men *un abrazo* usually involves a loose embrace and hardy slaps on the back.

Abuelita: an affectionate form of address for a grandmother. The frequent use of the diminutive suffix in Mexican Spanish (ito, ita) comes not only from its European mother tongue but also from the predominant Mexican indigenous language, Náhuatl. In Spanish the diminutive expresses both affection and something small. Náhuatl has a similar suffix which reflects some of the same sentiments in addition to reverence and curtsey.

Achichincle: (Náhuatl: a lackey) a hanger-on, someone who follows orders unconditionally. Politicians are noted for having many *achichincles*.

Agua que no has de beber, déjala correr: if you don't have to drink the water, let it flow on. In other words, mind your own business.

Aguas de sabor: flavored water. Lemonade-type drinks made with different fresh fruits, water, and sugar.

Alfonso García Robles: (1911–1991) a Mexican diplomat who, together with Sweden's Alva Myrdal, received the Nobel Peace Prize in 1982. The Prize recognized Robles's work as the driving force behind the treaty that established Latin America and the Caribbean as a nuclear-free zone.

Amigo/a: friend.

Amorcito: little love. Sweetheart, darling.

Antojito: an *antojo* is a whim. The diminutive form therefore is a little whim; hence, a snack, a tidbit.

Antro: a seedy bar or night club.

Atole: a hot drink made from corn flour, water, and *piloncillo* (unrefined cane sugar). It can be flavored with cinnamon, vanilla, strawberries, or chocolate.

Barrio: a neighborhood. As opposed to a *colonia*, a *barrio* is usually a smaller and more cohesive geographic area of a town or city.

Barbacoa: meat, usually mutton, wrapped in maguey leaves and flavored with spices and sometimes *pulque*; it is cooked overnight in a brick or clay oven buried in the ground.

Basura: garbage, trash.

Bienvenido/a: welcome.

Bóveda: is an ancient masonry technique which uses bricks or adobe to form a rounded self-supporting vaulted ceiling. The technique was employed widely in Spain and was brought to Mexico in colonial times. It is still used in contemporary Mexican architecture.

Buenos días: good morning.

Cabrón, Cabrona: (vulgar) asshole, son of a bitch; bitch.

Cacomixtles: (Náhuatl: half-cat). Ring-tailed cat. A member of the raccoon family, its preferred habitat is arid mountainous regions, although the animal abounds in my verdant garden.

Calabaza: pumpkin; *calabacita*: zucchini, summer squash.

Caldo de pollo: chicken broth; can contain rice, pieces of chicken, vegetables.

Cantera: a quarried, volcanic rock that is mined exclusively in various regions of Mexico and Central America. It can be found in a variety of colors and textures. Its characteristic softness makes it ideal for detailed carving.

Caray: wow, darn, good heavens.

Cascarones: tinted eggshells filled with cornstarch, confetti, and glitter, which are thrown or smashed over revelers' heads during pre-Lenten Carnival.

Cecina: thinly sliced, salted, and partially air-dried sheets or strips of beef or pork.

Chambelán: an escort for a young woman (*la quinceañera*) during the celebrations of her fifteenth birthday.

Chaparro (Chapo): short, shorty. Often used as a nickname for a short man. The most famous *chaparro* is El Chapo Guzmán.

Cheve: a beer.

Chicharrón: crackling; fried pork skin, pig skin.

Chili piquín: very hot pepper; can be up to forty times hotter than a *jalapeño* chili. The flavor is described variously as citrusy, smoky (if dried), and nutty.

Chingón: (vulgar) whiz, hotshot. It is derived from the verb *chingar* (to fuck).

Chipotle: (Náhuatl) a *jalapeño* chili becomes a *chipotle* when it is left on the bush until it dries out and becomes deep red in color. It is then smoked for several days, which leaves it with a distinctive flavor and the appearance of a raisin or a prune.

Chorizo: spicy pork sausage. Mexican *chorizo* differs significantly from the Spanish sausage of the same name. The Mexican variety is uncooked and usually flavored with chili and other spices. Spanish *chorizo* is cured and is more like salami; it is flavored with paprika.

Colonia: administrative section of a town or city. In Mexico, *colonias* normally have names and are more official than *barrios*.

Comida corrida: an inexpensive three-course lunch of homemade local food served in small restaurants or *fondas*. The courses are not large, and the menu often changes daily.

Crema y nata: cream and the milk skin that rises to the top of the milk; i.e., those at the top of social ladder.

Curandero: healer, medicine man.

Dama de honor: maid of honor.

Déjala: leave her alone.

Delicados: Popular, inexpensive brand of Mexican cigarettes. They have been on the market since 1908.

Derecho Penal y Civil: criminal and civil law.

Desmadre: (negative) disaster, mess, disorder; (positive) wild. An entire page of the Mexican Spanish Dictionary is devoted to the creative use of the word *madre*, which means "mother," in colloquial Mexican Spanish.

Día de la Candelaria: Candlemas Day, February 2nd.

Dieciséis de septiembre: September sixteenth, Mexican Independence Day. The celebration begins the evening of September fifteenth when in town squares across Mexico, the local leader shouts out the cry of independence, first heard in 1810 in Dolores Hidalgo, Guanajuato. Fireworks follow.

Dígame: tell me.

Don, Doña: a title of respect and affection. Usually used for men or women of a certain age and with the person's first name only.

Dulces de camote: candy made from sweet potatoes.

El Colegio del Reino de Dios: The College of God's Kingdom. The word "college" in Mexico may refer to a high school as well as an institution of higher learning.

El Refugio: The Shelter.

Enchiladas: fowl, meat, cheese, or vegetables wrapped in a tortilla and covered with a spicy sauce.

Encino: oak tree.

Ensalada de nopal: a salad made with cooked chopped cactus paddles, tomato, onion, lemon juice, chili, and fresh coriander.

Escamoles: the edible larvae and pupae of ants harvested from the roots of the *Agave* cactus plant. They were a pre-Columbian delicacy and are still a gourmet treat.

Esquela (de defunción): obituary notice published in a local newspaper for a fee.

Evangélicos: Mexico is over eighty-five percent Catholic. There has been, however, an increased participation in recent years of Evangelic sects. Their growth is greatest in Chiapas and along the northern border.

Fiesta: a party or celebration.

Flaco/a: thin, skinny. Often used as a term of endearment as is gordo/a, meaning chubby.

Flor de calabaza: zucchini flowers, deep yellow in color, used in *quesadillas*, soups, and sauces.

Fresa: strawberry, (slang) naïve, preppy young man or woman, not complimentary.

Frijoles: any of various dried beans used in Mexican cooking, black beans being the most common.

Gringo/a: in Latin American countries refers to someone who is foreign or English-speaking, particularly from the United States, usually not complimentary.

Gripa: the flu.

Guacamole: (Náhuatl, *āhuacamoll*: avocado sauce) *guacamole* is traditionally made by mixing mashed ripe avocados with chopped onion, *jalapeño chili*, fresh *cilantro* and lime juice. But many varieties of the concoction exist in Mexico as in the rest of the world.

Guapo/a: beautiful, handsome; *guapísimo/a*: very beautiful, very handsome.

Guadalajara: a well-known mariachi song composed by Pepe Guízar in 1937. He wrote the song in honor of his hometown, the city of the same name and state capital of Jalisco. Apart from the many renditions by famous Mexican singers, the song was also recorded by Elvis Presley and Nat King Cole. The lyrics of the first stanza are as follows:

> Guadalajara, Guadalajara.
> Guadalajara, Guadalajara.
> You are the heart of the province,
>
> You smell like the pure early rose,
> Like the fresh green river,
> You are homeland of a thousand doves.
> Guadalajara, Guadalajara,
> You smell like pure moist soil.

Guayabera: a man's cotton or linen shirt distinguished by pleats that run the length of the garment. Worn untucked, *guayaberas* are popular in the Caribbean, Central America, and Southeast Asia.

Hermana: sister.

Hermanito: little brother.

Hijo de la chingada: (vulgar) son of a bitch.

Híjole: wow, good grief.

Horchata: a cold drink made from ground rice, cinnamon, sugar and water.

Hospicio: an orphanage, poorhouse, old people's home, hospice.

Hostería: an inn, but can be a restaurant too.

Huachinango: red snapper (the fish).

Huevos rancheros: fried eggs are placed on a fried tortilla, then covered with a spicy tomato sauce. Alma likes a little crispy

Mexican chorizo sprinkled on top. The dish is served with refried beans. In the Mexican countryside, a big breakfast like *huevos rancheros* is eaten midmorning after working up an appetite. The main meal of the day in Mexico is eaten mid-afternoon between two and four.

Huipil: the most common traditional garment worn by Mexican indigenous women. It is a loose-fitting tunic, often beautifully embroidered and/or decorated with ribbons.

Huitlacoche: corn mushroom. It is a fungus that grows on organic corn. Much prized, it is used in *quesadillas* or soup, or as a base for a sauce to flavor chicken or fish. It is sometimes called the Mexican truffle.

Jardín: garden, yard or even a small patch of green.

Jesús me salva, Jesús me bendice: Jesus saves me; Jesus blesses me.

La Gordis: term of affection for a chubby woman.

La Casa de la Esperanza: literally, The House of Hope.

La Virgen de Guadalupe: on the morning of December 9, 1531, a Mexican peasant named Juan Diego saw a vision of a maiden on a hillside in Tepeyac (once the site of a temple to the mother goddess Tonantzin; now a suburb of Mexico City). The woman identified herself as the Virgin Mary and asked that a church be built in her honor on the site. When the Archbishop asked for proof, Juan Diego appealed to the apparition. She told him to look for flowers at the top of a usually barren hill. He discovered roses on the spot which were unknown at the time in Mexico. Wrapping them in his cloak, he returned to the Archbishop. Upon opening the cloak, the flowers fell out and an image of the Virgin Mary henceforth known as La Virgen de Guadalupe was found on the fabric. Her shrine in Mexico City is the most visited Catholic holy site in the world.

Las Hermanas de Santa Margarita: Sisters of Margaret, a fictitious order of nuns but similar to orders found today in Mexico.

Licenciado/a: someone with a degree from a university in law, business, or administration.

Lima: sweet lime.

Limpia: *limpiar* is to clean. *Una limpia* is a spiritual or ritual cleansing.

Los amigos de nuestros misioneros: Friends of Our Missionaries.

Los Militantes de Jesús: fictitious conservative religious organization although similar groups are very real in modern-day Mexico.

Macho: male animal or plant, vigorously masculine or aggressive.

Madre mía: Holy mother. Oh God, oh dear.

Madrina: godmother.

Maestro/a: a title and term of respect given to primary and secondary school teachers.

Manchego: cheese made originally in the La Mancha region of Spain from sheep's milk. Official manchego cheese is aged. The more commercial Mexican variety made from cow's milk has a buttery texture which makes it melt perfectly in a *quesadilla* or *torta*.

Mariachi: musical style originally from Western Mexico that dates back to at least the eighteenth century. A modern mariachi group can consist of as many as eight violins, two or more trumpets, and guitars. Singers are chosen for voice quality and musicians for their talent and training. Historically made up of men, today female mariachis can also be found. The groups wear the traditional costume of horsemen (*charros*) from the state of Jalisco: tight trousers, short jackets, boots, wide bow ties and large sombreros. The suits are adorned with silver ornaments.

Masa: white, yellow or blue grains of corn are boiled with water and a small quantity of lime. The mixture is left to soak overnight, then rinsed and either ground by hand or machine. The result is a thick dough used for making *tortillas* and many other recipes.

Más Papista que el Papa: more righteous than even the Pope.

Memoria: children's board game, which challenges the memory.

Menos mal: just as well.

Metiche: busybody.

Mezcal: (Náhuatl, *mexcalli*: oven-cooked *agave*) often associated with the state of Oaxaca, mezcal is a distilled alcoholic beverage made from the heart of the *agave* plant. Its characteristic smoky favor comes from cooking the *agave* in pit ovens over hot rocks. Some mezcals, like some tequilas, are aged.

Mierda: shit, crap.

Mi premiecito: my little prize.

Miscelánea: a neighborhood store mostly carrying dry goods. Also referred to as a *tiendita*.

Mocho/a: a sanctimonious person.

Mole: (Náhuatl, *mōlli*: sauce) *mole* is the generic name for a number of sauces used in Mexican cuisine, as well as for dishes based on these sauces. They are mixed with fowl, pork, beef, and/or vegetables, and vary in color and ingredients. *Moles* can contain fruits, a variety of different chilies, nuts, seeds, cocoa beans, and such spices as black pepper, cinnamon, and cumin.

Muchachas: girls.

Mucho gusto: pleased to meet you.

Náhuatl: has been spoken in central Mexico since at least the seventh century AD. It was the language of the Aztecs, who dominated a large part of central Mexico preceding the Spanish conquest. Their influence made Náhuatl the most prestigious language in the area. In pre-Columbian times the language was written on deer hide and plant fiber and had a pictographic and ideographic writing system. At the conquest, with the introduction of the Latin alphabet, Náhuatl also became a literary language, and many chronicles, grammars, works of poetry, administrative documents, and codices were written in it during the sixteenth and seventeenth centuries. Náhuatl is still spoken by an estimated one and a half million people.

Nana: nanny, nursemaid.

Narco: drug-dealing gang member.

Niño/a: boy or girl.

Novios: sweethearts.

Oficial: a person of rank in the police, army, or government.

Órale: all right, okay, come on.

Padre: father.

Pajarito de la suerte: little bird, usually a canary, who selects fortunes.

Palancas: levers, i.e. connections, influence.

Pan dulce: sweet breads, rolls often eaten for breakfast or a light supper.

Parroquia: Catholic parish.

Patita fea: ugly duckling.

Patrón: boss.

Pendejada: (vulgar) stupid remark or idea, crap.

Pendejo/a: (vulgar) a stupid person, a jerk.

Perita en dulce: can refer to a sweet woman but is often used negatively to refer to a woman who is difficult.

Peyote: small, spineless cactus with psychoactive alkaloids, particularly mescaline. The plant is believed to have curative properties and is used to treat such varied ailments as toothache, pain in childbirth, fever, breast pain, skin diseases, rheumatism, diabetes, colds, and blindness.

Pierna: leg.

Plan de Iguala: a declaration formulated by Agustín de Iturbide in which Mexico declared its independence from Spain.

Plata o plomo: shorthand for saying a choice is between giving a bribe (plata: silver) or getting shot (plomo: lead).

Pobrecito: poor thing.

Porfirio Díaz: (Oaxaca, 1830 – Paris, France, 1915), a military man, was president of Mexico seven times. In total he governed the country for thirty years. He was forced from power by the advent of the Mexican Revolution.

Preparatoria: high school.

Privada: dead-end street, can be gated.

Procuraduría: Attorney General's Office.

Puesto: a position, a job. Also, a stall selling anything from food to black-market DVDs.

Puta: a whore.

¡Que milagro! What a miracle! Often used when one hasn't seen a friend for a long time.

¿Qué te pasa? What's wrong?

Quesadilla: a folded tortilla filled with cheese, vegetables, or a combination thereof and then grilled until the tortilla is toasted, the cheese melted, and the ingredients warm.

Queso añejo: an aged cheese traditionally made from skimmed goat's milk, although cow's milk is preferred today. It is rolled in paprika which adds spice to its salty, sharp flavor. It is often grated over a pasta or tortilla dish.

Queso fresco: a fresh, creamy, un-aged white cheese used as a topping for *antojitos*, *frijoles*, egg dishes.

Quinceañera: girl celebrating her fifteenth birthday.

Quinceaños: celebration held to mark a girl's coming of age (at age fifteen).

Ranchera: a genre of traditional Mexican music dating from before the Revolution. It later became closely associated with the *mariachi* groups from Jalisco.

Rebozo: a woman's shawl.

Ropero: a free-standing wardrobe or closet.

Salsas: in Mexican cuisine *salsas* (which are not always sauces because some are not cooked and some served cold) are infinite in their variety. A basic ingredient is almost always chili: be it one variety or several—fresh, dried and/or smoked—with or without seeds or veins. The chili can be toasted, grilled, fried, boiled, or in its natural state. *Salsas* often incorporate herbs like the Mexican pepper leaf (*hoja santa*), coriander, or worm seed (*epazote*). Fruits and vegetables such as *jitomate* (red tomato), *tomate* (green tomato), mango, or papaya can be used. Garlic, onion, and lemon juice are almost always present. Nuts and seeds also are common ingredients. The components can be chopped, crushed with a mortar and pestle, or liquefied in a blender.

San Miguel Arcángel: The Archangel Saint Michael.

Santísima Madre de Dios: Holy mother of God.

Seguro Social: the Mexican government institution that provides health care, childcare, and pensions, among other benefits, for those registered in the system by their employers.

Señora: married woman or any woman over a certain age.

Señorita: young unmarried woman although even seventy-year-olds are often politely referred to as *Señorita*.

Si nos dejan: "If They Let Us,"the song was composed by José Alfredo Jiménez Sandoval (1926–1973), a Mexican singer-songwriter who composed in the Mexican country-music styles of the *ranchera*, *huapango*, and *corrido*. His songs are part of Mexico's musical heritage. According to the singer Miguel Aceves Mejía, the composer didn't play an instrument, didn't know the Spanish word for "waltz," or even what key his songs were in. Nonetheless, he composed more than a thousand songs, all known for their lilting melodies and appealing lyrics.

Simpático/a: charming.

Sencillo/a: natural, unaffected.

Solamente una vez: "Only Once," a popular song composed by the Mexican composer Agustín Lara (1897-1970), who is recognized as one of the most popular songwriters of his era. His work was widely appreciated not only in Mexico but throughout Latin America, the U.S., and Japan. He was married to the movie star María Félix.

Sopa de sopa (sopa seca): a first course in which miniature pastas are first browned in oil, then cooked with chopped onion, tomato, *chipotle* chili, and a little garlic until all liquid is absorbed. The dish is served with cream, avocado, *queso fresco*, and bits of fried *ancho* chili on top.

Sopes: a snack appropriate for morning, noon, or night. The size of a small fist, the base of a *sope* is made from toasting a circle of *masa* on a *comal* (clay or metal grill). It is then topped with refried black beans, crumbled *queso fresco*, lettuce, chopped onion, red or green *salsa*, and cream. Sometimes other ingredients like chicken or *nopales* are added. Like an open-faced sandwich, the variety of ingredients is endless.

Su servidor: your servant, flowery phrase to ingratiate oneself.

Tacos al pastor: slices of marinated pork are skewered on a spit and then slowly roasted on a vertical rotisserie called a *trompo* (lit.: spinning top). An onion and a chunk of pineapple are placed on top of the spit. When ready, the meat is then thinly sliced off the spit and served on small tortillas with finely chopped onions, cilantro, and pineapple. These are eaten with a *salsa* often made with *chili de árbol*, garlic, lime, or pineapple juice.

Talavera: authentic Talavera pottery comes from the town of San Pablo del Monte in Tlaxcala and the cities of Puebla, Atlixco, Cholula, and Tecali in the state of Puebla. This is because these places have not only been producing the pottery since the sixteenth century, when the technique was introduced by the Spanish, but also the quality of the clay found there is ideal. Much of the pottery was originally decorated only in blue, but colors such as yellow, black, green, orange, and mauve have become common.

Tamales: are a traditional Mesoamerican dish made from *masa* and pork lard. There are savory and sweet *tamales*. The savory variety can be filled with meat, chicken, cheeses, vegetables; a red or green sauce spices up the mixture. Sweet *tamales* can be filled with different fresh or dried fruits. Both are wrapped in a corn husk or banana leaf and steamed.

Tejana: a woman from Texas.

Telera: a flat, oval-shaped bread roll used for sandwiches. The interior of the roll is soft; the outside, crispy.

Telenovela: a limited-run television drama popular all over Latin America. The content is similar to that of a soap opera.

Tequila: is a regionally specific distilled beverage made from the blue *agave* plant found primarily in the area surrounding the city of Tequila in the highlands of the state of Jalisco. The white version, known as silver tequila or *blanco*, is not aged. Rested *(reposado)* or aged tequila *(añejo)* varies in flavor, aroma, and color. It is light to dark amber depending on the type of wood used for storage and the length of aging.

Tía: aunt, or can be a close friend of the family.

Tlacuache: (Náhuatl, *tlacuatzin*), a type of opossum. The size of a house cat, with a long, pointed nose, round ears, short legs, it is grey in color. The female has a pouch for her young. The animal can look bigger than it is because of its long hair. Slow but inquisitive, the *tlacuache* is nocturnal and often heard scrambling over roofs in search of potential food. A large part of its diet is insects and other invertebrates, but it also eats eggs, wild birds, fruits, and berries.

Tomate or Tomatillos: green husk tomato used in many *salsas*.

Torta: sandwich; Tor-to-ta, a very big sandwich.

Tortilla: a staple of the Mexican diet. A circular flat bread made from *masa* (see above). It can be formed by a press or by hand, cooked on a grill at home, or bought in a tortilla shop where a machine does the work.

Tostadas: fabricated with fried, baked, or toasted *tortillas*, *tostadas* are usually topped with refried beans, shredded chicken, shredded iceberg lettuce, thinly sliced white onion, tomato, cream, crumbly cheese, avocado, and salsa. They can also be topped with cooked *nopales* or other vegetables.

(Ser) Uña y carne: (to be) flesh and fingernail. That is, inseparable, or figuratively, thick as thieves.

Vete al diablo: go to the devil, go to hell.

Zapote negro: called "black persimmon" in English, this variety of *zapote* is native to Mexico and Guatemala. The size of a tomato, the fruit's pulp is a rich, dark brown color with a custard-like texture. The flavor is mild and nutty. Traditionally, the ripe fruit is blended with orange juice for a light, refreshing dessert.

ABOUT THE AUTHOR

S.B. Urquidi, American by birth, is a long-time resident of Mexico. Having worked as a marketing executive for an international company and later been part-owner of a book store & café in the legendary town of Tepoztlán, Morelos, Urquidi has become well-versed in the landscape, culture, people and expat community of her adopted country.

Her first book, *Love in Fire and Blood*, began the Alma Jaramillo series. Published in 2017, it received favorable reviews both from those familiar with Mexico as well as those just looking for a good read.

87897822R00171

Made in the USA
San Bernardino, CA
08 September 2018